THE ONE AND ONLY

When everything you've always wanted isn't enough

STUART V. GOLDBERG

ICHOR PRESS

 Published by Ichor Press. Printed at Grace Printing, 2050 W. Devon Ave. Chicago, IL 60659.

For those that provided the kaleidoscopic color to the solitude -- the writing of this book was accomplished in appreciation of:

Rhea Goldberg - late night master-editor
George Clooney - for accepting the novel in Lake Como, Italy
Jamie Foxx - for believing in a brother
Emmanuelle Chriqui - muse
Don Frye - one-of a kind
Andrei Arlovski - poetry in motion
Kenneth C. Griffin - first rhapsodic review
Doug Simmons - manuscript editing
Matthew H. Kaplan - cover photography
Mohammed Abueida - my Arabic brother
Dave Sargaent - global marketing; author's photo
Holy Doufkir - muse
Melanie Saldivar - muse
Allen Zelleski - story contribution
Joe King - providing a writing oasis
Roger Welp - ace wingman; actor-extraordinaire
Daniel Kuhlman - trailer director
Howard Gordon - visionary
Jon Mendenhall - trailer editing
Rino Burdi - sartorial splendor
Jimmy Guadagno - stylist virtuoso
Justin Berzon - research wizard
Lydia Fisher - publishing maven
Mark Hoffman - for the prayers
Titus Eapen, Ajith Eapen, & Carlos Irizarry - Grace Printing guardian angels
Marcey Clemens & John Scaletta - Digital Studio web-site masters
Sam Adam Jr. - a fellow legal-warrior whose brilliance fueled me on

Disclaimer: All characters appearing in this work are fictional. Any resemblance to real persons living or dead, is purely coincidental.

First Edition, February, 2010. ISBN # 9780981979410

Dedicated to the loving memory of

Laurel Amy Goldberg and Edward Blumenthal

ONE

Winding along a foggy road in Cotswald, England, a silver Bentley Brooklands pulls up to a tiny storefront in Antique Row. In his ritualized, meticulously cut to fit, peaked-lapel suit, elaborately knotted- and pinned-tie, and dark sunglasses, Rene Sorrell times his entry into the antique shop just as the guard is locking the door. Sizing up Rene, the guard holds the door open. Immediately going to what he wants, Rene opens a glass case containing a twenty-inch high, copper-red and white, porcelain Ming vase decorated in scrolling flowers. He finger-swipes it and then tastes his finger.

A sophomoric salesman comes over, takes off his horned-rim glasses and points them at the Do Not Touch sign, "I guess you didn't see the sign." Smirking with a self-important, condescending smile, he closes the case, "There's no tasting the antiques."

Recognizing Rene as one of the finest collectors of Asian art in the world, the shop owner rushes over in horror and intervenes with heightened apology. "Mr. Sorrell, Mr. Sorrell, sir, please..." the small, tight-lipped, Asian shop owner reverentially bows, "please forgive him." Appalled, the owner turns toward the salesman so only he sees his wrath, "I'm so sorry." Flicking his fingers, he dismisses him. As the salesman walks out, a definitive cock of the Asian's head tells the guard what to do. The guard locks the front door. The Asian reopens the case and withdraws the vase.

"Mr. Sorrell, come, come." The shop owner waves Rene to follow him and the guard. Rene is escorted to a draped back room. Unlocking an antique safe with a key from a chain around his neck, the owner produces a second identical vase, places it next to the first and boasts, "You know what you're looking at, don't you?"

Sitting back in the red-lacquered, lattice chair, Rene folds his arms. "The two finest Ming vases in the world. Fourteenth century," he quips, "from the palace of Emperor Hongwu. The only peasant to ever become the Emperor of China." Leaning forward, taking out a black alligator billfold, Rene's eyes steel, "How much?"

They're..." the shop owner swallows, summoning his confidence, "they are five...five million dollars each." Holding his breath, he proclaims it, "They are the only two of their kind in existence."

Rene takes out a black fountain pen embellished with platinum. He writes a check for ten million and tenders it.

The shop owner finally breathes.

Like it was a rival near the throne, Rene intentionally knocks the second vase off the desk shattering it on the marble floor. He picks up the remaining vase, stands and stares at it in his palm, "Now, it's the one and only."

TWO

A Bombardier long-range jet cruises at Mach 0.85 over Nepal's Kathmandu Valley. Just hours after Nepal's lawmakers abolished the country's 239-year-old monarchy, sixty bare-chested tribesmen cross the holy Bagmati River bearing a pearl-white 1912 Hispano-Suiza roadster secured to long tree trunks as they ascend the rocky route to India. The jet dips to get a better view of the priceless piece of bounty that slipped away from the royal palace. The jet's pilot, Don Frye, 45, a thick black-mustached, Greco-Roman warrior disguised as a good ol' country boy, taunts a preoccupied Rene Sorrell seated next to him, "Ten million dollars for a vase that somebody was once using for a lamp? And then you donate it to The Metropolitan Museum of Art. Why'd you buy it to just give it away?"

Rene stares out over the endless blue sky, "To be able to hold infinity in the palm of my hand."

Don Frye drops the jet for a closer look at the Hispano-Suiza motorcar. "From the government of Spain, to the royalty of Nepal -- to us. The only thing to make it out as fast as the deposed king. What are you going to do with it, it doesn't even have wheels?"

Rene watches his hired men thick-step along with the pristine, turn-of-the-century race car, "Wheels aren't of much use along an escape route. There's no roads where they're going."

Don Frye reaches back and pulls out a tobacco tin. "I got you something you've always wanted." Wild-eyed, he rattles the tin in front of Rene. Rene opens it to reveal a key chain with a picture of the Mona Lisa. Don Frye puts a CD disc in and cranks up Nat King Cole's song *Mona Lisa.* He broadly arcs the plane to the music as he sings along with Nat King Cole, teasing Rene, *"Is it only cause your lonely...they have blamed you for that Mona Lisa strangeness in your eyes?"*

Rene holds Don Frye's eyes. They both laugh.

Hours later, as the sun sets over the Irish Sea, the jet lands on a small runway of the only airport of a self-governing crown dependency in the middle of the British Isles. Exiting the jet first, Don Frye squints up at the red triskelion flag of the Isle of Man. He shakes his head, "How do you live in a country whose flag is three bent legs, and its head of state is a woman called the Lord of Man?"

Rene rolls a customized, cherry-apple red motorcycle down the plane's ramp, "No tax and no speed limits, that's how."

Shadows abound as a nighttime rain pounds a fully lit racetrack as a lone MV Augusta F4 1100 CC motorcycle, spinning circles of rain, rounds a corner and heads into the straightaway. Leaning on a wing of the jet, his cowboy hat dripping rain, Don Frye holds a stopwatch as the MV Augusta F4 rockets by at 195 mph. Clad in black leather, dropping one knee and then the other, Rene waltzes the cycle into successive tight turns. Feeling the vibration of his cell phone, Don Frye takes it out and answers it. He waves a lit flashlight at Rene as he comes around again. Not slowing down until the last second, the motorcycle skids wildly to a stop next to the jet. As Rene removes his helmet, Don Frye grabs it from him, "Hey partner, why don't we make it really dangerous and just turn off the lights." As Rene takes his helmet back, Don Frye holds on to it, "Remember you're mortal." He hands Rene an Isle of Man ten-pound note.

"What's this?"

"Flip it over. That's where you're going. "

Rene turns the ten-pound note to see a red brick castle with fortified towers.

"Peel Castle." Don Frye smirks, "That's how it looked in the eleventh century. Now, its practically a grave yard." He points at Rene, "Don't forget to throw the money on the Fairy Bridge when you go over it," he holds Rene's eyes like he's done a hundred times, "otherwise it's bad luck."

Rene tucks the bill inside his leather jacket. "Fairy Bridge?"

Don Frye shrugs, "It's haunted."

Dissecting the apexes of the rolling hill's turns on his motorcycle, Rene roars along the nighttime coastline approaching the causeway connecting the Isle of Man to a small islet called St. Patrick's Isle. Arcing around a tight turn, the tower of a rundown, red sandstone Viking castle comes into view. Running late, Rene fires up the rpms and whines the MV Augusta into higher gear. In front of him, suddenly coming out of a dark, bushy path, the red taillights of a farmer's truck back into the narrow, tree-lined lane. Rene skids to a stop on the wet pavement.

The truck stops in Rene's path blocking the road. The forceful rev of Rene's engine booms alerting the truck of his presence. The truck's motor sputters and stops. As the truck's motor cranks trying to start, Rene waits. He flashes his brights. The truck's red taillights blink hazard flashes. Rene skirts forward and starts to go around the stalled truck, but the space is too tight. Putting the kickstand down, he gets off the bike and walks toward the truck. Just as he gets near the driver's door, the motor suddenly goes on and the truck takes off.

Looking at his watch, Rene dashes back to his bike.

At the entrance to the harbor, the motorcycle rumbles over the old floorboards of the wooden swing bridge to Peel Castle. Midway over the water, Rene smiles seeing letters and notes pinned to the trees lining Fairy Bridge. He flies by them.

Just ahead, on a rocky outcrop overlooking the Irish Sea, sits Peel Castle. Entering the castle walls, Rene whizzes past the ruins of several red stone buildings and targets the rear of the castle where floodlights highlight the shadowy brick walls of one of the castle's towers. As he rounds the tower, a line of black limos and rainbow-hued exotic cars catch his eye. He parks in between them.

Walking past black-vested, masked armed guards with Uzis, Rene enters the tower. The tight, circular brick room is empty except for two-dozen chairs facing a podium. The chairs are occupied by the crème de la crème of the art underworld -- their jealousy finding pleasure in their rival's misfortune. Walking up the cobble stone aisle, surrounded by the most eccentric wealthy collectors, their faces familiar, Rene nods. His adversary, stately, long white-haired Andre Pope, 68, ageless English nobility in a baseball cap, sarcastically pats an open seat next to him. Rene prefers to stand. Once Rene's father's partner in their textile business, Andre is now a fierce competitor.

Enjoying the moment, Andre rubs it in, "You're a little late."

"The Blue Mauritius?"

Andre Pope nods, "The stamp just went for twelve million."

"Someone overpaid."

Andre laughs, "Tell him that." He points at a silver-haired, pockmarked, arthritic German arms dealer of elegant brutality.

Standing soldierly with the aid of a silver-tipped cane, Ernst Stauken, 52, seeing Rene coming toward him, places the dark-blue, two pence stamp in his wallet.

Rene catches Ernst Stauken at the front door.

Enjoying himself, Stauken leers sarcasm, "Run into a little trouble with traffic?" He bumps shoulders with Rene and walks out.

"Well..."Andre shrugs, taunting Rene, "there are other things being offered."

Rene looks at the crowd gauging whether he's going to sit down. He leaves.

Opening a slanted door of his yellow Lamborghini Murcielogo, Stauken painfully draws himself in. Idling along, his wheels crunching gravel, Stauken pulls up alongside Rene's cherry-red motorcycle. The Lamborghini's twelve cylinders rev to a roar. Stauken makes the mistake of waiving his wallet with the stamp at Rene and takes off, tires burning. Rene's stomp ignites the MV Augusta. Arrogantly, his fingers flick five seconds before he starts. Echoing the boom of a F22 fighter jet, in seconds, the red motorcycle pulls up alongside Stauken. Fading right and then dipping left, riding the crumbling rocky edge of the cliff, the motorcycle overtakes the Lamborghini.

Racing down the coastline approaching the causeway, the

men exchange leads. The Lamborghini's massive horsepower gives it dominance in the straightaway. Stauken purposefully runs his wheels on the cliff's edge shooting stones back at Rene. Rene swerves right through a cloud of gravel as the cycle's windscreen cracks.

Wheel-to-wheel as they approach the narrow old bridge, the two rivals jockey for position. Hitting the wooden slats of the Fairy Bridge, Rene's hand reaches inside his jacket, pulls out the Isle of Man ten-pound note and flings it into the air.

Stauken seizes the delay to pull ahead.

At a 180 miles an hour coming around a turn, Stauken is suddenly faced with an unattended tractor left out on the road as a sheep farmer locks up a gate. The yellow Lamborghini smashes into the trailer, flips over and ignites into flames.

Rene screeches to a stop. He jumps off, letting the bike slide along the roadway. Running to aid Stauken, Rene sees the wallet with the Mauritius stamp is laying flipped open inside the car. He opens the Lamborghini's door and reaches for Ernst Stauken's arm. The car explodes blowing Rene off his feet.

Andre Pope is the first of the others to arrive. Running at fast as he can, he rushes to get to Rene. Out of breath, Andre lifts him up, "Rene, are you alright?"

Rene moves Andre's hands away and brushes himself off.

Andre steps back from the heat of the inferno.

Rene stands mesmerized, staring at the fire. "Don't you want to know if I got the stamp?" Face-to-face, Andre glares at him. The fire crackles before them. Pushing it, Rene's eyes relinquish possessed confidence, "It's in there with him."

"Of course." Andre looks at him with reproach and just shakes his head. "How much more valuable does that make yours?"

THREE

Back in Manhattan, Rene elevates attire into art. Methodically dressed in a subversively decadent, black velvet tuxedo, crisp white shirt, crimson knotted-scarf, and ivory polka-dotted pocket square, he enters Sotheby's. He doesn't just enter, he seizes the room. Heads turn. The filled-to-capacity auction floor is seething with an atypical crowd. Art historians, connoisseurs, and museum directors elbow against unscrupulous dealers as they jockey for seats amongst the filthy rich.

"Hey, partner," Don Frye, in jeans, boots, and a Stetson that he refuses to take off, barks in his guttural growl to Rene as the crowd stares at them going up the middle to their reserved front row seats, "we got ourselves another all-star artistic vaudeville".

The usher offers Rene a nametag; Rene's glare dissuades him. Rene spots Andre Pope in the front row. Rene shakes Andre's hand and looks down at his own, letting him know he's checking to see if his diamond pinky ring is still there. While Rene stands discreetly assessing the crowd, Don Frye takes his seat and smiles at Andre. Andre hands Don Frye Sotheby's catalog of items up for auction. The cover of the brochure has a platinum picture of the most priceless timepiece ever made, the legendary banking and fanatical watch collector, Henry Graves' Patek Philippe super complication pocket watch. Don Frye smirks, folds the brochure and sticks it in his back pocket.

Andre stares daggers, "He's not getting it."

"Relax partner," Don Frye gently headlocks Andre. "You know why we're here." He gives up his trademark, broad mustached-smile, "For the rare and the covetable."

As the auction begins, an arresting, though understated, bespectacled-woman, with her hair in an over-tight French bun, captures Rene's attention. She is Saira DuFour, 28. A fallen angel whose delicate vulnerability and dynamic stillness paint her olive-skinned face with pathos -- yet, an alluring marvel of Moroccan-French-Irish and Punjabi blood. Her eyes carry the despair of someone that was about to be told the way it really was. Her red phone lights up. Saira's attention is diverted as she puts on her headphones to handle an emergency call from an undisclosed bidder for a rare painting.

Tookie Mills, 26, a lithesome, cheeky, ebony-skinned, spirited girl from Ghana, Saira's roommate, only close friend, and her runner at Sotheby's, takes the folded bid and asks in her flawless British accent, "Whom do we have?"

Saira shrugs, "Some dot-com idiot with more money than taste."

Dressed in an untucked but wide-belted men's tuxedo shirt, and skin-tight, three-quarter length, black satin Capri pants, Tookie puts a sylphlike leg up on the rung of Saira's chair and ties her bright-pink, high-top sneakers, "That's the way the world is going. Whew!" Tookie's bangled wrists go out as she does a jitterbug-step reading the outrageous bid, "This guy must really want this painting."

"You know what they taught us at Berkley," Saira scans the press of hip, young millionaires in the audience, "if more than ten-percent of the population likes a painting it should be burned. I'm flat broke, owe a hundred thousand in grad-school debt, and these trust fund, silver-spooned brats can't tell a Cezanne from a black velvet Elvis."

Tookie runs a hand through her wild mane of dark hair as she looks at the decked-out heavy hitters awarded the front row. "Hmmm." She pats the folded bid against her bee-stung lips as she checks out Don Frye. "The craggy one in the cowboy hat is rather endearing." She checks her hoop earrings, "I always wanted to live on a ranch."

"Ladies!" their Sotheby's manager, a hunch-shouldered, bushy eye-browed Filipino who jitters at any provocation, rushes over and points. All three of them watch as a trio of armed guards enter

Sotheby's secret side door escorting a velvet-covered item on a four-wheeled cart. The guards stay back, keeping the cart concealed. The floor manager sighs, "The world's been waiting over three hundred years for this painting." A knot of consternation between his eyebrows, he locks their eyes, "It's up next after the watch. Stay on top of it. Make sure our client doesn't lose it."

The Graves Watch comes up.

The bidding ignites. Paddles go up in the middle of the hall with fervent bids. As soon as the numbers hit a million, the experienced auctioneer focuses up front on Rene Sorrell and Andre Pope. They bid only in millions. Raising his fountain pen as a gesture, Andre is unhesitating. Rene's two fingers touch his pocket square offering more. The crowd tightens behind them, watching as the bids volley back-and-forth. Competing with Andre, Rene is distracted watching the two Sotheby's employees, Saira and Tookie, zeroing in as guards escort a cart with the velvet-covered item to be next in line. As the cover is removed, Rene leaves his seat. Walking along the wall, getting closer to the near-square, fifteen-inch, numinous oil painting, Rene's eye catches something and he smiles.

The auctioneer's hammer slams. He points at Andre Pope. Andre gets the platinum Patek Philippe pocket watch setting a record at twelve million.

Don Frye's look questions Rene's loss of the watch. Sitting down, Rene holds up a hand silencing Don Frye. He concentrates on Saira as the guards wheel the small oil painting toward the podium.

Saira holds her hand against her buzzing earpiece as her eyes dart back-and-forth from her manager to her lit-up phones. Scribbling fast, Saira pens a new bid, waves Tookie back, and sends her rushing to their second row floor trader with their orders.

Whispers hush across the ballroom and drop to deadened silence as the next item the auctioneer is watching is carried on stage. Their attention stolen, the eclectic crowd stares as the auctioneer lifts his half-glasses and scrutinizes the painting placed on the easel. His back to the audience, his head drops as his eyes close enjoying the moment. Ecstatic, he turns and faces the audience, "Ladies and gentlemen, five to ten million works of art were produced by seventeenth century Dutch artists. Up until now…" he goes and stands behind the glazed tiny painting, "only thirty-five of these masterpieces were known to exist. In 1660, in Delft, Holland…" he pauses for affect, "The Hague's London sculptor, John Larson, acquired this from the artist himself. This painting…" he points at the brilliantly chromatic oil, "was listed in the estate of Mr. Larson as merely a miscellaneous tronie of a man's head." His voice booms, "It remained undiscovered for three hundred and fifty years. Not just a tronie," he bows before it and sweeps his hand, "but a calling card. The artist's self-portrait."

A shifting of chairs is heard as paddles pause to be raised.

"Ladies and gentlemen, Sotheby's is proud to give you…" the goateed auctioneer parades across the stage with their prize, "the missing Vermeer." His chubby thighs swish corduroy against each other as he turns back-and-forth, "Not just a Vermeer," he flaunts the glazed Golden Age self-portrait of Johannes Vermeer, "I give you the Sphinx of Delft. Johannes Vermeer himself."

The phantom Vermeer that has haunted the art world for centuries sucks the air out of the room as chairs creak forward. The evocative, leering stare of the half-shaded face of a long brown-haired, twenty-four-year-old, adorned in an oversized, flamboyant red beret, captivates the audience. Hands go over hearts as breaths are held. The auctioneer returns to the podium and places the painting on the easel.

Rene is the first to go after the painting. Before the auctioneer can begin, Rene stands, holds up both his hands and flicks them three times. To the crowd's dismay, the bidding starts at thirty million. For a moment the floor is stunned, and then Andre Pope holds up his pen and a full hand, raising the bid by five million. A raucous frenzy takes hold of the hall faster than the auctioneer can restore order.

Sweating, loosening his tie, Sotheby's aging-by-the-minute floor manager looms over Saira, prompting her, with circular waves of his hand, to be faster. Saira's fingers frenetically hit triple banks of lit phone lines like a keyboard. The Filipino manager points at one private number lit up in red. Saira concentrates on the one call. In headphone contact with her most important caller, Saira signals his bidding. The manager pushes clerks aside, opening a path for Tookie as she races back across the floor to retrieve the higher bid.

Standing again, Rene bids it up. So does Saira. Rene squints at her and shakes his head. Saira does a slow burn in his direction. She shrugs him off as an idiot. Rene discreetly waives a finger, no. Saira takes it as an insult, it fuels her on.

As wooden chairs are heard to push back and fall, the hall ignites into a menagerie of rising buyers catching the fever. All decorum is lost as custom and formality bend to disorder. No one waits for the auctioneer. Impassioned purchasers abandon paddles and shout offers.

"Ladies and gentlemen! Please." Catching his breath, the frazzled auctioneer tries to regain control. "Ladies and Gentlemen!" Tapping the microphone, the auctioneer is out-shouted as multi-million dollar offers envelop the hall. The bids hit the record breaking one hundred million mark. At the last second, Rene quietly sits down. The auctioneer looks definitively at Andre Pope. Andre stares at Rene. Rene gives him nothing. Andre follows Rene's lead and sits too. The hammer slams as the auctioneer points at a five-foot, blue-haired Chinese woman with a commodity trader's contract of rose gold around her neck.

Caught between aggressive bidders and Rene's distractions, Saira loses the painting. Saira yanks off her headset and goes straight for Rene. Don Frye loves it.

Saira weaves through the crowd and gets right in front of Rene, "Mr.…" She looks for Rene's nametag. Of course, he has none. "Mr. Asshole, you just ruined my career." Flushed, she spins on her heels leaving. Saira's billionaire dot-com client, furious over the loss, wastes no time. Before she can get there, Saira's phone flashes red. Melting down, Saira's floor manager pushes Saira aside and fields the call. He moves the phone away from his ear futilely trying to suppress the gush of vitriolic slanders.

All the manager can get in is, "Yes sir, I know, sir. But sir..." holding the phone against his slicked down, bible-black hair, he wipes his forehead with a hankie, "but..."

The never rebuffed dot-com brat insists Sotheby's dismiss her.

The floor manager slowly places the phone on its hook. As he releases it, his hands stretch toward the ceiling and ball up, "Oh-my-God!" He motions for Saira. Losing an extra four million in commissions, the floor manager takes off Saira's headset and unplugs her phone. His stubby fingers motion for her ID card, "Goodbye."

Tookie runs over and holds Saira.

The manager points at Tookie, "Get back on the floor."

Standing in her way, Tookie won't let Saira leave.

As the auctioneer starts the bidding on the next item, clerks rush orders to Tookie. The manager's voice cracks as he raises it, "Now, Tookie. Or you can go too."

Staring him down, Tookie spins and goes to leave with Saira.

"No," Saira stops her. "We'll lose the apartment."

Offers are called out by the auctioneer.

"Go," Saira manages a feeble smile. "Get back to work."

Her glasses watery, holding a paper bag of all of her things, Saira stands at the back door of Sotheby's and stares. Standing in the chilling rain, her breath fogging, she looks at where her bicycle used to be. The lock is cut -- the bike stolen. Her head drops. Soaked, she walks the Sotheby's paper bag over to a garbage can and gets rid of it all. Not seeing a cab, she resignedly walks down the block to an unsheltered bus stop.

Saira looks down the empty street. Not a bus in sight.

Holding herself, trying to stop shivering, Saira turns back and squints seeing something turn the corner. Her finger wipes her glasses. A silver Bentley Brooklands pulls up with her bicycle dangling out of its trunk. The fogged passenger window rolls down.

Rene holds out his hand.

Arms-crossed, Saira doesn't flinch. She rather die then get in his car.

Don Frye goes to get out for her. Rene's hand stops him.

Rene gets out and stands in the steady rain. He holds the door open.

Saira is intransigent. A cement statue bolted to the ground.

Rene shakes his head at her stubbornness. "I couldn't let you buy it. It was a forgery. Vermeer was left-handed and signed his name with a swift brush stroke that followed the light." Self-amused, he gives up a smile. "That painting had a right-handed brush stroke."

Thunder booms as a flash of lightning crackles overhead. The rain gets heavier. Now, they're both soaked. Like a cat whose paws are wet, Rene doesn't like it. He digs deeper as he steps closer. "Vermeer never painted himself. He was too private." A confident shake of his head negates it, "That wasn't a Vermeer."

Saira's is unwavering. To yield would be unthinkable.

"Besides…" Rene steps closer and delivers it like he's parting with a protected secret, "I've got a real one back at my home. Want to see it?"

Saira's face gives up a scintilla of pathetic amusement.

Rene's head drops with self-effacing embarrassment. He laughs, "I know, that's a lot like…do you want to see my etchings."

FOUR

From closed floor-length drapes, a stream of sunlight finds its way across a king-sized bed. Her sable hair over a pillow, Saira is asleep. A muffled, "How about that," stirs her. Saira awakens and clutches herself. Her eyes flutter as she takes in where she is. She evaluates the half-unmade bed -- its lavish, ultramarine quilt is pulled up covering the other side's pillows. She exhales a sigh of relief. Voyeuristically she takes in the inner-sanctum of Rene's room. The grandeur intrigues her. Covering her body with a white sheet, tiptoeing across the cool crème marble, she explores further.

Her eyes are drawn to an oil painting on the far wall. A child dressed in a burgundy, velvet-vested suit and tie, stands autonomously. As Saira walks, her eyes hang on the painting. Entering a massive closet, Saira's hand runs along the finest of wool and silk suits. Opening an armoire, her fingers skim along colored cashmere sweaters. Across a counter, rows of gold and platinum watches glisten. She wraps her sheet tighter, lays one on her wrist and smells its black alligator band. Bottles of cologne beckon her. She smells each one. Her eye catches a silver-framed picture of a young boy sitting in a Daytona race car next to its driver and a beauty queen. She picks it up.

"How about that," beckons her more clearly. She walks to a covered cage. As she peeks inside, a beautiful, all-white parrot speaks, "Be quiet, I wanna' go to sleep."

Saira chuckles. Hearing footsteps, spinning, her sheet drops. She puts the picture frame back, grabs the sheet, runs back to bed and pretends to close her eyes.

Rene enters the room impeccably attired in a navy pinstripe

suit, pink shirt with white collar, slate-blue and dusty-rose striped tie, sapphire-stud cufflinks, and magenta pocket square. He soundlessly approaches and stops. The quickly pulled sheet exposes a seemingly endless, beautiful leg and perfect toes. Rene smiles to himself.

Saira's eyes slowly flutter open.

Rene leans over her and softly entices her, "Close your eyes." His fingertips trace along her temple as he bends close to whisper, "Stay as long as you like."

Saira's eyes follow his exit. Her mind races. His cologne stays with her as she drifts off.

There's a knock on the bedroom door.

As Don Frye peeks through the door, Saira waives him in. "Mornin' ma'am," barelegged, in a Stetson, cowboy boots, and long denim apron, he carries a silver breakfast tray and lays it on the bed.

Saira looks for her clothes.

"Your clothes will be back soon."

Her look questions his familiarity.

He motions toward the fireplace. "Remember at the fireplace...?" He winks, "You were chilled. I left you a little sherry before you went to bed."

"And you are?" Saira fights a smile taking in his outfit.

"Don Frye," his moustache lifts, "your chaperon." His bear-claw hand goes out, "nice to meet you, partner." Leaning in to shake hands with her, Don Frye steps back out of respect. Enjoying the moment, he points under her plate. Saira sees the envelope. "Mr. Sorrell is sorry you lost your job. You've got an interview in an hour."

The Bentley is waiting for Saira as she comes outside.

As Don Frye drives her to the Upper Westside, Saira investigates, "There was the most evocative oil painting on the wall outside his closet. In seventeenth century art, children were painted as miniature adults. That child...? Who was that?"

"That was Rene just before…." Don Frye stops himself.

Saira holds his eyes and continues. "And the boy in the race car? I…I recognize his father. He was a famous race car driver, right?" She sees Don Frye smile in the rear view mirror. "Were those his parents? His mother was beautiful."

"Thanks," Don Frye responds. Saira stares at him as he explains. "Those were my parents. Rene's parents died in a automobile accident when he was nine."

"A drunken driver?"

"Yeah…" Don Frye sighs heavily, "his father." He looks back at her in the mirror, "Rene wasn't ready to be that brave at nine." The Bentley stops. "We're here." Don Frye hops out and opens her door. He winks at her, "Good luck, partner."

Looking up at the modern steel and glass office building, Saira enters. Security at the door confirms her appointment and sends her to a bank of elevators. Fifty stories later, the elevator opens revealing a shiny, black granite hallway lined with paintings that should be hanging in the Louvre. She stops to examine one. A secretary interrupts her, pointing her down the hallway to enormous, bronze, Asian temple doors. Saira tries to knock, but there's no knocker. She looks around, there's no one. Saira straightens her suit, adjusts her glasses, and tucks back her hair. Drawing a deep breath, she opens the doors to a magnificent walnut-paneled room. At the back of it, before a lit, massive fireplace, in between Venetian bronze torcheres, is a silver-gilded Louis 14th desk. Seated at it, is Rene.

"Why am I not surprised?" she murmurs a little too loud.

"Ms. DuFour," Rene nods. Red velvet club chairs, originally from a French bank, are in front of his desk. Rene motions her to sit, "What do you know about rare art?"

She sits. "Not enough…" she leans back, "so it seems."

Rene's hand waves her on.

"I acquired a Fine Arts Degree with Honors in 17th century European art at Berkley. Then I semestered at The Art Institute documenting Delacroix and Caspar David Friedrich, and interned at The Getty, logging Chinese Ceramics and Porcelain. I got my masters at Syracuse University in Chinese bronzes. Then I beat out sixty-three applicants for my dream job. I was…" she exhales, "at Sotheby's for two weeks."

"School's out. Let's see how you do on the track." Rene stands, takes two, similar, muddy-green vases down from the mantle behind him and puts them before Saira. "One is priceless Pre-Columbian, the other, Pier-One. Drop the fake."

Saira holds a vase in each palm. Smelling each one, she expounds, "Pre-Columbian clay was porous. The fakes tried to imitate it by using special clay that was artificially aged, by boiling it in meat broth, refiring, or even sometimes storing them in sewers." Rene's eyes hang on her. As her right hand releases a vase, Rene lunges for it. She catches it herself and smiles, "They're both priceless Pre-Columbian. Mr. Sorrell…" her eyes challenge him, "you like to take chances."

Rene sits, and withdraws his alligator billfold. He takes out his black fountain pen, writes a check and slides it to her.

"This says a million dollars," she says in shock.

"You just passed your job interview. That's your first year's salary." Rene holds his pen up, "I'm going to change your life. If this was a magic wand," he keeps her eyes, enjoying the effect he perceives he's having, "and you could ask for anything, anything you wanted. What would it be?" Self-possessed, effusing charm, he half-smiles, "Be careful what you ask for."

Saira sits expressionless, drawing Rene in. Her continued silence goads him. The cat lets go of the mouse. "Did you really think it was going to be that easy?"

Caught off guard, Rene doesn't know what to say.

Saira takes his pen. "Did you ever hear of pentimento? You take a palate knife," she runs his pen over her palm, "and scrape off the layers of paint to get to the artist's original charcoal sketch. Mr. Sorrell…." She looks at him with challenge. Her arms extend and take in the opulence of his office, "Who are you without all of this?"

Rene leans back, "Excuse me?"

Saira hands him his pen back. Standing, she beckons him, "Change places with me."

Rene squints, enjoying her mettle. He gets up and sits in her chair.

Standing over him, Saira runs the back of her hand under his chin, "No man shaves that close. You have a barber straight-razor shave you every day." She messes his perfect hair up, "A three hundred dollar haircut," she cocks her head, "that's my share of the rent each month." She looks at his watch, "Give me your left hand."

Rene holds it out.

She unbuckles his watch and lays it out, "Patek Philippe's Sky Moon Tourbillion. Rose Gold. They make one a year for a million dollars." Her hand grabs the lump in his pocket; "I figure a flush guy like you carries fifteen thousand cash on any given day."

Rene takes out his wad, "Twenty-five to be exact. The bills crisp and facing up."

"Take off your suit jacket." He does. She feels the material, "Ten thousand dollar Vicuna, custom-made." He nods. Her fingers motion for his tie.

Just as he undoes it and Saira's sliding it off, Don Frye knocks and enters. Don Frye's eyes go wide seeing Rene's condition. He turns to keep from laughing, and then matter-a-factly informs Rene, "We've got a problem."

"Well, thanks for your time, Mr. Sorrell." Saira slides the million-dollar check back across the desk. "You owe me thirty-nine dollars for a new titanium bike lock."

Their eyes follow her out.

"Hey partner," Don Frye gets in close with scrutiny, "you all right? I've never seen that look on your face before." He hands Rene back his tie. "Well, I figure that qualifies for a rodeo-rope." Rene's hands go out like he's clueless. Don Frye grins, "She had you out of the chute and roped in seven seconds or less."

Rene double-Windsor knots his tie, puts on his suit coat, and addresses Don Frye's admonition. "What's up?"

Don Frye looks out the fiftieth-floor windows, "It's going down in Cuba."

Rene takes out his cell phone, "Get the boat ready."

The raging chorus of three gas turbine engines generating 17,000 horsepower erupts from a narrow and angular, black-glossed super-yacht that looks like it was built for a special-forces billionaire.

FIVE

The massive interior of Christie's Auction House is abuzz with the news that a publicly undocumented Faberge egg made for the Rothschild family in 1902 has surfaced and is up for auction on the day's agenda. Since all of Karl Faberge's fifty-four priceless jeweled eggs had been long ago delivered to the Imperial Family in Russia, none others had been thought too exist. American billionaires, English Lords, French art aficionados, and Russian oligarchs pack the auditorium. In a corner, at a bank of phones, are the newly hired employees Saira DuFour and her roommate Tookie Mills. A triple-bleached-blonde administrator, untouched by femininity, hands her two new employees a folded bid and scoffs, "I don't know how you two got so lucky your first day here."

Saira opens the bid, rolls her eyes and passes it to Tookie. Seeing that it's labeled 'Anonymous Bidder', Tookie shakes her head, "Here we go again."

The auctioneer is passed a spectacular, diamond-encrusted, translucent-enameled, pink egg. Holding it up, he opens the egg -- from inside the egg, a crowing cockerel pops up and flaps its wings. The audience roars. As soon as the bidding starts, wooden-numbered paddles push up. Holding her hand against her earpiece, Saira signals Tookie to cast her bidder's due.

"Saira...." Tookie stares as she unfolds the bid, "This says, 'I want it. *No limit.*' Who the hell have we got?"

Saira shrugs and waves Tookie on, hurrying her to the floor.

Bids shoot up all across the floor. Saira encounters serious opposition. The bidding lasts for more than five minutes as the remaining six determined bidders fight to acquire it. Every bid triggers Saira's constant raise. The opposition is worn down by Saira's unyielding determination. Her undisclosed bidder's 18 million dollar offer prevails.

Under the salesroom's cheers, Christie's administrator walks over the glistening pink egg, with a dazzling, diamond-encrusted gold clock in its belly, and holds it out to Saira.

Saira pulls off one earphone and stares at the egg. "What?"

"He wants you to bring it to him personally."

Excited to see the purchaser, Saira and Tookie look through the crowd for his identity. Tookie jumps on her toes, "Where is he?"

The administrator points to the mass of shoulders in the middle of the packed hall, "Look for paddle number one-twenty-nine."

Tookie excitedly whispers to Saira, "Can I come too?"

Saira nods. Carefully cupping the Faberge egg against her chest, Saira threads through the crowd. She sees a smiling face and heads toward it.

Andre Pope nods at her, "Congratulations miss, you broke the record." As Saira preciously holds out the pink Faberge' egg to him, Andre touches it like it was the Torah, "I just had to see it, to touch it." Andre looks past the Faberge prize and assesses Saira, "This time I'm not the lucky man." Smiling, he directs her toward the middle of the auditorium.

Saira locates the designated spot. A circle of Russians crowd around the seat obscuring paddle number 129.

"Gentlemen…" Tookie steps ahead, "let her through."

The crowd parts. Saira finds paddle 129 on an empty seat. Resting under the paddle is a titanium bike lock.

SIX

Six young women, in pajamas and nightshirts, hold their breath sitting cross-legged in a circle on the floor as Saira tells them the history of what they're looking at. In the center of the group, a desk lamp's light is focused on the most luxurious bauble ever produced -- the pink Faberge egg. In glasses and her hair up, Saira educates, "Peter Karl Faberge, a Russian jeweler, was the supreme craftsman of his era...perhaps any era ever. Russia's Tsar Alexander III gave Faberge the order to design the first Imperial Easter egg as a special gift for the most important holiday on the Russian Orthodox calendar. He told the master designer, it must be fitting the majestic beauty of the Czarina of Russia and an example of the love I have for my wife." Little by little, Saira slowly opens the pink egg. As the girls try peeking inside, Saira closes it with a smirk.

"What'd the Tsar put inside?" A redhead, in purple rollers and an avocado mud-mask asks, "A diamond ring?"

Tookie smiles and teasingly winks at Saira, "Not yet."

Exasperated, Saira continues, "Faberge was told to put a special surprise inside the egg for each Easter. To this day, Faberge's magnificence of jeweled art has never been rivaled. Fifty-four Imperial eggs were created. Only forty-six survive today."

"What happened?" one of her roommates asks.

Saira continues, "The grandeur of Russia and the fairy tale Romanov Royal Family were doomed. The ruling Romanovs soon were assassinated in their palaces. Following the Russian Revolution, Faberge fled to Switzerland while the palaces were ransacked and the treasures moved to the Kremlin Armory. To Stalin and his lackeys, they were reminders of Imperial excess. To the Russian Royal Family they were precious gifts commemorating Easter." Saira picks up the solid gold, diamond-encrusted, pink egg, "To me it's the most romantic thing I've ever heard."

The redhead rolls up her sweats and inches closer, "What's this one called?"

Saira let's her carefully touch it, "Its called the Rothschild Faberge egg because it was hidden off the market over a hundred years by the Rothschild heirs."

"So what's..." a spiked-blonde in a oversized college sweatshirt, nervously asks, "what's it worth?"

Saira stands with the egg, "It broke all records as the most expensive Russian art object ever sold at auction." The nervous blonde goes to double-lock the apartment's front door. Tookie draws the drapes as they all hang on Saira waiting for more. Walking out towards her room, Saira casually turns, "Eighteen million or so."

"Dollars...?" Spooked, the spiked-blonde looks at the door and then at the other girls. "We don't even have an alarm system."

The girls all get up and trail Saira down the hall.

"And the bike thief..." Tookie persists, "Mr. Bentley? He just gave it to you to hold for him?" She shrugs not getting it, "When you gonna' see him again?"

Saira keeps going.

The redhead in the mud mask anxiously asks, "He's not coming here is he?"

Saira's hand goes up dismissing them. Closing her bedroom door, she leans against it and exhales, "That's a lot of questions."

Standing barefoot in a white terry cloth robe, her dark-brown eyes close up to the washroom mirror, Saira asks, "Who are you..." she smirks, "Mr. Bentley?" Having no answer, she spins on her heels, snatches her leather-bound diary, carries it to her bed and falls asleep before she can document the day's events.

A sleeping Saira tosses and turns. Pulling up one quilt after another, she kicks them all off. Sitting up in bed, she takes off her eye mask and goes to her closet. Standing on her tiptoes, she takes one shoebox after another down from the closet shelf. From the last shoebox she unfolds layers of tissue paper and takes out the pink Faberge egg. She takes it with her and opens each drawer of her armoire. Going back to middle one, she secretes the egg in her underwear.

Saira gets back in bed.

Fluffing her pillow, switching one then another under her head, she gets back up. She gets the egg, puts it under her pillows and lies back down. Her feet twitch and swish under the covers. A slamming door on a car outside startles her. Her hand fumbles for her night stand drawer and comes out with a flashlight.

She scans the room. Nothing.

Sitting up, Saira withdraws the egg and turns the flashlight on it. Diamonds shimmer off her wall. Rotating the egg, she smiles making the sparkles of light twirl. She sets the egg on the pillow next to her and stares at it, "Czarina Fedorovna, he must have loved you very much." After staring at it for a while, Saira smells it and sets it back on the pillow. She whispers to it, "Good night." Cupping it against her breast, she pulls up the covers and goes back to sleep.

The next afternoon, as Rene and Don Frye walk out of Rene's Upper East Side Manhattan townhouse, a grey Brinks armored truck pulls up next to the Bentley.

It's engine idling; the truck just sits there.

As Rene and Don Frye walk towards the Bentley, the driver of the Brinks truck points at them. A Hispanic unformed-guard jumps out from the passenger side.

Rene and Don Frye stop walking.

Gun drawn at his hip, his other arm wrapped around a small cardboard box, the Hispanic uniformed-guard scans the street, and then walks toward Rene and Don Frye. Pushing Rene behind him, Don Frye reaches inside of his coat as the guard approaches.

Seeing Don Frye's wary, quick movement, the guard stops. "I'm from Christie's." He shows his identification.

Don Frye takes the box and opens it with his pocketknife. His mustache lifts as he gives it to Rene, "She's got your number."

Inside it is a straight razor, shaving cream, a shaving cup, and a brush. Rene opens the shaving cup. Inside it is the Faberge egg.

SEVEN

A nervous-coughing, shoulder-twitching, thickset, African American man looks at the Italian beef sandwich bag in his hand as he watches red digital numbers tick away in an elevator in the Time Warner Center as it whooshes towards the top floor. Ex-New York Vice Cop, Tony Stokes, 46, whose retirement started early when he was facing indictment for creating false police reports and extorting art gallery owners, can't resist the smell and opens the bag. Just as he bites into the sandwich, the elevator door opens revealing the 16,000-foot duplex penthouse of Andre Pope. Two-story windows boast the best view of Central Park in Manhattan.

In a reincarnation of antiquity, the first step in lands one on a thousand-year-old stone floor. As if in a waking dream, the interior is more an anthology devoted to Eastern spiritualism than a residence. The living room is a recreation of an authentic Himalayan temple, its walls covered with colorful allegorical paintings. Sacred religious artifacts and monuments of Krishna, Shiva, Vishnu, and Buddha prevail, attempting to propitiate the Gods. Dressed in a white silk shirt, smoking jacket with his family crest embroidered in gold, and black silk pants, his arms crossed, Andre looks at his watch, "You're late." He immediately spots the sandwich in Stokes' hand. "What do you plan to do with that?"

"Enjoy it."

"This isn't a cafeteria."

Stokes sticks the sandwich in the pocket of his green Army surplus jacket as he assesses Andre's home. "Nice place. I read in the paper how you flew in a Chinese Fang Chooey expert to bless it,

That true?"

Andre rolls his eyes at Stokes, "It's pronounced Feng Shui."

"Yeah…." Stokes sniggers, "They tell you where to put your bed so you can sleep." Following Andre down the mahogany-paneled, stone hallway, Stokes picks up a sterling-framed picture off an end table and walks with it through the apartment.

The men go into Andre's study.

His back turned; Andre is preoccupied with a framed map of a tiny island in the Indian Ocean east of Madagascar. A red marker pinpoints Mauritius. While Andre stares at the map, Stokes feels the sandwich grease on his hand. Searching his pockets for a napkin, he finds none. He wipes his hand on the chiffon drapes. He eyeballs the revered possessions covering the walls, and interrupts Andre's rev-erie. "I thought it was extinct. Where ya' going to mount it? A tri-colored bird would look good in here."

"What…?" Andre looks at Stokes in utter disbelief. "It's a stamp not a bird."

Stokes continues, "I was as close as I am to you, and all he talked about was the Blue Mauritius Pigeon."

"That means you're an idiot and Rene knew you were there."

Jingling coins in his pocket, Stokes holds out the sterling-framed picture. In it, two men stand in front of Buckingham Fountain with their arms around a stunning, graceful, auburn-haired, Celtic woman with light skin and freckles. "This guy looks just like Rene. Is this you on vacation with Rene's mother and father?"

"Where'd you...?" Andre yanks it out of Stokes' hand, "Give me that. Who moves things in a person's home?"

"Sorry."

"Stokes…." Andre lays the picture face down. "I want Rene Sorrell's informant. That's what I pay you for. Information that other people don't have." Andre squints. He spots something different about his silk drapes. He goes to inspect them. "The word is, a Florentine con artist, who's been arrested by Interpol and did time for fencing stolen art, tips Rene off as to rare items hitting the market. After the informant calls, Rene's been seen making deposits into a numbered account at the Credit Suisse. With one of the Blue Mauritius stamps destroyed, now the other two are worth much more." Andre holds up the stain on the chiffon drape and shows Stokes.

Stokes shrugs, "Check your housekeeper." Swishing his thighs back-and-forth, Stokes looks out at Central Park. "Nice view."

"Take a good look, it's the last time you're going to see it from here." Andre walks him out. "I want to know about the last two stamps before Rene. Understand?"

Stokes nods. "I gotcha'. Don't worry."

"Stokes…." Andre puts an arm around the big man, "They really do turn off your lights when you don't pay your bills." He stops at the door, "You're suspended from the police force, you smoke pot with your dog, you're unemployed, and you've got a Russian girlfriend who needs a visa." Andre takes an envelope of cash out of his jacket and puts it in Stokes' hand. "If you don't get me what I want…" Andre holds onto the envelope, "you got nothin' coming but hard times."

EIGHT

Turning a nondescript brass key, Rene unlocks a safe deposit box. Carrying the box to a table, he sits before it and folds his hands before his lips. His eyes close remembering the moment he became fascinated with collecting.

There was this sea-foam-green, ostrich leather jewelry box that was always tucked away hidden in his mother's armoire. When he asked why she kept it there, his mother told him, "It was private." He remembered how she said it was their secret and then unlocked it with a key. All it had was an old envelope with two colored stamps. He remembered laughing when he saw it wasn't even addressed to her. Holding it like a sparrow in her hands, she let him touch it. Guiding his little four-year-old fingers, she ran the tips over edges of the stamps. "Feel it?" she asked holding his eyes. "This has traveled over a hundred years and all across the world. You're feeling history."

Rene opens the safe deposit box. Putting on white cotton gloves, he takes out a graying, three-by-five-inch envelope penned in sepia-colored ink. Not just any envelope, The Bordeaux Cover. Received and hand postmarked 'Bordeaux, France', the envelope contains not just the One-Penny Orange Queen Victoria Mauritius stamp, but also the Blue Mauritius Two Pence stamp next to it. Regarded as 'la piece de resistance de toute la philatelie', the envelope is the most coveted item in philately's entire stamp world.

Rene carefully places The Bordeaux Cover in a protective glassine envelope, puts it in a fitted titanium case, and zips it into his black alligator valise. His cell phone rings. Rene tries to answer it and loses the call in the vault. Locking the safe deposit box, he leaves.

Seeing Rene hurry out, the female bank manager approaches. "Mr. Sorrell, sir.... Is everything all right?"

Rene nods.

Seeing the phone in Rene's hand, she asks, "Would you like to use my land line?"

"No, thank you." He holds up his hand in passing, "I'm fine."

Standing in a teller's line, in a flesh-colored, personal injury foam collar brace, oversized pilot sunglasses, and with two American Girl doll boxes under his arms, Tony Stokes watches as Rene goes over to the bank's lobby windows to make a phone call.

Rene talks for twenty seconds and rushes out to his Bentley.

Stokes looks around at all the overhead security cameras and smiles. Recognizing a security guard as an off-duty, moonlighting NYPD vice cop, Stokes goes over to him. "Waz' up, Dante?"

Dante grins. He looks at the large American Girl boxes under Stokes' arms, "Looks like you're pretty flush. I heard those dolls cost a fortune." Dante stares at the brace on Stokes' neck, "You milkin' a personal injury case?"

Putting his arm around the security guard, Stokes soul-brother handshakes Dante passing him two hundred dollars in the handshake. "Show me the surveillance room."

Dante radio clicks his walkie-talkie alerting the guards he's leaving his post. The duo walks into the bank's surveillance room and Stokes smiles at the wall-to-wall video monitors showing every angle of the bank's interior.

"There," Stokes points at the spot where Rene was on the phone. "Replay that." Dante replays the tape re-tracking Rene as he walks out of the vault, waives off the bank manager and then goes to the lobby windows to make a phone call.

"Freeze it there."

Dante freeze-frames a still of the image.

"Blow it up for me, will ya?"

Dante digitally enlarges the cell phone in Rene's hand. The tenth blow up reveals a full screen image of the keyboard of Rene's phone as his finger hits the keys. Stokes jots down the called number.

Stokes slaps a high handshake clasp on Dante, "Thanks."

"Thanks nothin'. Can you cut me in on the action? Ya' know being the man is a short hustle. You know what NYPD pays. Shit."

Ignoring him, Stokes dials Andre Pope. "I got' em."

Early the next morning, sitting in the back of an idling Black Range Rover with dark-tinted windows, Andre Pope waits outside a Tribecca adult bookstore as a limping, diminutive Florentine, Pascali Debartolo, 39, wearing a pork-pie hat with a crisp orange feather, comes out and squints at the flood of daylight.

Stepping out of a doorway, Stokes bumps Debartolo from behind, "Lost your library card?" Debartolo's brown paper-wrapped porno books and X-rated DVDs fall to the ground as Stokes shoves him into the Range Rover as its door opens.

"What the hell...?" Debartolo looks at the strange duo in the Range Rover. He focuses on Andre since he's closest. "You're too old to be the police that's for sure."

Stokes slaps Debartolo's face to catch his attention.

"He's not, but I am." Stokes flips out his revoked NYPD badge. "You got three choices." He holds the little man's eyes. "You catch a beating right now and go to jail. You can tell us what we want to know. Or..."

Impatient, Andre Pope interrupts the Tony Stokes Show and gets to the point, "Listen, we know who you are, where you live, and that you work for Rene Sorrell. "

Debartolo asks cavalierly, "What's choice number three?"

Stokes yanks open the Range Rover's door affording Debartolo the chance to run. As Debartolo evaluates his chance of escaping without harm, Stokes opens his jacket and exposes the NYPD-issued red pepper spray hooked on his belt. Stokes' eyes dare him, "It's less than lethal." He grins, "That means I don't have to put my hands on you to catch you."

Andre hands him his card, "I want to know what Rene knows. I pay better."

The little man gets to limp away this time.

NINE

A silvery, 116-foot mega-yacht, with the nautical design of a peregrine falcon diving in attack mode, slices through nighttime waves of the Atlantic Ocean. The thirty million dollar, one-of-a kind, Wally 118's carbon fiber superstructure's propulsion system, driven by three massive gas turbines, roars across cerulean waters at 100 mph toward the twinkling lights of Havana, Cuba. Docking at the Marina Hemingway Harbor, Don Frye and Rene leave the mega-yacht in the trusting hands of their Israeli ex-military crew.

Entering Cuba, they tender their passports.

As the armed customs agent goes to stamp their passports, a bearded man in a Cuban army lieutenant's uniform slips a blank piece of paper over the passport's page.

The blank sheet is stamped.

"You were never here," the bearded man winks and directs them to follow him. "I'm Tiburon," he shakes their hands, "it means shark. Forget everything you've heard about Cuba. Cigars, Russian missiles," he shrugs, "bearded-men, prostitutes, and sugar. We're a lot more." As the anthem Suite de las Americas trumpets in the street, Tiburon threads Rene and Don Frye through the colorful carnival activities packing the cobblestone historic streets of Havana.

Two centuries of neglect offer an open-air museum of colonial architecture. Restoration leans on decomposition. Pastel-hued, crumbling neo-classical mansions, whose balconies boast decorative Moorish wrought iron, marry ugly 1950's prefab high-rises that shadow the stained glass windows of French colonial homes. All the while, everything is fading under the Cuban sun, heavy with the thick salty air, and blanketed with the pungent odor of tropical vegetation.

A gold leaf, 56-foot high sculpture, The Statue Of The Republic, the third tallest statue in the world, draws Rene's attention.

Don Frye scrutinizes his friend. "You've got that look in your eyes again."

Rene grins staring at the statue. "I want that for our lawn."

Don Frye elbows him, "I'm not talking about inanimate objects." Rene's stare questions him. Don Frye teases, "You know *who* I'm talking about. Ms. DuFour."

They follow Tibron into an old, marble amputeed-mansion. The Moorish Palacio de Valle now serves as a restaurant for corrupt policeman, thugs, and bandits. Going up the crumbling steps they see what was once an elegant sculpted stairwell, now covered with red letters stenciled-in, extolling Fidel. As they go through the door, Tibron assures them, "Your host will be here soon."

Shortly after Rene and Don Frye sit at a corner table and watch cabaret dancers, in shimmering pink silk sequins and feather headdresses, dance the bolero, rum drinks are sent over. Don Frye looks for the hot prospects that sent it.

All he sees are bearded dark faces.

As Don Frye scoops ice out of his water and drops it in the rum, two sultry, curvaceous, barely post-teens, in half-an-outfit of sprayed-on pink gauzy cotton, come over, speak to them in broken English, making it clear by their gyrations that they want to dance. One of the precocious girls tries to get Rene to slip off his jacket.

Rene's look dissuades her.

"A true gentleman," Don Frye goads a hesitant Rene, "ought to dress well, shoot well, and dance well." Expressionless, Rene is immobile. "C'mon partner," Don Frye eases him up, "give a buddy a little support."

Rene gets tugged to the dance floor.

The precocious girl runs her hands up Rene's sides as she

dances, "Caliente." She nibbles his ear. Rene pushes her away. Slighted, her head flings back her mane of caramel hair as she leaves.

His dance partner sitting on his lap, Don Frye joins Rene back at the table. "Well, partner..." He nods his head at a phalanx of bearded Barbudos sauntering over, "your Cuban dancing career is over."

The smallest man speaks Cuban as he approaches.

Don Frye looks to his glued-on dance date, "Who's your short, fat friend?"

Struggling in fragmented English, she answers, "You...disrespecting our best Cuban rum." Still infatuated, she feels Don Frye's rock-hard, high cheekbones; "We never put ice in. We drink...and offer it to the Gods at room temperature."

Don Frye disregards the group of Barbudos closing in on them, "Bummer." Moving in his seat to the music, he shakes his glass cooling the rum and drinks it.

A taller Cuban, that looks like a barber pole in American track shoes and an awning-striped shirt, steps forward. "Why're you here? Who are you?"

"Two famous Americans," Don Frye answers straight-faced as he puts still more ice in his drink. He points at Rene, "He's Ralph Lauren and I'm Benjamin Moore. We're here to open a paint distributorship." Provoking them, he shakes the ice in his glass for a toast, "Your whole country needs a good coat of paint."

As the tall Cuban moves in close on Don Frye, Rene stands to push him back. Smiling, Don Frye holds Rene's wrist down to the table, "I got this one, partner." He gently relocates the honey in his lap and slowly stands.

The squat Cuban whips out a machete from behind his back.

Don Frye front snap kicks him through a plaster wall. Shifting quickly behind the barber pole Cuban, Don Frye grapples his lead-pipe arm around the man's neck. In seconds, the tall Cuban is choked out unconscious. He drops.

As the entire crowd moves on Rene and Don Frye, machine gun fire rakes the ceiling and walls. “They’re our guests! Vamoose!” A pretentious cross between an aardvark and albino rat, Bartholomae Blanco, 40, commands them. Che Guevara in a derby, brandishing a gold Rolex on each wrist, Bartholomae Blanco, aka Benny Blanco, is one of the wealthiest men in Havana’s underworld. A Cuban drug dealer claiming to be Creole aristocracy, he enjoys welcoming his expected guests, “Mr. Lauren, Mr. Moore,” he repeats, going along with the joke, “how do like my country?”

“Time for a change,” Don Frye chirps in looking at the miscreants on the floor.

“Today’s banditos,” Benny Blanco shrugs, “tomorrow’s President.” He sits down with them, “And if the history of our country has shown us anything...a Cuban President is only a day away from fleeing to Mexico or the Bahamas.” Blanco turns his attention to Rene, “Is my ride here?”

Rene nods and motions for what he wants.

Blanco signals for one of his fireplug posse to pass him something. A sugar cane worker’s rusted lunch box is passed forward. Unlocking it, Blanco takes out a wrapped sandwich. In cellophane, between the slices of bread, is the Blue Mauritius Stamp.

Rene takes out a tweezers and diamond tissue paper. Don Frye passes Rene a jeweler’s loupe. Pinching the stamp delicately with the tweezers, Rene holds it up and examines it. The dark-blue, primitive nature of the 1847 image of Queen Victoria on the Two Pence Stamp reads, ‘Post Office’. He runs his fingertips lightly over the stamp and tastes his fingers. Smiling, he nods as to its authenticity, places it in the diamond tissue paper and slips it in his alligator billfold.

“Documentation beats conversation,” Blanco grins. His ten-ringed fingers flick, “Now...where is it?”

Rene’s head motions outside, “It’s in the back of the army truck that brought us.” Rene cocks his head with respect, “How did you manage that?”

“The Cuban Army, while it’s got an ironic sense of history...”

Blanco grins, "also embraces creative capitalism." Blanco eyes Rene's diamond pinky ring. "Wanna' sell it?"

Rene shakes his head no. "It was my grandfather's."

Don Frye notices more Barbudos outside and elbows Rene. Rene asks Blanco, "How do we get out of here safely?"

"The same way you got in."

"What about the bandits?"

"Don't worry, amigo," Blanco slaps Rene on the back, "*We* are the banditos." He goes outside to examine Rene's side of the barter.

Armed Cuban soldiers throw off the tarp covering the back of their infantry truck. Blanco's eyes go wide seeing the luminescent, pearl-white 1912 Hispano-Suiza. "The barbaric Spanish conquerors came here..." he spits on the ground, "decapitated the Indians and soon thereafter enslaved half a million Africans. And just when the African slaves learned how to machete their aristocratic landowners, you Americans flooded our country with your crime syndicate. And then," he eyeballs Rene, "your CIA killed our Che Guevara."

Don Frye flashes a look to Rene that it's time to leave.

Winding himself up, Blanco's crazed eyes threaten to change his and Rene's deal. He climbs aboard the Hispano-Suiza and smells the leather of the driver's seat. "Fuck it, I got what I want." He unzips his zipper, "A hundred years ago, Spain's bony-ass King, Alphonso XIII, the butcher of Spain, slipped away from his royal palace and fled his country in this car." Blanco urinates out the side of the car, "Now I'm pissing out of it." He pulls the tarp back further and looks down at the car. "Where's my wheels?"

Rene looks at the sordid crowd. "When we're home safe, they're home safe."

"Whew..." Blanco zips up, "I was holding that for a hundred years. My friend..." Blanco jumps down, "if I didn't trust you, I would have had you killed the moment you set foot on our Cuban soil." Blanco pulls an ass-wrinkled envelope out of his pocket, "Your competitor wanted me to give you this instead of the real one."

Rene looks inside the envelope. He smirks seeing the counterfeit Blue Mauritius stamp. "It's good work."

Blanco motions for more.

"The wheels and spare tire are on my boat."

"Okay. What do you want me to do with the stamp?"

Rene hands back the bogus stamp. Walking out, Rene turns, "Mail it to me."

Back at the harbor, they board Rene's boat. Blanco carefully loads the Hispano-Suiza's red-spoked wheels into the army truck, and eyes Rene's mega-yacht, "How fast will she go?"

Rene studies Blanco's gaze as it drifts to the Cuban Border Patrol boats docked in the harbor. "Seventy knots. Flat out, that's about a hundred miles per hour."

Blanco looks at Tibron. Gauging, Tibron rubs his beard and then nods. Blanco simpers, "You're fine. Stay low."

"Stay low...?" Don Frye stares at Rene as Blanco spins on his heels and leaves. "What's that supposed to mean?"

Rene rushes to get the boat ready. He calls out to his crew, "Fire her up!"

Rene's phone rings. It's his informant, Pascali Debartolo. "How'd I do boss?"

Rene's eyes squint as he thinks. He can't fight a smile. "Make Andre happy. Tell Andre Pope I fell for it."

Don Frye and Rene grin.

Looking at his boat's captain, Rene whirls his hand in a circle. The three-man, Israeli Army trained crew goes to their stations. The detonation of 17,000 horsepower ignites. Turbine engines shoot water into the air as the high-speed mega-yacht roars out of Havana.

Across the harbor, two Cuban Border Patrol boats fire up and take off after it. The crack, crack, crack of fired canons echo in the air as mortar shells whiz across the yacht's deck. Don Frye shelters Rene. Shock waves of up-shooting water spray on the sides of the Wally 118's carbon fiber bow. The boat rocks with the volleys.

The super-yacht's turbo-charged propulsion system kicks in at thirty knots. Howling across the water, its bow propelled up over the waves, Rene's yacht shoots ahead. The chase soon becomes futile -- the heavy Cuban Border Patrol boats are no match for the Wally 118's raw speed. As the super-yacht flies out of Cuban waters, the border patrol boats keep firing.

Don Frye watches the shells drop short. "It's a good thing the Banana Republic only has access to banana boats."

TEN

A wild-haired, Pakistani limo driver is taking a conservatively dressed Saira, in a navy pant suit and belted, white trench coat, to the airport. Constantly looking back in the mirror, studying her unique facial features, the driver wants to ask her ethnic background, but instead makes easy conversation, "Christie's must really like you."

Trying to focus her excitement, checking her purse, fumbling through papers, Saira finds her Christie's itinerary and asks, "What airline am I flying?"

Fluffing his pompadour of hair in the mirror, the driver smiles, "You're not." He points to a private runway. "That's your plane."

Saira checks her itinerary again. It does say 'Paris, France'.

The driver jerks to a stop, rushes out and opens Saira's door.

As Saira ascends the jet's stairs, she looks back for the limo driver. He's gone. Holding her breath, Saira steps aboard a glistening, sleek, white private jet.

"Good morning, Ms. DuFour," a flight attendant's smile greets Saira's sigh of relief at being on the right plane, "right this way."

Saira looks for the other passengers. There are none. Anxious, she's chatty. "I'm so excited, I couldn't sleep all night. Paris has always been my dream ever since I was a little girl." She looks to the attendant, "We are going there, right?"

The flight attendant gives up half a smile, "Yes."

As Saira gets settled in the plush, over-sized leather seat, the pilot's voice comes on over the intercom. "Good morning, ladies and gentleman." Saira looks behind her, she's alone and the plane's door is closing. "Make sure your seatbelts are securely fastened..." the pilot's voice animates with élan, "this baby can fly."

Saira nervously offers a smile as the attendant watches her buckle up. Turbines blast on. In seconds, the jet screams off the runway and in less than two thousand feet is airborne. Holding onto the armrests, Saira's pushed back in the seat.

"Now..." the captain's voice soothes, "just relax. Your flight will be six-and-a-half hours of floating through cream."

Saira's look questions the flight attendant as she goes by. She gives no response.

"The weather in Paris," as the captain speaks, intercom static obscures his voice, "is picture perfect at seventy-five degrees and balmy. For those of you going shopping, Paris is home to the best fashions and great collectibles. You can find those hard to get milk bottles from Sussex, Mongolian harnesses, plastic Jesuses, gilded Eiffel Towers, and coveted Betty Boop dolls." Covering her mouth, Saira starts to crack up but contains herself seeing the flight attendant's subdued serious professionalism in serving her bottled water and a croissant. The captain continues, "For our art aficionados, a scenic river boat tour along the Seine offers the best discount art bargains."

Saira mumbles, "Christie's wouldn't want me to miss that."

The attendant comes over. "Ms. DuFour, did you need something?"

"No." Saira shakes her head, "Nothing, thank you."

Saira looks up waiting on the ceiling's speakers. No more words. Fidgeting, just as Saira finally settles in, the pilot continues, "And for those of you traveling to Paris for a romantic getaway...."

Saira stares at the attendant. The attendant is stone-faced.

"For those independent thinkers who believe in synchronicity, serendipity, and fate. Anything is possible in Paris. The next man you see may be your one and only."

Dressed in a tailored pilot's coat and captain's hash-marked flight hat, Rene exits the cockpit. He comes straight for Saira. Her head drops as she closes her eyes in disbelief. Smiling, he stops next to her. She takes off her glasses and neatly folds them in their case, "Am I being hijacked?"

"Au contraire, Mon Cherie," Rene sits down next to her, "you're being courted."

The jet slices through nighttime clouds.

Rene is sleeping next to Saira in a dark cabin. Saira awakens and takes it all in. She turns on her overhead light and studies Rene. He turns toward her but remains asleep. Saira notices a slight straight-razor shaving cut on his cheekbone.

Amused, she smiles and turns off the light.

ELEVEN

Amongst the frenetic clamor of jackhammers, arcing cranes, and the myriad of trucks fueling the constant reconstruction of what was once the southeast Paris railway yards, Rene walks serenely along the Seine River past the futuristic Paris Rive Gauche development. An antiseptically white-coated, thick-bespectacled, animated Pakistani research biochemist from the French Red Cross, Dr. Akbar Sharif, hurry-steps next to Rene accompanying him on the excursion. "Who said Paris can't adapt."

Rene smiles, "Is that them?" He points up ahead, where a group of fifty, white-shirted, East Indian children, with doctor's stethoscopes around their necks, are being escorted out of a renovated flour mill now containing the neo-classical façade of the newly re-built Paris Center for Immunology Research.

"Yes, yes, of course," Dr. Akbar Sharif answers and continues enjoying his own self-styled architectural tour. "Mr. Sorrell, this was a stale wasteland until your donation." His open palm displays the array of buttoned-up, boxy, glass-and-steel office buildings, cutting-edge apartments, and cleverly converted industrial structures amid an asparagus patch of cranes, concrete mixers, and forklifts. "Of course, in our always opinionated city, some people criticized us and opted for more parks, but Paris is like a zoo. People come in all different shapes, sizes, and blood types. A zoo can be interesting if you organize it well." Excited, the biochemist takes off his glasses to clean them. His eyes twinkle up at Rene. "Thanks to you, Mr. Sorrell, we have shown we can modernize Paris and the practice of biochemistry." He shades his eyes from the sun and points where the fifty children are headed, "And to connect it all, we built the world's longest pedestrian bridge." Elbowing Rene, Akbar Sharif dances his furry eyebrows, "And our kids will be able to say they rocked it."

Rene turns his attention to a 1,000-foot, figure-eight-shaped bridge standing without any pilings due to the architectural artistry of intersecting its tensioned steel and suspension system.

Dr. Sharif beams, "Are you ready for the children's thrill ride?" He waves to a team of engineers guiding the children at the base of the steel bridge. Sharif blows a whistle. Rene smiles as the fifty, petite, dark-skinned East Indian children march in synchronized unison onto the bridge's oak planks. Akbar Sharif continues, "The Eiffel Company made it in their factory, it crossed Paris on a barge, and it was hoisted in two hours. It's amazing isn't it, it's called the Passarelle Simone de Beauvoir Bridge. We French like to give things majestic names."

"Sure," Rene shakes his head hastening him on. "Tell me about the children." Rene watches as the children position themselves in the center of the bridge.

Dr. Sharif gloats, "We've brought them from all over. Pakistan, India, Punjab, The Philippines, Indonesia, Sri Lanka, Singapore -- wherever we could find them." He double-steps to keep up with Rene, "You've indemnified all of their lives." Dr. Sharif blows his whistle. Raising their hands above their heads, the children sway from side-to-side. As the bridge gets wobbling, their laughter is wildly contagious. Rene lights up. Sharif carefully monitors the seconds on his stopwatch and then blows his whistle once more. The children all drop to seated positions, with their legs crossed. Sharif points at the structural engineers. "Now, they measure the time it takes the bridge to stop moving. The shorter the time, the more effective the support dampers."

Bending his forefinger against his thumb, the engineer flashes the perfect sign. Sharif puts his arm around Rene. Rene edges away from his touch. Sharif explains, "This was their present for undergoing two days of research tests."

Rene gets lost in the children's laughter, "Think they'll remember it?"

"Forever."

TWELVE

A light, dry, Parisian late summer wind blowing in through the open windows of his black Silver Spur Bentley, finds Don Frye, in jeans, a Crimson Tide football bomber jacket, and his Stetson, waiting in front of the Four Seasons George V Hotel.

A spring in her step, Saira comes out of the beveled-glass doors of the hotel and waves at Don Frye. Before she makes it to the car, he opens the back door for her. Seeing no Rene, Saira pauses before getting in, "And my cordial hijacker?"

"Business."

As the Bentley turns down the tree-lined Avenue des Champs-Elysees, Don Frye looks back in the mirror at Saira. Leaning forward on the edge of her seat, her head turning left-then-right not to miss a thing, she soaks up the city. He catches her eyes, "Welcome to Paris." Mesmerized, Saira can't stop smiling. Peeking through the pockets of greenery, she studies the throngs of tourists rushing to a myriad of fashion's superstores.

Circling around the Arc de Triomphe, Don Frye dodges the mass of mini cars whizzing by, switching from lane to lane to enter any of the connecting twelve avenues. "Here, they call this a round-about." He scoffs, "I call it a circle jerk."

Saira catches his eyes. He shrugs apology for his words.

He takes her for a scenic tour of Paris and turns down The Right Bank of the Seine. Crossing an old wooden bridge, Don Frye purposefully enters an aging quarter of Paris called Le Marais. Mansions deserted by the Parisian elite of the eighteenth century still remain. Bookstores and restaurants boasting Hebrew posters and storefront signs herald a different world. The streets narrow as they pass by cracked houses surviving the century. Driving down Rue des Tournelles, Don Frye's eyes hang on an imposing, florid, Romanesque synagogue with Moorish echoes. Tablets of the Law join with the Paris City Coat of Arms crowning the pediment. He pauses in front of it. "Rene's grandfather took us here years ago when we visited him for the first time." He studies Saira in his mirror, "This is where his people came from." He marvels at the old temple, "We sat squeezed in between hundreds of old people in these incredible cast iron galleries designed by the guy ten years before he built the Eiffel Tower."

"Gustave Eiffel?"

"Yep."

Saira studies the temple, "I didn't know Rene was Jewish."

"Neither does he," Don Frye smiles. "His grandfather, Simone Sorrell, definitely was. It meant nothing to his father. He was outside on the phone the whole time. Rene was the precious only grandchild...but his grandfather was a stubborn old timer and a heavy hitter in the banking business and couldn't bear to leave his Paris. Rene's father brought him to New York when he was six. Then three years later, everything changed."

"So...who raised him after the accident?"

"His grandfather and..." he beams, "my parents. We lived in the coach house. Rene moved us into the big house and wouldn't let us leave. Half the time he slept on the floor with my dog next to the fireplace in my room." Spying on her in the mirror, Don Frye watches Saira smile. The Bentley leaves the Rue des Tournelles' old sector. "The big baby cried every night for almost a year."

"Cried?"

"My father eventually found a way to get him to stop."

Hanging on his every word, Saira's beckoning hand implores him to continue.

"Every Sunday afternoon, my father would take a different

convertible out of the garage, and we would all cuddle up in the front. We'd put the top down, fly down the highway, sing, and feel the wind kiss us."

"Sing? Sing what?"

Don Frye searches around in his flight bag next to him and takes out a disc. He sticks it in the Bentley's dash. As *Handy Man* plays, he harmonizes with James Taylor's words, *"Hey girls, won't you gather around."* His voice drops lower as he croons, *"Yeah baby, I'm your handy man."* As he continues, Saira covers her mouth with amusement. *"I'm handy with love and I'm no fool. Fixing broken hearts I know that I truly can."* Looking back in the mirror, Don Frye dips his sunglasses. *"If your broken heart should need repair, ohhhh darlinnnnn'..."* he hams it up and holds the note, *"I'm the man to see."* He reaches back and grabs Saira's hand to sing along with him.

She gives in and does. They harmonize. *"Come-ah, come-ah, come-ah, come. Yeah, yeah, yeah."*

Saira and he crack up.

THIRTEEN

Sitting in the window, Saira stares out at the last flush of a Paris sunset. A ripple of rain blows as evening starts. Alone in her hotel room, a sole vanilla candle flickers in the background. Bundled up in her George V Four Seasons white terry cloth robe and teal silk pajamas, she listens to Michael Buble sing *Home* in her earphones as she paints her toenails magenta. Watching night's flow of red taillights fusing up the Champs-Elysees, down past the Arc de Triomphe to the Eiffel Tower, Saira daydreams.

She stares at the phone on the desk. She goes over to it and dials the operator.

"Oui, Ms. DuFour?"

"Do I have any messages?"

"No, you do not. Is there anything I can help you with?"

Saira sighs, "No. Well…." She picks up the room service menu from the desk, looks at the prices and then decides against it. "No, thank you. Good night."

"Bonne nuit a toi aussi."

Twenty minutes later a knock startles Saira. She darts to the front hall mirror. "One second," she calls out. Adjusting the collar of her robe higher, she checks herself out. Unlocking the door, she turns back to the mirror. Taking off her glasses, she let's her hair down. She peeks through the peephole. It's room service.

"Bonsoir madame." Holding a vase of long-stemmed, white cymbidium orchids, a room service waiter, in a black waistcoat and bow tie, wheels a silver cart into Saira's room. He holds out the vase, "Where would you like this?"

Saira points to the desk. "There will be fine."

The waiter sets up the elegantly appointed table. The pop of champagne turns Saira around from smelling the orchids.

"Christie's paid for all this?"

"No…." The waiter fights a wry smile. "It's compliments of Monsieur Sorrell."

Clutching the neck of her robe, Saira goes to her door and opens it. As the waiter fights a snicker, she peeks down the hallway. It's empty.

"Ahhmm," reaching inside of his coat, the waiter hands a small envelope to Saira.

Saira opens up the envelope and takes out a card. It reads, 'Enjoy your privacy'.

The waiter stands at attention. "Will there be anything else, Ms. DuFour?" Saira goes for her purse. He holds his hand up. "It's all taken care of. Bonne soiree."

"Thank you again." Saira walks him out. "Good night."

Her client lists, Christie's catalogues, glossy object d'art photos, and research charts before her, she prepares for the Paris art auction. Lifting her glass of champagne, Saira looks at the white-faced orchids and melancholically toasts an imaginary partner across from her, "To our first night in Paris." She shrugs and sighs. A fork in one hand, a financial chart in the other, Saira enjoys her meal. Sipping the last of her champagne, she leaves the table, smells the orchids one more time, walks over to her bed and props up her pillows. Sitting up, Saira's eyes drift to the phone on the desk. It's still not blinking.

She falls asleep half-propped up on her stack of pillows.

As an August noon Paris sun kiss dries the wet streets with sultry warm air, Saira strolls aimlessly down the Champs-Elysees. Window shopping in a navy-blue skirt suit, white collarless shirt, and blue and white-capped heels, Saira's arm swings her white patent-leather purse as she strolls past magnificent shops devoted to perfume, purses, shoes -- and even exotic automobiles. She stares at an East Indian family all holding hands as they cross a street. The proud father cradles the smallest child in his arms. Across the boulevard, a young European couple leans on a lamppost and kisses.

Saira enters one of Paris's hidden covered passageways.

Her eyes go wide staring at the breathtaking chandeliers hanging from the gilded, arched-skylight ceiling of the Galerie Vivienne designer shops. A short way down the gallery, Saira hesitates at the entrance of the side-by-side doorways of an art gallery and the Chanel boutique. Something catches her eye. Chanel wins out.

Inside the store, a short-hair-bobbed, perfectly appointed, elderly saleswoman approaches, "Oui mademoiselle?"

Saira points at a hat in the window. "May I see the blue one, s'il vous plait."

The saleswoman smiles, goes into the back and brings out a pastel hatbox.

Taking off her glasses, letting her hair down and smoothing it back, Saira tries on a perfectly shaped, navy-blue, wide-brimmed, straw capeline hat. Turning all angles in the mirror, Saira revels in it. She holds it out hesitantly, "How much is this?"

"You have very good taste," the elderly clerk answers. "It's perfect for a refined girl like you." The woman subtly flashes Saira the price tag.

The cost beyond her means, Saira disappointedly smiles, "Thank you very much."

The clerk tries to keep her there. "Possibly something a little less dramatic?"

"No," Saira's touch lingers over it a last time. "If I'm ever getting a hat in Paris, it's got to look like that. Well...another time," Saira turns, looks back and leaves. Outside, her eyes catch the handsome profile of a dark-haired, well-dressed man window-shopping across the street. Squinting through the passerbys, she thinks its Rene. She starts to waive as he turns around.

It's not Rene. Seeing her wave, the man smiles.

Saira goes to an outdoor café and stands in line, waiting to be seated. Looking around, she soaks up everything. The cosmopolitan chic and European faces intrigue her.

After she's seated, the waiter comes over. "There's a gentleman who'd like to buy you lunch." He points to the crowded line of people waiting at the front. The dark-haired man waves back.

Saira uncomfortably smiles, "Tell him thank you very much, but no thank you."

"Madame, s'il vous plait." The waiter doesn't leave. "He was very insistent."

A tall, leggy blonde, with shopping bags dangling from each arm, kisses the well-dressed, dark-haired man in line. As they leave, through the empty space in the line, Saira spots a black-helmeted man in dark sunglasses, black leather, boots, and blue jeans on a Ducati motto GP motorcycle. Rene dips his sunglasses.

Saira can't fight smiling, but doesn't get up.

Rene spins a tire-smoking, donut-wheelie on the motorcycle. The crowd all stares at Saira waiting on her response.

She gets up and walks over to Rene, "Do you always get what you want?"

Rene smiles and pats the back seat.

The motorcycle does an arcing waltz through the French countryside. On back, holding on tight, Saira's arms are around Rene's chest. Adeptly shifting gears, Rene courts her with the Ducatti's primal sound, precision turns, and brute speed. As they approach the Seine River, the motorcycle stretches to board Europe's longest suspension bridge. Accelerating as they climb the steep span, Rene smiles feeling Saira hold him tighter. Reaching midway across, he slows down and stops, allowing Saira to take in the breathtaking view of the Pont de Tancarville. They both share a quiet moment. Noticing her arms are still grasping Rene, Saira self-consciously lets go. Rene's foot stomps the Ducatti back on.

As a dull-grey mist rolls over the French countryside, Rene's motorcycle winds down a long, tree-lined cul-de-sac. At the end of the road, Saira sees a picnic set up on a patch of fine French grass. Turquoise- and white-striped cushions rest atop an orange blanket. A white wicker basket sits in the center. Stark bone china plates, sterling silverware for two, with Baccarat crystal flutes nearby, stand ready for the chilling wine. Saira whispers in Rene's ear, "How did you pull this off, Mr. Sorrell?"

Don Frye steps out from behind a tree. "Man discovered fire," his voice booms, "and Southern Fried chicken begat civilization." From behind his back, Don Frye withdraws a black cast-iron skillet, "It ain't the fiddle, it's the fiddler. Are you ready to witness the art of fried chicken?"

Rene helps Saira off the motorcycle. He unzips his black leather and sits down on a cushion. He pats the blanket for Saira to sit. As she does, Rene opens the wicker basket and withdraws a pastel hatbox. "Everyone should have something to remember a trip." He gives the hatbox to Saira.

Her hands freeze opening it. She looks up at Rene in a moment of amazement. Opening the hatbox, she lifts out the navy-blue, wide-brimmed straw hat she couldn't afford.

Rene beams, "Happy Paris."

Seeing she's speechless, Don Frye intervenes, "Lemonade, beer, or champagne?"

Saira takes off her glasses, lets her hair down and tries on the hat. "Mr. Sorrell," She leans over to Rene and whispers, "What am I going to do with you?" She kisses him, "Thank you."

Don Frye dons his apron, "Who's hungry? Raise your hand?" As Rene and Saira do, Don Frye walks away and prepares the fryer.

"So," Rene leans in, "how long are you going to keep calling me Mr. Sorrell?"

Saira tucks the hat back in its tissue and goads him, "Until I know you better."

"Alright," Rene pulls her cushion closer to him, "what do you want to know?"

Saira half-laughs, "I don't know where to start. Everything." Her hands take in the lavish picnic setting, "Why?"

Rene baits her, "If you have to ask, you can't handle it."

Saira folds her hands across her chest, "I can handle it." Their eyes lock. Her hands go out, "I know nothing about you." Rene's look defies her. "Okay..." Saira speaks first, "what's your profession?"

Rene enjoys a moment of silent exaltation. "I have none."

"Trust fund baby, huh?" Saira raises her eyebrows waiting.

"Started out that way. My father had a textile empire and aspirations for me that were typical of his world. It was kind of a suit of close-fitting clothes that he had put together for me since birth." He smiles, "I always try do the opposite of what people expect of me."

"So," Saira persists, "planes, Bentleys, motorcycles, office buildings, rare paintings...?"

"I have simple tastes. I am always satisfied with the best."

"So what is it...? You're a gangster?" She holds his stare, "How'd you do it, Mr. Sorrell? You were smart and bought cute little Internet stocks in the nineties?"

"Hardly. I just took a lesson from Harry Winston." Rene's knows he's got her locked on. He enjoys the attention. "As a child, Harry Winston got a quarter from his father and bought a shiny stone at a flea market and later sold it for eight hundred dollars." He smiles, "As many millions in stones that Harry Winston accumulated, whenever he walked around, he still had to have a pocket full of diamonds to jingle in his hand. He had to keep a token of his past close," Rene shrugs, "as a reminder."

Saira hangs on him waiting for more. He complies.

"As a child walking the streets of New York, I was disturbed by the smoke escaping out of the cracks in the street."

"The subway steam?"

He nods. "I thought it was gas. I figured it was underground everywhere. As an adult, I just found a way to open the cracks. When all my contemporaries were investing in conventional speculation like the stock market, commodities, and real estate, I bought up cheap land. Swamps, marshes, landfills, abandoned coal, oil, and fossil fields all over the world." Realizing how much he's revealing, Rene looks at Don Frye to see if he's watching. He is. Rene shrugs at Don Frye and continues, "Then I hired the brightest Quants..." he explains, "scientists to take advantage of the technological breakthroughs in horizontal drilling and seismic survey data enabling the industry to evaluate geological formations in three dimension."

"Three dimension?"

"It's like looking at a Cat Scan versus a regular X-ray." He shrugs feigning modesty, "I guess you could say I own a lot of natural gas. It was the ultimate clean investment."

"Mr. Sorrell, you're what they call an environmental anomaly." Saira rubs it in Rene's face, "Cars, planes, boats...."

"Who said I had a boat?"

Don Frye brings over crystal flutes with drinks on a silver platter. Saira looks up at him, "You always have his back, don't you?"

Don Frye half-smiles, "He gets cranky when he doesn't eat. Rene's idea of roughing it is slow room service." He eases her up and takes her over to the fryer. "Are you ready to receive the secret?" Don Frye guides Saira's hand as she picks up the chicken with a pair of tongs. Saira steals a look back at Rene. Don Frye notices. Don Frye assuages her; "I've never seen him like this before."

Saira's eyes hold his for the truth.

Don Frye smiles and nods. He dips the edge of the chicken in the oil to gage the sizzle. He holds Saira's eyes and instructs, "If the oil sizzles, its ready." He takes the tongs and gently moves the pieces around, “You have to pretend their babies taking a bath.”

Rene, Don Frye, and Saira enjoy the feast.

After the meal, when Don Frye moves away to read a book under a tree, Rene resorts to comfortable domain. “We need a game plan for tomorrow’s auction.

“For the Double Lucky Charm?” Saira interjects.

Rene nods. “A necklace of twenty-seven beads made from the most translucent emerald green jade ever mined.” His voice elevates to exhilaration, “I’ve hunted it for years. But there will be a lot of competition. The Russians and Asians will be there. The new Russian art collectors all own banks and hate to be beaten. And when they acquire their art, they like to horde it in offshore warehouses in impregnable darkened rooms.”

“And the Asians?”

“The Asians,” he laughs with respect, “believe one can put a price on gold but jade is priceless. On top of that, they’re convinced it has magical healing powers for the possessor and they’ll go to any end to hunt it.”

“So,” Saira asks, “is it true that five hundred diggers toiled for months to clear a mountain in Burma to unearth three stones of jade the size of marbles?”

“Yes, but those little marbles were worth almost a million dollars each. The diggers even had virgins wading through the river alongside the mountain to attract the gems to the surface.” He looks into her, “To this day, Chinese brides drink out of a jade cup during the confirmation of their wedding vows. But my favorite is the emperor who was buried in a suit of jade to assure his immortality.” He grins, “Think we can find his tomb?” Rene leans in, “Here’s what we’re going to do tomorrow….”

As Rene mentors her, Saira takes Rene in from head-to-toe, studying him as he tells her his strategy. In the distance, Don Frye smiles seeing Saira soak up Rene’s lessons on acquiring art.

FOURTEEN

A fully transparent, massive cloud of swirling glass panels, resembling a gigantic cocoon soaring over the trees of Bois de Boulogne's park, is the site for the long awaited Christie's Paris art auction. The new Louis Vuitton glass museum makes the Louvre look staid. Inside, bidders are wall-to-wall as Christie's France Auction House emerges on the Paris art market scene. French retail tycoons vie with Europe's richest. Chinese billionaires struggle with Middle East oil barons and ministers. Vodka moguls bully Russian oligarchs. Everyone is jockeying for coveted seat placement close to the stage.

Andre Pope is the first row, right in front of the auctioneer. Rene's seat, number eight -- right next to him, is empty. Seeing the auctioneer approach, Andre stands and looks for his arch competitor.

Along the walls, there's a flurry among the bank of phone stalls. Christie's multi-linguistic operators field phones lighting up with anxious international bidders waiting for the auction to start. Not at her Christie's post, Saira is nowhere to be seen.

A hush goes over the crowd as the auctioneer takes the stage. He walks back-and-forth holding up the evening's prized item. Voices still as halogen lights illuminate the viridescence of The Double Lucky Charm jade necklace. The auction starts.

As the packed auditorium's sophisticated art aficionados traditionally bid with subtle signals to the auctioneer: an eyebrow twitch, a nod, the twirl of a finger, the tilt of a fountain pen, and a removal of one's glasses -- way in the back, a turbaned-woman in Punjabi dress fervidly waives her paddle, upping each bid.

Art world etiquette forbidding standing up for a better view, the A-listers at the front are stuck craning their necks for a look at the mysterious, turbaned, olive-skinned, dark sunglass-adorned, double body-guarded bidder, seated in the last row which is considered as Siberia in the art world's hierarchy. Adorned in gold necklaces, bangles, and rings, dressed in a pearl-buttoned, semi-transparent, turquoise kameez with slit seams, over golden-weaved salwar trousers whose legs are wide at the top and narrow at the bottom, the loose garment covers her physique but certainly not her physical appeal.

The competition is relentless.

Making vigorous use of his paddle, fanning the face of others in front of him, a stoop-shouldered, dyed black-haired, rough-hewn Russian oligarch's lieutenant, resembling a boxer with a wide-spread broken nose, tries to out bid the turbaned woman. With each of the Russian's bids, Christie's phone bids counter volleying bids from a female Chinese paper-recycling billionaire. It's like a Wimbledon match with three players fighting it out. The collectors looking to the bank of phones, to the Russian, and then to the back of the room at the mystery woman. Left, right, back. Left, right, back. Each time it meaning half a million dollars more.

The Chinese phone bidder and the Russian fight to the end, ultimately conceding to the turbaned, mystery woman's unrelenting pace. As the hammer finally comes down, the crowd applauds the mysterious bidder. As private art dealers scurry to swarm her, Christie's dispatches staffers to surround the winning bidder. While the floor supervisor carries the jade beads, Andre Pope trails closely behind him. The Christie's supervisor hands the beads to the turbaned bidder. She takes off her dark sunglasses.

It's Saira.

Andre pushes through past the floor supervisor.

Saira's guards block him. "That's okay," Saira raises a hand, stopping them. Andre approaches her as the beads are being passed.

Andre looks to the floor supervisor, "May I?"

The floor supervisor looks at Saira. She nods her ascent.

Andre takes the beads, places them around Saira's neck, kisses her cheeks, and winks, “Now, you’re double lucky.”

Saira pulls up her silk-embroidered duplatta scarf, covers her head, turns on her heels and exits with her guards trailing.

FIFTEEN

As Saira walks down Boulevard du Montparnasse's narrow corridor past colorful café's and pocket bistros, she shows her map's red-circled spot to a thin, vividly-dressed Frenchman walking a scruffy three-legged dog, "Excusez vous, ou est le restaurant?"

Rising his eyebrow, the Frenchman points down the street at Brasserie Coupole, "It's not a restaurant, but a brasserie. Bon jour," he bids as he leaves, stopping a short distance later to watch Saira's determined high heel gait.

Saira spots the restaurant's green awnings, cuts across the street and enters. As a puffed-up maitre d', wearing a white carnation on his lapel, escorts Saira through the crowd, past the elaborate wall mosaic panels, decorated mirrors, and belle époque chandeliers of the most famous brasserie in Paris, he directs her towards the second slightly smaller room in the back.

As they pass a table, a hand catches Saira's.

Andre Pope stops her, "You won't be happy in the back room." Saira lights up seeing Andre. Elegant, in a black turtle-neck and black and grey plaid cashmere jacket, Andre sweeps his French beret while bowing his head, "Mademoiselle, won't join me?"

The maitre d' smirks and disappears.

"Well..." Saira looks around, "I don't want to intrude."

Andre gently tugs her hand guiding her to sit across from him. His outstretched arms take in the beautifully painted walls, decorated mirrors and Veronese-painted ceiling, and then rests his eyes obviously on Saira, "I love being surrounded by beauty."

"Mr. Pope, I do believe you're flirting with me."

Andre leans forward, "I couldn't let the mysterious Punjabi princess be exiled to the back. The best dining experience is in the front. You get to discreetly people-watch everybody in the mirrors." He continues to charm her, "Brasserie Coupole follows a strict hierarchy. Regulars and VIPS are seated in the first room, locals in the second room in the back…and tourists," he winks, "are sent upstairs."

"Looks like you rate."

Andre shakes his head no. "I speak perfect French." He rubs his thumb and forefinger together symbolizing money.

They both smile.

Andre sits back, "This is my favorite place in Paris. Coca Cola is banished. Using cell phones is forbidden. The food is like your grandmother's, the wine is fair, and the waiters are rude and inattentive as ever. But…" he smiles as he opens his arms, "look around." Andre scans the walls covered with the paintings of once-struggling artists. "You are surrounded by some of the greatest examples of sheer brilliance and beauty that most people never see." He points, "Monet, Chagall, Balthus, and Picasso were all regulars here and painted the walls to pay for their meals."

A waiter approaches and speaks to them in French.

Saira's accent is perfect. "Pied de Porc Farci Grille and for desert, Millefeuille."

Andre smiles to himself while studying her unusual, yet perfect, proportions of her face. As the waiter leaves, he asks, "Are your parents from France?"

Saira takes a moment to answer. "My mother is from Punjab." Saira notices that makes Andre smile. "And my father…" she takes a breath, "was French-Moroccan and worked for the American Embassy. And...I'm afraid that's all I know about him."

Andre winces, "I'm sorry, I didn't mean to…"

Saira interrupts, “And you, Mr. Pope?”

“Please,” his hand touches hers, “It’s Andre.”

“Oui,” she titters. “Why did you smile when I said Punjab?”

“We’re almost kin. My grandfather was a British officer stationed in Bombay when he married my grandmother.” He enjoys saying it, “They say she was Indian nobility.”

“Do you have any children?”

Andre nods and holds up one finger.

“Do you get to see him?”

“Occasionally.”

An attractive, voluptuous Alsatian woman walks by and openly flirts with Andre. He politely nods.

Saira gets a kick out of it. “So…” she prods, “do you have someone special?”

Andre’s slow to answer, “I did.” Nostalgically, he takes in the whole brasserie, “We used to come here.” He changes the subject, “What about you and Rene?”

Saira surrenders a shrug and coquettish smile. She dodges his examining gaze, “You two seem to have a lot in common.”

“We both love perfection.” Head in his palm, Andre makes it plain he means her, “And the opportunities there are to find it.” He tries to read her, “There’s no one like Rene. He’s quite spoiled, you know.” His eyes twinkle, “But, that’s the secret of his attraction.”

Saira teases, “You know what they say….”

“It takes one to know one.”

They both snicker.

As the waiter brings a breadbasket, Andre moves the white rose, sitting in a slender glass bottle, from the center of the table. His finger jerks. Pricked by a thorn, it instantly bleeds. His chair shoves back as he stands. His face pales.

"What happened?"

In a second, Andre withdraws a pre-packaged bandage from his inside coat pocket and has got the finger instantly wrapped. He breathes slower and deeper.

Saira leans in, "Are you okay?"

Andre sits down and laughs at himself. "Forgive me, I'm a little hemaphobic."

Saira reaches out and tenderly cradles the bandaged finger. "Are you sure?"

Andre nods, and smiles, quickly making light of it. "So..." he looks around and leans in, "he's told you about it, hasn't he?"

She looks clueless, "What?"

Andre whispers, "The stamp." He waits as the waiter places down their meals. After he's left, Andre continues with a whisper, "The Blue Mauritius."

Saira enjoys the distraction and whispers back adorably, "They left that one out of our education at The Art Institute."

As they dine, Andre captivates her with his story, "Joseph Barnard, a young English stowaway on a French vessel bound for Madagascar, was discovered and thrown off on this tiny little pip-squeak island in the Indian Ocean." He tilts his head, "Mauritius. He married there and while earning a living as an engraver and miniature painter, in 1847, he got the fortuitous chance to engrave the profile of Queen Victoria on Mauritius's first stamp. Five hundred were printed, most of which were used on invitations sent out by the wife of the Governor of Mauritius for his Inaugural Ball. But," he holds up a bread stick, "there were no formal instructions for the apprentice engraver. To the great fortune of stamp collectors forever..." he bites the bread stick, "the stamp was engraved with an error. They were all engraved 'Post Office' instead of 'Post Paid'."

"How many are left in existence?"

Andre holds up only three fingers. He smiles with the irony, "The one I gave Rene's mother forty years ago before they got so valuable. And...two others that Rene and I are both competing for."

"So, you've known Rene all his life?"

"When he was a child, I spent every holiday and Thanksgiving with he and his parents." He shrugs with self-assurance, "I like to think that I know him better than anyone." He smiles paternally and slides his card to her. "If you ever need me."

SIXTEEN

The newly formed Federal Democratic Republic of Nepal's national anthem plays as a line of seven black Range Rovers approach the royal palace's gates. Nepalese children waive their new country's crimson and blue pennant flag as the motorcade enters the palace grounds and proceeds through a line of armed guards. Seated in the back of one of the bulletproof cars, Don Frye leans into Rene. "Let's not bring up our snatching the past king's Hispano-Suiza roadster. Their country is still on the terrorist list."

"We didn't snatch it, we helped him liquidate some of his debts." Rene's eyes go wide as he goads Don Frye, "I heard they still have the Mercedes that Hitler gave to the King's father."

An armed guard turns around from the front seat and glares.

"Shhhh," Don Frye elbows Rene, "I'm not kidding. Not a word. They don't have much of a sense of humor here. It was the Crown Prince that killed the King and the rest of the Royal Family six years ago because he accused him of misbehaving at a party."

"Misbehaving?"

Don Frye nods solemnly.

"What happened to the Crown Prince?"

"The military swore him in as King."

As the procession of cars pulls up to the prodigious gold- and silver-latticed door of the Kathmandu Royal Palace, black-uniformed guards with machine guns encircle the Range Rovers. Rene looks back as Nepalese uniformed soldiers scurry to close the palace gates.

The guards escort Rene and Don Frye out of the car. "But..." Rene turns to Don Frye, "now it's a democracy."

Don Frye looks around as they walk between two columns of expressionless guards in military uniform. "At the moment."

"That's why we're here." Rene puts arm around Don Frye, "We're helping out."

Inside the sprawling, pink pagoda-roofed, former palace of the dethroned King of Nepal, Rene stands on stage, dressed in a black tuxedo and bow tie, before hundreds of Nepalese children in multi-colored uniforms and vibrant Nepali hats. Burnished gold walls boast centuries of collected treasures -- the gifts of kings and despots, from Hitler to Mussolini. While armed guards are stationed at every door and along the sumptuous walls, Buddhist priests and nuns thread through the cross-legged children sitting on the marble floor. Gone are the monarchy's deposed King, his family flag and unfortunately, the air conditioning that comforted the Royal Family. The entire palace's latticed- and grilled-windows are propped open, while huge fans whirl, re-circulating the baking Kathmandu mid-summer air. Don Frye, sitting along the back wall with decked-out Nepalese dignitaries in traditional black Nepali hats, fans himself with his black Stetson.

All eyes are on Rene as he starts. "Once upon a time there was this white-haired, master craftsman from Mandalay...and every morning when he entered his workshop, he stubbed his toe on a lump of stone which he had used for years as a doorstop."

The kids' laughter fills the room.

Rene revels in the kid's joy. "Cursing with pain, the master craftsman flung the stone out the window. Then..." Rene smiles drawing them in, "one day, his young..." Rene steals a peek at the children; "dark-skinned apprentice stood over it, looked more carefully at the bothersome stone and decided to dig it out of the mud so he could practice his cutting skills. The young boy lifted it up and set his grinding machine to it." Rene's hands animate circles in the air, "Clouds of crystal dust flew in the air and..." his pause holds the kid's attention, "a small, shiny emerald-green patch emerged. The master rushed over, took the stone and helped his apprentice create..." Rene's words come out slowly revealing it like a secret to a magic trick, "a necklace of twenty-seven perfect imperial jade beads." Rene withdraws the string of jade beads from behind his red pocket square.

The kids all oooohhh!

Holding the beads up, he parades them. "And that rock's emerald patch became the most expensive piece of jade in the world."

The nun's hands wave commanding appreciation. Children flutter the room with their orchestrated applause.

"So…." Rene looks out over the rows of uniformed children, "What's the moral of the story?"

Total silence.

"The lesson is…." Rene smiles at the bronzed, little stoic faces, "*Those that see the invisible, can do the impossible.* And…" he smiles holding their stares, "anyone is capable of magic."

Two armed soldiers approach Rene. He winks at Don Frye. Rene hands the soldiers the necklace of jade, "This is my gift to the Democracy of Nepal."

The applause flutters again and again and stops.

"Sir…." A button-nosed girl in a purple wrap raises her hand, "What are the beads worth?"

The sweltering air seems to stand still.

Rene smiles and then pauses. "Over ten million dollars."

A brazen, elfin, eight-year-old boy lights up, stands and asks, "What's it like to be rich?"

A nun rushes over. Her yank-down chastises him.

An uncomfortable stillness muzzles the grand hall. For the first time Rene hears the grating scrape of the huge fans churning behind him. In the brief silence the humidity seems oppressive. Uncharacteristically, Rene takes off his tuxedo, hangs it on the mike, and stands in his white shirt and bow tie. "I'm sorry…." He strains to hear the child over the fans whorl, "What's your question?"

The child looks to the nun standing over him. She looks to Rene. Rene's nod is accepting. The child stands up again. His voice chirps louder this time, "What's it like to be rich?"

Rene is silent. His head drops as he considers the question. He undoes his bow tie. "I asked myself that same question when I looked in the mirror this morning." His head slightly shakes off the ironic realization. "What's it like...?" Drawing a lifetime of breath, Rene's eyes search the grandeur of the palace. His voice resounds as his hands go out to the grand room's riches, "It all disappears."

Rene takes his jacket off the microphone stand and walks out. Don Frye follows him and stops at the feet of the child. He puts his Stetson on the boy's head.

SEVENTEEN

As the Bombardier jet slices through the nighttime clouds over a midnight-blue Atlantic Ocean, Saira sits alone and stares out the window as she bids Paris adieu. She looks at her straw capeline hat on the empty seat next to her. Her fingers trace over it. A simper comes over her face as she thinks about her Punjabi princess outfit and winning bid in the Paris auction. She sighs and sits back in her seat pondering how she'll ever adjust back to the life of a Christie's phone clerk. As the jet's powerful engines hum, she pulls up her RS-monogrammed cashmere blanket and her eyes close.

A few hours later, she awakes to find Rene sitting next to her. He has a brown paper bag in his lap. "Did I wake you?"

She shakes her head dreamily no.

Rene tucks the blanket up over her shoulders. "Do you need anything? Are you hungry?" He sees her glance at the bag. " No," he smiles, "that's not your dinner." His eyes go wide as he leans in close to her and whispers, "It's grab bag surprise night."

Saira wipes the sleep from her eyes. "Excuse me?"

A little full of himself, Rene folds his arms and sits back in the jet's cushy leather seat. His demeanor oozes charm and total confidence. "I want to ask you something." Rene waits for her Oh My God What Could Be Next Stare. She gives it to him.

"I want to take you on a date."

Saira shakes her head with his craziness. Her hands take in the plane. It all.

"No, Ms. DuFour. Not on Christie's time." He stares into her, "Just you and I." His eyes twinkle as he holds out the paper bag, "Grab bag night."

Saira's eyes squint at him assessing his hypnotic madness.

"Saira," his alchemy in full tilt, Rene's laser focus and mellifluous tone woos her, "inside the bag are a bunch of little pieces of folded paper. Each piece of paper has a destination on it." He holds the bag in his palm. His slowly spoken words bewitch her, "Reach in. Wherever you pick in the world, we'll go."

Her hand in mid-air, Saira hesitates. Rene nods. As if under a spell, Saira sticks her hand in the bag. Her fingers swish around the paper pieces. She pulls one out but is afraid to open it.

"Go ahead, Saira..." he coaxes her, "open it."

She does. Unfolding the slip of paper, she reads it aloud, "Los Cabos, Mexico." Saira slowly offers it to Rene. Her eyes seek his and ask for validation.

"Good choice," Rene smirks. He looks at the slip, "Looks like we're going to The One and Only Palmilla." He takes the bag. "Where heaven embraces the earth."

"When...?" Saira asks entranced.

"Right now," Rene answers her. He picks up the intercom phone and instructs Don Frye, "Los Cabos, Mexico."

The jet arcs south for its destination.

Witnessing the Pacific Ocean marry the Sea of Cortez, their jet declines, skimming down across the Baja Peninsula's eleven hundred mile strip of land to its tip. Mesmerized, Saira stares out the window at a verdant oasis. Azure waters greet mountainous desert. As its wheels screech down on smoldering asphalt, the jet lands at a machine gun guarded private runway tucked away in a corner of Cabo St. Lucas. Rene, Saira, and Don Frye are chauffeured in a black Hummer down a two-lane highway surrounded by uninhabited wilderness.

As the sun sets painting everything burnt-gold, their driver enters the guarded, massive, twelve-foot, whitewashed gates of The One and Only Palmilla Resort. Swaying gigantic palm trees, hugging huge birds of paradise, line the meticulously manicured burgundy and yellow floral route of the main driveway to the stone-tiered lobby. When the Hummer stops, a welcoming staff of five men and a woman, dressed in bronze-buttoned, double-breasted, beige waistcoats with crimson sashes, place their hands over their hearts and slightly bow.

Rene hops out. Holding the door for Saira, he helps her down from the Hummer. "I got you an ocean front room. I'm sure you'll love it." The staff quickly gathers up Saira's luggage as Rene gets back in the Hummer. Standing alone, Saira tries to comprehend Rene's agenda. Rene lets the window down. "Bye." He gives up nothing but his charming smile, "You'll be picked up for dinner at eight."

"Picked up?"

Rene smiles.

Saira watches Rene leave. As she looks at the staff with bewilderment, a cart pulls up. The cart's driver, a stumpy, over-tanned Ecuadorian, introduces himself as he puts his hand over his heart and bows, "Ms. DuFour, I'm your butler, Raul." After escorting her up two flights to the top floor of the villa, Raul passes his card, "I'm on call twenty-four hours whenever you need me."

Saira pushes large wooden doors open to reveal a sumptuous suite. Slipping off her shoes, she wiggles her toes amidst the chocolate leather strands of the woven rug that covers the earthen-tiled floor. Her fingers touch the wrought iron screens, delicately patterned like lace, separating each of the rooms. She goes out on the veranda, explores the wrap-around view, and plops down on the cushy mattress of the oversized, awning-striped sun bed. Staring out at the endless turquoise water, Saira leans back and sighs. As her eyes focus on the revolving hurricane fan overhead, she takes out her phone and calls her roommate. It rings, but no answer. Saira leaves a message. "Tookie, pick up, pick up. Help. I'm in Mexico. I'm at the One and Only Palmilla Resort. On a date. It's breathtaking. And sooooo romantic. Call me, I need your advice."

Saira changes into four ounces of brief pink cotton that's pretending to be a running outfit. Running in the baked air along the beach's rocky shore past thatched huts and sun-bleached white row-boats up on the sand, she pushes her stride harder as she stretches to gauge the vast length of the Palmilla Resort. She's out of breath; it's longer than she thought. As the rising tide diverts her path further from the water's whooshing edge, Saira's cell phone rings.

It's Tookie on speakerphone.

Tookie's processing her hair and has it wrapped up in her make-believe Peter Pan hat made out of the day's New York Times headlines. At the kitchen table, watercolor painting her self-designed royalty playing cards, she puts down her paintbrush and in her British accent queries, "Why are you out of breath?" Her hand on her hip, Tookie teases, changing her tone to sarcastic, "And why are you answering the phone when you're doing what you're doing?"

"I'm running along the beach at sunset."

"Princess DuFour…." Tookie pushes the sarcasm, "It must be nice. It's been freezing all weekend in Manhattan." She breathes out. "I can see my breath in the apartment. Running along the beach...? I thought you were in Paris."

"Well, I was sleeping and he put this bag in my lap."

Tookie interjects, "While you two were in bed?"

"No, silly. Listen. On the plane back, he had me stick my hand in…"

Tookie interrupts again, "I'll bet."

"Stop. Inside a paper bag were slips of paper with different cities on them. And whatever city I picked…." She sighs, "Never mind. I'll explain later. Now, we're on a date."

"I should hope so. He's flying your pretty little ass all over the world. Now you're in Mexico? God, I love that guy's style. Is the tall, good-looking cowboy with him? Do you have the right clothes? Palmilla is ultra-posh. What're you going to wear?"

Saira reviews only having business attire hanging in the closet, "I don't know." Her mind turns to her Parisian hatbox, "A hat."

"A hat...?" Tookie retorts, "This guy always looks like he came to town to kill a guy." Tookie resumes painting her cards, "Listen to your gypsy fortune-telling roommate, I'll bet he's going to have a dress sent to your room. By the way, *where is* Mr. Bentley?"

"Somewhere...." Saira humors herself, "Somewhere else."

"What do you mean somewhere else? You have your own room?"

"Ah-huh. I...I..." Saira lifts up one track shoe after another as a she dodges the bubbling, rising tide, "I don't know what to do."

"What to do?" Tookie's voice grabs Saira through the phone. "Agghhh!" she exhales with frustration as she bites the stick of her paintbrush. "I tell you what to do." Her British accent elevates, "Stop sleeping in different rooms."

"Tookie...." Saira laments that all too familiar insecurity. "I'm serious. I don't know what to do."

"Excuse me?" Tookie's tone changes to irritated. "Saira, I don't want to hear it. I've heard it all before."

Saira is silent. She looks down at her soaked track shoes. Seeing the rising high tide, she recedes back into the shadowy cave of a nearby hill and sits on a rock. "Everything's been perfect. But I...I guess I don't know...I don't know how to be happy."

Tookie exhales in frustration, "He's made you happier in three weeks than anyone in your whole life. "Saira DuFour...." Her words come one-at-a-time like to a child, "Don't-you-ruin-this." Her tone turns chiding, "You two haven't done it yet, have you?"

"No..." Saira answers miffed, "nothing."

"What do mean *nothing*?"

Saira attempts to extricate herself, "Physical intimacy's not the problem. It's just that, Saira edges away from the depth of the cave, "I'm afraid he doesn't really know me. If he did, what would he see? Rene Sorrell has such a rich, layered history. I'm a whisper in a burned-down orphanage." The sun sets and so does the last bit of light. Saira looks at the dark walls of the cave, "If I disappeared this minute, there's no proof of my existence."

Tookie throws in her hand of cards; "I can't take it any more. Stop it! Stop looking for ways to sabotage your happiness. Saira DuFour, if you mess this up..." Tookie picks up the handset to the speakerphone, points into it and admonishes her, "I swear to God I'll throw your clothes and entire butterfly collection in the street."

Holding the phone, Saira leaves the mouth of the cave.

Tookie rapid-fire drills, "Do you love him? Have you ever felt this way before?"

Saira doesn't answer.

Tookie limits her silence, "You can't think about it."

Saira becomes a fading shape on the beach.

As Saira vaults up the steps to the top floor of her room, she slowly opens the door. Saira drops her head, "Oh Tookie, Tookie, why are you always right?" She holds her hands to her mouth and stares. Inside, laid out on the bed is a magnificent peridot-green, full-length, grape-skin tight, evening dress with a deep V plunging neck-line. While rising pleats intersect across the waist, foot-long tassels inch down from the thighs to the hem. Matching open-toed, five-inch, Christian Louboutin heels rest at the foot of the bed.

"Yeah Tookie," holding the dress against her body, Saira steps in front of the room's full-length mirror and answers softly, "I think I may love him."

EIGHTEEN

As a full moon ripples on water, Rene sits naked in a lotus position on a rock that seems to float on a grey-black drape of starless sky seamed at the horizon by rippling cerulean water. Flanked on either side of him are the wide spread leaves of palm trees resting over the rocks defining the sides of his infinity pool. The murky shadow of his bare back and buttocks mirrors back in the tranquil flatness of his infinity pool as the white-capped whooshing spray of waves splash up twenty feet from beneath him on the shore. Open palms resting on his knees, Rene sits bare, meditating out over the infinite darkness. Moments later, he turns and dives back into his pool.

Dripping wet, Rene steps into his glass fortress.

Standing in front of a full-length mirror, dressed in the vest coat of a tissue-fine, three-piece, black silk suit with a grey stripe, Rene runs his hand through his silver-laced, swept back hair. As his hand loops the black and grey polka-dotted tie around his spread collar, Sea Island cotton, white shirt, he stops to look at himself. Thinking about what lies ahead of him, he takes a deep breath.

Putting on his suit coat, Rene makes his mirror face and is distracted by the uneven points of his dusty-rose pocket square. He fluffs it perfectly, and picks up two, magnificent, Lima bean-sized, ruby cufflinks. Slipping the cufflinks into his cuffs, he holds them out making sure they are exposing the exact same amount of white. His finger running over the suede panels of his jewelry drawer, he chooses the perfect watch for the occasion, making sure it's one Saira has never seen. On his wrist he drapes his eighteen-karat white gold, Grand Complication Patek Philippe Minute Repeater.

Rene stares at his nightstand's global Atomic clock and waits to set his watch. A red digital flash announces the time. He sets the time precisely to the nanosecond.

NINETEEN

As night falls, Saira descends from her room. Every few steps down, candles illuminate her way. An elegant, open black carriage, drawn by two white horses, is at the bottom of the steps. Standing alongside the carriage, her tuxedoed-butler, Raul, waits to assist her. As she approaches, Raul's right hand covers his heart as he slightly bows his head and opens the carriage door. Leaving the entrance of the Palmilla Resort, torches, set in huge cement vases, blaze against the blackness of the night. Candles flickering in over-sized hurricane glasses mark the carriage's path every twenty feet.

As Saira's carriage slowly clops along the winding, candle-illuminated, shadowy path of Palmilla's lush grounds, Don Frye jumps in. He's in a t-shirt and jeans, and of course, a cowboy hat. Raul quickly turns back. Don Frye taps Raul's head with the Stetson, "Keep your eyes on the road lit'l buddy."

Don Frye lightly kisses Saira's cheek and presents her with the gardenia blossom he picked, "Good evening, darlin'." Saira smells it and chuckles as Don Frye puts his ostrich cowboy boots up on the rail and relaxes back. "Don't worry, pumpkin, I'm not going to dinner. I have this little senorita in Cabo San Lucas that makes a mean heuvos ranchero," he shrugs, "and she's got these two little girls that just won't leave my side. Matter-of-fact if Rene knew I was here he would kill me." He checks out her dress, "Wow." He snuggles elbow-to-elbow with her trying to disguise the reason he's there, "I just wanted to see if the dress fit. We got it in Paris. Mr. Perfectionist had me carry him to seven stores until he got the color he wanted."

Saira smiles, but then sighs.

"What…?" Don Frye shakes his head pretending he's not understanding. He's aware of her trepidation, but attempts to distract her. "You don't like the dress?"

"No, that's not it. I absolutely love it. I never had anything like it. It's just…." Saira straightens the folds of the dress and looks up as the clouds part the full moon exposing it. "It's just that we're…." She sighs, "He's so accomplished. And I'm so…."

"What?"

Looking at the dress, Saira fishes for time. She insecurely shrugs, "Different. He's got everything. And, I'm..." she looks down at the dress and struggles to smile, "Cinderella in a borrowed dress."

Don Frye delicately holds her chin, "No, you're not." He waits until she feels his affection, "You're family." Slowly clopping ahead on immaculate pavement, past manicured grounds, the carriage steadily climbs the hill. Wishing he could stay to see Saira's reaction a little further up the road, Don Frye eyes the bend of large palms coming up. "It's time for me to disappear." He jumps out.

"Wait." Saira steps down as the carriage stops. She comes over to him and hugs him, "Thank you, Don Frye." She turns, modeling the dress, "Do you really like it?"

"Darlin', you're gonna' give his heart a limp." He steps into the dark foliage, disappears, "Oh…" and then comes back out, "forgive me for cutting your bike lock?"

Saira nods, fighting smiling. "How'd you do it?"

He gives her his trademark moustache smile as he turns away, "Cupid's arrow."

In less than a minute, from the saddle of the hill, the carriage turns the wide bend and Saira goes into shock. On the top of the hill is an unearthly, flickering, incandescent glow. Hanging on an edge with overwhelming views of 360 degrees of surrounding water, rolling green mountains and the homes set in them, is a candle-lit, spectacular house enveloped with glass skin. Transparent, it appears to be drowning in water, the ocean, and dark-blue sky.

A layer of mirroring water covers the edges of the rectangular glass box stretching it out to unite the surface with the endlessness of the Atlantic Ocean. The roof contains a succession of stainless-steel louvers and slats opening the ceiling to the moonlit night. Within the transparency of glass and water, the walls, ceiling, and floors, are all glass floating in a symmetry in which everything dissolves. And so does the furniture within -- tables, chairs, couches, and the master bed's frame, are all steel-supported glass.

Dressed to kill, Rene is waiting at the door.

Saira does a curtsy bow, "Thank you for the dress, Mr. Sorrell," she says playfully, "it really wasn't necessary, but..." Saira whispers, softly holding and kissing his cheek, "I love it."

Rene lingers in her touch, smelling, storing her scent in his memory. Taking her hand, he guides her in. "It's the most beautiful you've ever looked."

Saira waits for Rene to walk ahead of her so she can check him out. She smiles and relinquishes under her breath, "You too."

Trying to be cool, Saira can't help but be overwhelmed by the house and its pure dramatic spectacle. "Oh my God," sneaks out. She's speechless. Rene lets her have a moment as he takes her in. Saira spins with the view, "I guess I did pretty good on grab bag night. Do you have other homes like this?"

"Other homes...not like this." He guides her through his glass castle. "I had it built so as to allow all boundaries to disappear." He takes her hand, "Enclosure without containment." Rene turns from the view and stares into her, "No frozen space of walls where the subject is cut off from the object." Shrugging, he laughs, making fun of himself, "At least that's what the architect told me."

Rene steps out on the veranda. A balmy wind kicks up.

The porous steel screens flutter like lotus petals. Waves slap the rocks below with kisses. Rene puts his arm around Saira as they step near the unguarded edge. "I've never shared this house with another sole." He stares out at the never-ending darkness, "It's like gazing into the mirror of eternity. Isn't it?"

She nods. Unsure of what to say, she extemporizes, "So, what's with you and possessing only one-of-a-kind?"

Rene doesn't answer.

He takes her hand and guides her back inside the glass house. A hundred flickering vanilla candles set the stage for the fathomless darkness behind. "I love the scent of vanilla, don't you?"

"It's my favorite," Saira coos. As they walk, Saira enjoys checking out Rene's black velvet, RS-monogrammed loafers. She doesn't let him see her amusement.

Inhaling the scent, Rene takes a deep breath and closes his eyes; "Madagascar vanilla began my love affair with fragrance. As a child, it was what my mother wore when she kissed me good night." His guard exposed, he sarcastically unravels, "The scent stayed with me all night. Long after she departed for cocktails and dancing."

Saira stops walking and stares at him.

Rene assesses his unexpected vulnerability and shifts mental gears. Guiding her through the house's transparent rooms, his mood mercurially changes. "Speaking of dancing…." Rene flicks a switch and the soulful croon of Barry White's words, *"You're the First, The Last, My Everything,"* fills the boundless walls.

Saira looks at him, assessing his zany mood swing.

Rene repeats what Don Frye told him, "A true gentleman has got to know how to dance." He takes her hand and tries to dance. He's not very good -- but, he gets her into his arms. Animated, Rene lights up singing to the verse, "*I know there's only one like you, there's no way they could have made two.*" He drops his voice sounding like Don Frye, "*Just you and me baby.*"

Saira cracks up. His effort works -- it breaks the tension.

As they enter the dining room, Saira looks at what's on the table and challenges Rene, "Okay. Where's Don Frye hiding? Did he do this?" Saira marvels at how Rene has procured an exquisite meal of Punjabi origin. Saira walks around the table surveying sterling plates of sizzling chicken tandori, rolled masala dosa on a banana palm leaf, idlis with coconut chutney, mata paneer, saffron rice, makke di roti, and crispy naan bread with mango chutney sauce. Mango lassi sits in a chilled crystal flute accompanying each place setting. Alongside it, is a white masala tea in a cup. For desert, is roz mali.

Saira just shakes her head and tries to fathom what's next.

Rene, a master of poise, seats Saira. Seated at an oval table, whose floor beneath it is illuminated, Rene and Saira dine. The clouds shift allowing the moon to spotlight different features of their faces with an infinite game of ephemeral reflections. They take turns revealing themselves.

Rene defies her, "Ask me anything."

"Okay...." Saira reflects, "Tell me about that oil painting hanging in your dressing room in New York. It's mesmerizing."

Rene is caught off guard. "It was..." he fumbles, "it was right before I lost my...." He stops himself.

Saira touches his arm, "I'm sorry, I didn't mean to...."

Rene puts his hand on hers, "Don't be, it was a lifetime ago. I've been alone my whole life."

"Except for Don Frye," Saira corrects him.

"Except for Don Frye." He smiles, "What else?"

"Okay." Saira lightens the mood, "Why a parrot?"

"They only talk back what you teach them."

Saira gives him a look. "What's with the perfect shaving?"

"I'm tired of half-shaved men trying to look primal. They always look like they're posing for model comps or showing up late."

Smiling, she leans in with scrutiny, "Okay, now a tougher one. Why have you never brought anyone here? Why are you single?"

"That's two questions." Rene leans back and folds his arms, "I'd rather spend all of my life wanting something I didn't have, than having something I didn't want."

"That's your mantra, Mr. Sorrell." She can't help blurt it out, "*That's total bull.*"

He laughs. Rene leans forward, beckoning her with his hands, "Come on, is that the best you can do?"

"What's with you collecting only one-of-a-kind?"

"When something is priceless, you can ask any price for it."

Saira glares at him over his totally evasive answer. She shakes her head with amusement, "There's much more to it than that."

Her defiant spirit amuses Rene. He pushes his plate away, "Now, it's my turn. My Punjabi princess, tell me about your family. What was life like as a child?"

"It was perfect. It was all the things you'd want your child to grow up with. Loving, diverse, challenged with constant knowledge, my mother always there making me safe, and my father reading me to bed every night. Even though I wasn't the typical blonde, blue-eyed child; and my adoring mother was a devout Hindu with a temple in the house; and my handsome French-Moroccan father was a Protestant whose family never acknowledged my existence -- I was raised as the most spoiled, constantly indulged, and revered child in my family."

Rene squints assessing her truthfulness.

Quiet mounting exasperation consumes Saira. She leans forward toward Rene, "Well, that's what I wished I could tell you." She studies his scrutiny. "But there is a Punjabi saying: Raising a daughter is like watering your neighbor's garden." Her look defies him, "None of what I said is true."

Rene is unfazed. He looks at her with sincere devotion.

She's mystified by it. "Say something."

"For me," he stares adoration, "character is born from the management of life's disappointments -- and you've done it masterfully. Saira DuFour, I think you're a serene, breathtaking beauty with dynamic stillness. Yet the most beautiful women are rarely the most enchanting." Rene tries baiting her and waits for a response.

Saira gives him nothing.

Rene stares into her, "But one like you, an intellectual beauty unswayed by the foible of vanity. One whose glamour is born from true character, integrity, and grace -- possesses it all."

Hearing Rene's affection forces her to return to herself. The balance of Saira's self-love and self-hate won't let her trust it. Saira can't help herself, she unravels, "I've got a father who never saw me, and probably never even knew about me. And a mother who thought I was disposable. My entire childhood, I never saw two happy parents. I went from orphanage to foster family back to the next orphanage. All I learned from my childhood was an amalgam of different languages and dialects. Hell was other people."

"Ooh, I think the shrinks call that a little misanthropic."

"Mr. Sorrell.... " Saira moves her pointer finger up-and-down, "Don't throw stones if you live in a glass house."

Rene waits and then smiles. "We're perfect for each other."

"Prove it."

"In much the same way as you, I lost my parents. And, I never forgave the world for it." His face loses all guile. "When I acquire something that is one-of-a-kind -- I hold it for all of eternity. The family I never had is replaced by the power to have," he raises one finger, "the power to possess one thing for infinity. If it's the one and only remaining Ming vase...I have it for all of its past life and all of its future...to the exclusion of everyone else in the world. Whether it is a nanosecond or forever, I've possessed it. I have possessed it."

"But that's all an illusion. "

"No." Rene takes the saltshaker's top off and spills grains of salt on the glass of the table. His fingers flick almost all the salt away. Carefully, he makes sure to leave only six grains. He separates one to the top, one to the bottom, one to the left, and one to the right. He points to the grain at the top, "That's as high as the heavens and universe will go." He points to the grain on the bottom, "That's as low as the bottom of the sea." His finger moves to the grain on the left, "That's as far back as time immemorial." His finger slides all the way right, “That’s as far into the future as possible.” He squeezes the last two grains into the middle, next to each other, “Saira Dufour, that’s you and me -- time has no measurement for us. Here we are, exactly in the same place and at the same moment,” his arms extend out to the night’s vast darkness, “in all this majesty of an eternity of time.” He leans in closer, “I’m not going to waste it.” Rene wipes all of the salt off the table and folds his hands, “I have a confession to make.”

Saira holds her breath waiting for her bubble to burst.

“I stacked the deck.” He plays with her silence. “Every piece of paper in the grab bag read Los Cabos, Mexico.”

“Why?”

“I wanted you here.” Rene studies her lift her glass of water. As Saira is about to drink, she pulls back and puts the glass down. She spills the water out over the table. There’s something in one of the ice cubes. Rene goes over to her with a pitcher of hot water. He pours the water on the ice cubes. A platinum ring, with a dazzling diamond the size of a grape, is frozen in one of the cubes. It dissolves.

Rene picks up the diamond ring.

Holding it out before her, he gets down on his knees, “This is not the largest diamond in the world, and it’s not the most expensive. But, the world’s most renowned diamond cutter cut it for an Ethiopian Emperor’s Queen. After the diamond cutter finished it, the Emperor didn’t want the most perfectly faceted diamond in the world to ever be duplicated -- he had the diamond cutter killed. It’s the finest cut diamond ever.” Rene puts the ring in his palm, “It’s the one and only in existence. Saira...” he stares intensely into her eyes as he slips the ring on her finger, “I’m asking you to marry me.”

Saira draws a deep breath and hesitates.

Rene hides the agony in his eyes and turns his head down to the side. He lifts up a charming smile and rebounds with humor, “Don’t worry, it’s not cursed. I kept the ring in my safe for fifteen years.” He touches the ring and moves it around, “It fits perfectly. That counts for something.”

Saira’s world races. Her eyes flutter. Words escape her.

"Saira, sweetheart, I know we've only known each other for twenty-nine days. But, I've spent a lifetime learning to recognize what I want." He exhales. "I want to spend the rest of my life with you."

Saira stares at the ring and takes a deep breath. "Rene, I..."

Rene kisses her lips ever so sweetly comforting her. "Shhh," he whispers, tenderly cupping her face. "I know...I know I'm being unfair. I'm expecting you to feel, to decide as fast as I do." Rene stares into her, waiting. Hoping for a glimmer of surrender.

Saira remains mute.

"That's alright," Rene exudes poise and confidence. "Stay with me one night. Tonight." He kisses her forehead, "Tell me tomorrow."

TWENTY

Floating upon white sheets, under weightless layers of ivory duvet quilts covering a magnificent glass bed; all is dark, as Rene wakes up next to Saira in his glass house. Lying on his back, his arms crossed over his chest, he turns his gaze upon her. She is unstirred. Emotional, he turns away. Face-to-face with the immensity of the dark-blue sea and seamless sky, Rene gazes into his mirror of eternity.

Then it happens. An amber line rifles across the horizon. Seeing it, Rene's eyes flutter and close.

Bare-chested, wearing only white linen drawstring pants, Rene slips out of bed. He goes straight to a hidden wall safe. His fingers type in red digital numbers that unlock the safe. He withdraws two things: The fading envelope revered as The Bordeaux Cover with its deep-Blue Mauritius stamp and red one pence stamp side-by-side; and a lone Blue Mauritius stamp, the Cuban-purchased one, wrapped in tissue paper. He lays The Bordeaux Cover envelope out on his desk's glass, tracing his fingertips over it as he did when he was a child. Lifting it to his nose, he smells it. Next, he unfolds the tissue paper of the lone, steel-blue stamp and places it in his palm. Staring at it, he closes his eyes and drops the stamp in a crystal ashtray.

He looks back at a sleeping Saira, strikes a match and sets the stamp on fire. As the lone Blue Mauritius stamp's sides curl with the flame, Rene returns to the bed. His hand reaches into his pocket.

He lays the diamond ring next to Saira on the pillow.

Kneeling next to her, he watches her sleep. He leans in breathing in her essence. A haunting orange ball pushes up against the horizon. The skin of the glass house is tinctured iodine as the day dawns.

Fearful, Rene whispers, “Good morning, baby.”

Saira doesn’t stir.

Rene reaches out to touch her face. His hand stops short and traces the outline of her face without touching her. His head drops. “God…” he sighs, confessing to a sleeping Saira, the world, and himself, “I’ve wasted so much time. I’ve spent a whole life living in this house alone.” His head down, he doesn’t notice that Saira has awoken and is now watching him. Crescents of tears form in his eyes. “I convinced myself I’d built my own eternity. And as far as I looked… I couldn’t find myself.” His hand covers his eyes. “I’ve chased the most coveted, rarest, one-of-a-kind,” he breathes out the pain, “and now…I know my whole life hangs on this moment.” Feeling her stare, Rene slowly lifts his head. “Saira DuFour,” he looks into her soul, “you are my one and only.”

Saira puts her fingers to his lips silencing him. She answers his proposal, “Yes.” She nods her head. “Yes.”

A wall of cobalt-blue lifts its curtain. As a burning amber ball rises over a blue sheathe of ocean, the glass house’s walls, floors, and ceiling, glow orange. Holding her fingertips softly against his lips, Rene savors every nuance of her face. His eyes locked on hers, Rene takes Saira’s fingertip and brushes it by his lips. Starting with her little finger, he opens his mouth, nibbles, kisses and tastes it, and moves on to the next fingertip. All the while, his eyes devouring every inch of the map of her face. Kneeling before her, as the sun covers them with orange, Rene takes Saira’s face in his palms, presses his nose against her forehead and inhales her essence.

Steadily moving down, he draws in the scent of her eyes and moves across one cheekbone to the other and back to her nose. He pauses to nibble it. His lips trace the bow tie folds above her mouth. Then he kisses her deliciously, fully on the lips. He moves to each of the corners of her mouth, lingering, gently biting her top lip, then the lower. Rene guides her out of bed and stands behind her. His hands cradle her face as he tilts it back to kiss her lips. As his kiss endures, his hands graze down over her t-shirt skimming over her breasts. Trailing down, his fingers go beneath her pajama shorts. His palms stretch teasingly over the front of her hipbones and retreat. While landing scores of kisses on the contours of her mouth, cheekbones, eyelids, temples, and ears, his hands slide under her shirt and up her bare skin. His fingertips brush over her nipples and slowly back down again.

He slides off her shirt.

While staying behind her, he covers her breasts with his hands and presses her bare back against his chest. His hands move upward and lift her hair. He leaves slow, wet kisses across the nape of her neck and then down her spine.

Saira's knees falter.

Tugging at the strings of his pants, he undoes them. As his pants fall, Rene guides her around and presses her body against his flesh. He kisses her again, slowly, taking forever to draw his lips away. Undoing the drawstring of her pajamas, he goes inside them and runs his fingers across bare skin. Her shorts slip off. As the rising sun's rays flush the house fiery red, Rene guides her onto the bed.

The brilliance of the sun and its reflection off the water, amber-flash blurs their melding bodies. Kneeling over her naked body, Rene's hands run under the back of her knees, thighs, and around her buttocks. Kissing her lips, his mouth traces down, exploring her breasts, then down her abdomen and between her thighs, touching and caressing every inch of her.

As the sun reaches higher, stronger, brighter, Rene lies on top of Saira and takes her. He again places her hand to his lips. With each slow, protracted thrust into her, he engorges a different finger in his mouth. Holding it in his mouth as Saira sighs, he rhythmically goes deeper inside her. On a golden-orange bed, hot, slow, sensual lovemaking ensues. Anointed and consecrated by the God of the Sun, Rene consumes his future bride.

TWENTY-ONE

The Mexican sun is at its searing peek in the Los Cabos sky. Lying on a turquoise-padded, double-sized lounge partially submerged in the whooshing tide at the shore's edge, Saira and Rene sunbathe, playfully touching fingertips in the ocean's surf. Saira peeks down at her hand. The facets of her ring light up the whole beach. Waves crash over the rocks sending a rush of water. Saira trickles her ring in the whoosh of bubbles.

As a pink and orange sun sets, a tanned Rene and Saira take a late afternoon nap inside the glass house. Lying naked beneath white sheets, Saira wakes up before Rene. She's fascinated. It's her first time watching him sleep. Tiptoeing across the room, lighting a wrought iron candelabra of vanilla candles, Saira studies him. Feeling a shiver, she goes to his closet, dons his coral blazer, and sits, analyzing him as he sleeps. She slides the sheets down a little. Rene stirs. Saira moves back. The sheets expose the curve of shoulders, sinew of his arms, and muscles of his chest. She arranges his hair one way and then another. He doesn't wake. She smirks, gets up and goes to her makeup kit. As Rene sleeps, she paints his toenails coral, steps back and snaps a photo. Saira starts to laugh and covers her mouth.

Showering, staring at his toenails, Rene bellows, "Saira!"

Saira comes skipping from the opposite side of the glass house. Barefoot, a towel wrapped high around her, she finds Rene naked, just as he is stepping out of the open-air rainforest shower. Wrapping a towel around his waist, Rene stops. Saira has a straight razor in one hand and a wad of shaving cream in the other.

"What are you planning to do with that?"

Saira flicks open the razor. "Do you trust me?"

"Have you ever done this before?"

She lathers Rene's face and puts a dot of shaving cream on his sunburned nose. "I've shaved my legs."

"Saira..." his expression turns totally somber, "I don't do well with blood. I hire professionals for these things."

Her fingers holding his chin up, she shaves up his neck, "He loves me." Then she shaves down, "He loves me not."

Getting dressed for the night, Rene sneaks across the suite and snaps a surprise flash photo of Saira sitting naked before her makeup table in a head full of pink rollers.

The next day in paradise finds Rene lying on his back in The One and Only Palmilla's world-class spa. His hair wrapped in a white towel, his eyes are closed as he's getting a micro-thin, 24-karat gold leaf, anti-aging facial. Saira sneaks in, holds her finger to her mouth shushing the attendant, and snaps a picture of Rene's gilded-face.

Beneath a black sky, as waves crash in the background, Rene and Saira, wrapped in a blanket, melt together in front of a fire raging from a pit on the rocky shore. Staring out at the black sea, they hold each other, listening to the crackling fire. Every once in a while, Rene catches Saira sneaking a peek at him. He moves her closer, inhales her sun-kissed scent, and kisses her lips.

The next morning finds Rene out of his control zone. Saira's convinced him to play golf. As a clearly overdressed Rene, in black silk pants, a white voile shirt, and alligator loafers, motors the golf cart toward the first tee, Saira scrutinizes his unease.

Rene notices. "I've done this before."

An ex-golf team player at Berkley, Saira puts a hand on the hip of her pleated, short-skirted golf outfit. "Oh yeah, when?"

Rene rubs his closely shaved chin, "I think it was in high school. And maybe once in college." He shrugs defensively, "I don't like to do things I don't excel at."

After losing the first hole, Rene feels Saira's scrutiny. Trying to ignore her, he swings so hard that he entirely misses the ball. A cramp sticking in his back, Rene painfully tries to stretch it out. Saira falls down laughing.

Golf clubs fly out of a golf cart hitting fairway bumps as Rene chases down a zigzag-running Saira across the golf course.

Mid afternoon, Saira's intent on replicating the black and white Palmilla postcard of a couple kissing in the waves. Stopping on the shoreline, in awe of the crystal-blue water splashing on the rocks, Saira holds out the fairy-tale pose on the postcard and pouts until Rene goes along with her lunacy. Waving over her butler, Raul, Saira shows him the postcard, "Could you please try to capture us like this?"

Raul reluctantly nods. "I can try."

Rene hesitates as sunbathers laugh, watching him trying to keep his loafers out of the rising tide.

Saira tugs him into the water. "I need this to show Tookie."

Raul tries to capture a staged photo of Rene and Saira lying on the beach about to kiss as the ocean's waves edge up the shore. Rene tries to direct the shot, but waves cover them, sloshing them back-and-forth as they crack up with laughter.

Later on that day, Rene's will finally prevails. He gets Saira to go horseback riding. As the sun sets, both dressed in flowing pastel linen, Rene and Saira ride through the oppressive mountainous heat. Rene leads Saira to the bottom of a ravine, revealing his self-designed playground. Entering the shade of a forest, Rene dismounts, guiding Saira's horse to a stone-tiled opening in the foliage. There, amidst over-hanging tropical plants, in the middle of nowhere, exists the contrived flight of Rene Sorrell's fantasy.

Following the narrow-tiled path, Saira takes it all in. Half-finished, surreal, concrete shapes of Rene's subconscious interweave with tall standing trees and bullying plants. Cement spiral stairways rise and go nowhere. Open and closed doors exist with no walls. Three-story, sculpted-pillars support nothing. Tall cylindrical columns contrast moss-covered, bizarre blocks. Swaying beams tilt rooftops. Like in a dream, the forms have no order or design. They simply take shape. Walls collapse onto each other.

"Whose property is this?"

Rene relinquishes a sly smile.

"You built this?"

" I call it..." Rene's hands take in an architect's Gothic and baroque hallucinatory dream unraveling, "the persistence of time."

Saira spins, witnessing the disjointed dwelling Rene designed so that its weight would shatter its walls. "What's it all mean?"

Rene lets her imagination run.

There in the dead stillness, a bird suddenly shrieks. Saira jumps, causing her horse to rear. Rene grabs the reins and hauntingly holds Saira's eyes. Her chest heaving in the thick air, she witnesses an obsessed desire come over Rene.

Saira defies Rene's possession and kicks her horse away.

Rene mounts his horse and chases her. Trotting briskly away, Saira tries to evade him. He catches her. Rene runs his fingers through Saira's flowing hair and teases her, sensually running his hands down her back and under her belt as they trot.

Goading her horse to a gallop, Saira tries to elude him.

Rene takes the challenge seriously. As he catches her, Saira kicks the horse into a gallop through high reeds. The soft wetness of the reeds stains and paints her linen green. A gossamer veil of mountain runoff curtains a pool leading into a rain forest. As they ride through the cool translucent water, the fine spray shears their clothes.

Rene gallops alongside Saira and pulls her onto his horse. He starts kissing her. As they enter the garden's lush greenery, Rene bridles his horse to a walk, dismounts and pulls Saira down on top of him. In the stillness of the jungle, beneath immense walls of lush vegetation, Rene ravishes her on the damp, moss-carpeted earth.

TWENTY-TWO

Sun kissed, her tanned skin glowing, her arms full of Rene's presents, Saira comes back home late to her Lower East Side Manhattan apartment. It's totally dark. As she turns the key and enters, lights flood on. All in pajamas and sweats, her roommates scream as they rush toward her to examine her engagement ring.

Tookie grabs Saira's hand. "Oh-my-God!"

The girls all go crazy and swarm her.

"Jesus!" The freckled-redhead grabs Saira's hand and stares, "I'm bicycling to work everyday from now on."

"Only one month and this guy commits like this. Wow!" The spiked-blonde tugs the ring and tests how snug it fits. "How did he know your exact size? Can I try it on?" Saira's look dissuades her. The blonde winces, "How soon do we have to look for a roommate?"

Saira shrugs casually, "You've got time."

Tookie squints and shoots Saira a displeased look.

The girls hover around Saira waiting for juicy details.

"Ladies...." Saira goes for her bags at the front door, "It's late, we'll have a debriefing tomorrow morning. Okay?"

None of them move.

Saira drags her bags by. "Good night girls."

In flannel pajamas, Saira's in bed, writing in her diary as a headphone-wearing, bubble gum-popping and pizza box-carrying,

Tookie comes in without knocking. Saira quickly closes her diary and tucks it under the covers.

"Not this time, Miss Sabotage," Tookie busts her. "You only write in your diary when things are unresolved." Tookie goes for the diary; Saira tucks it under the sheets with her feet. Tookie sits on the edge of the bed and drills Saira with her eyes, "When you went home with him in his car that first day, you knew what you were doing."

Saira's silent, she opens the pizza box.

Tookie closes it and challenges her, "Only it didn't work. He didn't touch you." Saira gives Tookie a pissed look. Tookie's British accent rubs it in, "They're always too boring, too smooth, too young, too old, too bald, too hairy, uneducated, know-it-all, too short, too tall, unsophisticated, too cocky, or..." Tookie grabs a piece of pizza, "too fast to try get you in bed." Tookie does her jitterbug step, "Only this one didn't touch you. "Ms. DuFour," she bites the pizza, "Everyone looks for someone to love. You look for someone to reject."

Saira grabs her nail polish and they sit on the floor, with the pizza in between. As her fine-boned, ebony hand orchestrates in the air to Andrea Bocelli and Luciano Pavarotti's *La Donna Mobile*, Tookie puts one of the earphones in Saira's ear. Sharing the song and pizza, they take turns painting each other's toes.

"Know what they're singing...?" Tookie rubs it in, "La Donna E Mobile. The woman is fickle..." she dabs the nail polish artfully, "like a feather in the wind." Tookie snatches the diary from under the sheets and flings it across the room, "You've spent your whole life writing about a man you never knew. Let it go."

Saira gets up and goes for the diary.

Tookie yanks the cord stopping her. "Mr. Bentley loves you. Enjoy it."

Saira pulls out her earplug and gets the diary. Putting it on her dresser, she brushes her hair in the mirror. "How does one ever know?"

Tookie's tone is barbed, sarcastic; "I never want to belong to a club that would accept someone like me as a member. That it?"

"I come by it naturally. All my parents had in common was twenty-three minutes of bliss. Maybe less."

"I know..." Tookie mocks her, "and they left you with a lifetime of damage." Tookie spins Saira around, "Mr. French-Moroccan consulate worker, who in one night got a chance to walk out of your mother's life, causing you to live in the past for twenty-eight years -- I'm tired of it." She holds Saira's wrists, "There's an African saying. It matters not much whether the knife cuts the melon, or the melon falls on the knife. In the end, it's the melon that suffers the wound. Stop throwing yourself on the knife."

Saira sighs and turns away from Tookie's scrutiny.

Tookie tugs Saira close, "Listen to someone who *does* love you, you been living your whole life paying them back." She cups Saira's face and smiles assurance, "It's time to leave that all behind."

Saira looks down at her hand.

Tookie lifts Saira's hand and stares at the engagement ring. "Sweetheart, you're going to have the most incredible life with a man that worships the ground you walk on. There's not a woman in the world that doesn't want that." Tookie kisses Saira's cheek, "Stop over-analyzing everything."

TWENTY-THREE

Larger-than-life, centuries old, ceramic soldiers stand guard outside the glass doors of the glazed iridescence of Manhattan's ten-story, terracotta-tiled, jigsaw-windowed Museum of Arts and Design. In the lobby, alongside the museum's signature lollipop columns, stand sandstone elephants with bronzed warriors on gilded seats under pink umbrellas. The museum's grand hall is packed with black tie guests celebrating Christie's Indian Art Auction for the ensuing week.

Waiters in vibrant paper-mache masks, crowned with orange, yellow, and blue turbans, and swaddled in purple silk shawls, force-feed champagne and chicken tikkas to the well-heeled art crowd sitting on cushions emblazoned with a psychedelic map of Mumbai. Crystal adorned cages with green parakeets, and dancing girls in exotic silks and slippers, punctuate the room. In the center of the space are bare-chested holy men, bathing in a pool spouting emerald water, performing rites and chanting, using tiny brass bells and large pearl conches as props. Tikka stalls offer a myriad of silver dishes with every imaginable hue of dye to dot the foreheads of the evening's guests.

Saira, her hair up in a French bun, dressed in the dazzling, peridot-green, tasseled evening dress Rene gave her; and a precocious Tookie, chic, in her self-designed version of a man's black tuxedo with tails, are hosts for the evening's event.

Andre Pope, with a red carnation matching the red bow tie of his black tuxedo, comes over to greet Saira. He kisses her on both cheeks. "You're absolutely glowing." He holds up the diamond ring. "I heard. Congratulations." Andre's eyes take her in as he sighs, "Rene Sorrell is the luckiest man in the world."

As he walks away, Tookie eyes Saira. "You want to tell me who he is?" She looks around, "Speaking of, where's Mr. Bentley?"

Saira perks up and stands a little straighter, "He said it was my night, and he wanted to let me do my thing." Saira shrugs, "Besides, he already saw me in this dress."

Tookie raises her eyebrows, "And out of it."

Sporting a shock of shoulder-length, center-parted, straight white hair, and large, black oval glasses, five-foot-two of flamboyant attitude, Freddy Kim, 44, Christie's International Director of Asian Arts, coaches Saira and Tookie about the night's charity event. "One fifth of the world's population is living on a piece of land the size of Texas. It's called Incredible India. They're the world's fastest growing free market democracy and they've got an appetite to match. Four of the ten richest people on the Forbes World's Billionaires list this year are Indian." He motions Saira and Tookie closer as he sees the museum's glass doors open to an entourage of Sikhs. He notices who has just come in. "That's him." Freddy Kim frenetically gives the signal alerting the orchestra. "Crucial in protocolary respect for Indian royalty is the gun salute." He educates the women, "It starts at nine for lesser ranked royalty and goes up to twenty-one guns. This guy gets the full arsenal."

Half a dozen bass drums pound a welcoming salutation of twenty-one drumbeats.

In a stunning, flowing black tunic with silver and gold brocade outlining its collar, and black silk trousers with a gold-embroidered military stripe down the leg, six-foot-two Maharaja Ravi Rajamar, 36, enters the room. Dark-hued, strongly handsome, with a close-trimmed beard and distinct moustache, penetrating ebony eyes, and his jet black hair covered with a white silk turban, adorned with a magnificent golden stickpin of an onyx-faced prince wearing a diamond- and turquoise-encrusted crown, the maharaja assesses the crowd with the bent blend of royalty and enfant terrible. His falcon-like gaze immediately focuses on Saira in the welcoming line.

Seeing the Maharaja approach, Tookie elbows Saira, "Your mojo is working."

Maharaja Rajmar cuts the line. He kisses Saira's hand while laser-locking her eyes, "I am only going to say this once. You are the most exquisite woman in the room." He walks away.

Having met the others in line waiting on him, the Maharaja returns back to Saira and Tookie. Tookie sees Saira stiffen. As Maharaja Rajmar is about to speak, Tookie tries to lighten the mood. A diplomatically-loose Tookie admires the Maharaja's regal attire, "Your Highness, I love how you dress."

Freddy Kim cringes. "Your Highness, I apologize. She...."

Looking at Tookie's eclectic formal outfit Maharaja Rajmar smiles at her spunk, "We haven't adopted fashion's basic black yet."

Tookie is obvious in staring at his turban's magnificently jeweled pin. Saira elbows Tookie. "Oh my God, please excuse her." Saira attempts discreet humor, "Yes, we think your pin is beautiful."

Maharaja Rajmar reaches to his turban and pulls off it's jeweled pin. His fingers resting on Saira's bare skin, he pins it on the strap of her dress, "The most beautiful things should sit next to the skin." Stunned, Saira is motionless. Excitable, Tookie sneezes. Saira's fingers run over the jewels. She unhooks the pin and offers it back.

The Maharaja steps back. "In our country, it's bad luck to return a gift. Especially with the right hand." He looks at Tookie and charmingly smiles, "And never, ever after someone sneezes."

Saira looks to Mr. Kim for help, he shakes his head not knowing what to do.

Tookie whispers to the Maharaja, "What do you want from my roommate?"

The Maharaja doesn't know whether to be offended or laugh. Ravi Rajmar whispers back, "It's a mistake to ask an Indian what he wants. He wants everything."

The ballroom lights dim.

Rainbow-colored beams of light explode on and crisscross the dance floor. The air is electric as the wild, primitive beat of Buddha-

Bar's *Bless You,* accompanied by the orchestra's snare drums, fills the room. Tookie rescues Saira and pulls her onto the dance floor. Before a towering, azure-blue, paper-mache Taj Mahal, they dance. As the beat gets fiercer, Tookie lets down her black hair and wildly tousles it to the beat. She sees the Maharaja staring at Saira. "He can't stop watching you. Looks my little shy Saira has bloomed." As Saira lets go and dances more liberated with the primal pulse of the music, Tookie takes off Saira's glasses, "See what a good schtup will do."

Saira motions for her glasses back. The music hushes.

Tookie slows down her dancing. She stops entirely.

Saira stares at her, "What…?"

Tookie is silent.

"What?"

Tookie hands the glasses back.

Saira grabs Tookie's hand as she starts to leave, "What're you doing?" Tookie smiles. Saira turns to see the Maharaja behind her.

The orchestra stops, letting the Maharaja speak to Saira. He gets in close to her. "They certainly don't dance like that in Punjab." At a loss for words, Saira is silent. She puts her glasses back on and tucks her hair in. "Ms. DuFour," Ravi Rajmar openly flirts, "how long has it been since you've been back to your home?"

"Not since I won a national scholarship to attend high school in New York." Saira pushes it, "Do they still have the caste system?"

Taking in her spirited audacity, the Maharaja slowly smiles. He nods, "The rich still live well in the midst of the poor."

"In the midst of or because of?"

"It all depends on your perspective." Defying her, his fingers brushing her skin, he adjusts the position of the gold and diamond pin on Saira's dress. "It seems no longer fashionable to speak of the soul of a nation. The spirit of India has endured colonialism, religious strife, the caste system, and corruption, and responded with thousands of years of culture, philosophy, scientific advancements, the largest percent of victories in wars," he smiles bravado, "eighty-three percent... and soon the largest population in the world. Yes, the rich live well in the midst of the poor. But, in sixty short years, we've accomplished the greatest transfer of political power in history. From a small elite to the vast majority of a billion people. But, very few seem to know that because..." he looks at the caliber of the crowd, "most Americans only travel to their own self-styled America within India."

The Maharaja conveys his fancy with a hard look at the band-leader. The music resumes. "May I have the pleasure of dancing with you?" Without waiting for an answer, he takes Saira's hand, holds it against his heart, and begins to dance. He makes it clear he's looking at her engagement ring as he guides Saira closer to the blue Taj Mahal. "Have you ever seen it?"

Saira shakes her head wishfully.

"Moghul Emperor Shah Jahan built the monument for his favorite wife who died giving birth to their fourteenth child. For the next twenty-two years Shah Jahan waged wars and depleted everything in the royal treasury," his head tilts mockingly toward the Taj Mahal mockup, "building his final testimonial of their love." The Maharaja holds her eyes. "Unbridled romantic love can be imprisoning."

As Saira moves away, the Maharaja twirls her closer.

"To put an end to his father's wasteful and reckless extravagance, Shah Jahan was overthrown by his own son and put in jail. The rest of the former Emperor's days were spent overlooking the completed Taj Mahal from behind the bars of his cell."

The song ends.

"At least he finished what he started out to do." She curtsies. "Thank you for the chance to dance with a Maharaja."

The Maharaja kisses her hand and won't let go, "Give me the chance and I'll show you limitless limitation of limits."

TWENTY-FOUR

Walking up the sweeping, art deco-railed, crème marble staircase of his limestone, five-story, neo-Italian Renaissance mansion on the Upper East Side, Rene stares out at the window at the frozen architecture of a Manhattan night's frost covering his garden. Slightly tipsy, holding a Scotch, dressed in a black cashmere, hooded-sweatshirt and matching pants, his fingers trace along the gilded frames of a row of priceless canvasses and stop before the dramatic, cornflower-blue of his most treasured painting. The poetic timelessness of the soulful eyes of Vermeer's Girl with a Pearl Earring leers back at him with the certainty of love sickness.

"Don't be petulant." Rene rattles the ice in his crystal tumbler and takes another swallow of Scotch. "I know, you're not used to sharing me." He sets the tumbler on a sixteenth century Grecian urn. "What's that...?" he raises his hand to his ear, softly asking the ruby-lipped, vestal maiden. "You're right. Who needs the Mona Lisa when I have you." Rene shrugs, holding his hands out in apology, "But a guy only gets to take one girl on a honeymoon." He squints closer into the transparent, elusive colors on the surface. The pearly light of the exquisite interior scene of ordinary life in Vermeer's canvas defies him with a world more perfect than the one he possesses. With a half-hearted smile, he blows a kiss to his adoring muse, "Sweet dreams."

Rene opens the brass-handled, double doors of his master bedroom, walks across the spacious room towards a king-sized, floating grey slab that seems to hang in mid-air. Suspended entirely by magnets, the Dutch architect-designed levitating bed doesn't move in the slightest when he plops down on it. Rene flips a switch.

On the wall across from him, Rembrandt's expansive Blinding of Samson slides to the right revealing a bank of video monitors. Illuminating the screens are the colored images of natural gas fields in a dozen countries. Unconcerned, Rene flips it off.

He gets up, slides back into his velvet slippers, sits on the end of the bed and ponders. Looking up at the skylight, the leaded-panes split the blue ethereal heavens in two. Rene throws his hands up.

He goes straight to the sanctity of his halogen-lit closet. In the sparkling light, Rene stares at himself in his full-length mirror. In the mirror's reflection, his eyes catch the oil painting of him as a child. Rene challenges it with his stare. He slides the painting aside revealing a safe behind it. Opening the safe, he takes out a frayed photograph. Rene stares at the fading picture of his parents coming home with a baby boy wrapped in a blanket. He downs the rest of his Scotch and sits on the floor holding the picture.

After midnight, a tipsier Rene holds the railing as he walks down a flight of stairs. Hearing the murmur of television, he stops at the cracked door of a bedroom. He opens the door. "Are you okay?"

Don Frye, a bowl of popcorn on his lap, nods.

Rene stands quiet, still in the doorway. "Are you sure?" Rene shakes the ice cubes in his drink. "Feel like a little company?"

Staring straight at the television, Don Frye waves Rene in. "You did the right thing tonight. You don't want to overwhelm her."

Rene sits on the window stoop and gazes out. "It's a clear night. No wind."

Absorbed with his movie, Don Frye murmurs, "Ah-huh."

Rene squeaks to the brindle bloodhound puppy sleeping on its back with its legs in the air alongside the crackling fireside. The willful puppy flips up and rushes over, nipping at Rene's pant leg. Rene makes a whirling hand movement above his head, "Beauregard hasn't seen the city from up above." Don Frye looks at Rene and assesses his mood. Rene struggles to free his pants leg from Bo's little spike teeth, "He's a willful one, isn't he?" Rene stares out the window at the early autumn frost on the garden. "Think he'll ever settle down?"

"He's a rare breed. Too soon to tell."

Don Frye gets up and waves Rene to follow him.

Whirling above inky clouds, a futuristic Sikorsky helicopter arcs with hushed speed witnessing a thousand fantasies rush by as Manhattan does its midnight dance. Floating through an empty-vaulted, azure night, the helicopter follows the green tongue of the Hudson River. Pilot Don Frye provides Rene, and the puppy in his lap, a crystal clear aerial view of a fairy tale Lower Manhattan and the stretch of the twinkling support lines of the Brooklyn Bridge. Hanging aloft, hovering above the glossy skyscrapers, the quicksand of countless flickering lights draws the helicopter up the Hudson River and across the canyon of the towering steel turrets of the Financial District. The puppy widely yawns.

"That's okay, boy." Rene pats Bo, "What's night got to do with sleep anyway?"

The orange-hued lights atop the Empire State Building serve as a turning point as Don Frye spins past Fifth Avenue skyscrapers and the Plaza Hotel. He lets the helicopter drift over the dark void of Central Park and roll on to the Upper East Side. Blades whorl as they pass Battery Park and go out towards Ellis Island and The Statute of Liberty. The rich-green, patinated statue transfixes Don Frye, "It's unbelievable. Not even a century of biting salty air or punishing sun has affected her. She's more beautiful than ever."

Pressing his head close to the window, Rene stares down at the lit-up statue. "I love her, Don."

"Yeah." Don Frye stares at Rene with uncertainty. "Saira?"

Rene nods.

Don Frye offers an easy smile, "Me too."

Rene's arms stretch to take in all the world has to offer, "I want to show her it all. Give her everything."

Don Frye's palm eases Rene's reach down. "Easy brother." He looks at Rene with four decades of intimacy, "Baby steps."

Rene exhales and closes his eyes. The steady flutter of the Sikorsky's blades, and the night in its silence comforts Rene. He leans back, trying once again to live an eternity in the single moment.

"Relax." Don Frye smiles. "You're on top of the world."

TWENTY-FIVE

In the last row, behind a packed chapel of parishioners attending the services within the soaring vastness of St. Patrick's Cathedral, Rene Sorrell, in dark glasses and a three-piece, slate, glen plaid suit with his signature splashy pocket square, scans the stark white-marbled walls wondering why not one piece of significant art is present in the chapel. As the New York University Choir sings *Ave Verum Corpus*, peddled keyboards and handstops shutter and pump the controlled volume and timbre of thousands of pipes from the cathedral's Grand Organ. The divine notes bounce and intersperse as they waft over the stony-walled realm. The medieval mystery of the sweeping, high-vaulted Gothic architecture serves as an ideal backdrop for the hushed conversation between Rene and the pork-pie-hatted, flea-bitten-mustachioed, art fence and chronic informant, Pascali Debartolo. Debartolo's pistachio-stained fingers offer a paper bag of nuts to Rene. Rene scoffs and pushes it away, "We're in church."

Debartolo loud-whispers, "It's in there."

Rene fingers through the pistachios and finds a folded cocktail napkin. Rene dips his shades and stares disdainfully at Debartolo's toe-fractured, faded-brown shoes. "I think you're either born caring the way your shoes look or you're not. Pascali, it's an ever present theme in your life."

Debartolo's nose twitches. "My shoes?" He looks down at the contrast of his shoes next to the piano-black shine of Rene's.

Rene unfolds the cocktail napkin and sees a postage stamp-sized, crayon sketch of a soft, visor-capped, wavy-haired Rembrandt. "You used a crayon? See what I mean." Debartolo laughs. Rene scowls at him, "And take off your hat. Show a little respect."

Debartolo licks his stained fingers and plumes the bright orange feather in his hat. "It's my trademark."

Rene scoffs.

Debartolo thumbs at Rembrandt's hat. "Look at him. What... every time he felt a self-portrait coming on, he grabbed a goofy hat?" Debartolo reluctantly takes off his hat, revealing a pink, bald dome floating in half a cantaloupe of mousey hair. He takes out a long silver comb and hums to the music as he rakes what's left of his curls.

"Shhh!" A disapproving, blond-haired suburban couple, that looks like they fell off a wedding cake, turns around and stares.

Rene scrutinizes Debartolo, "You saw it? You're sure." He holds the wrinkled napkin sketch out to him, "It was this size? No bigger than a postage stamp?"

Debartolo nods, "Rembrandt's self-portrait." He grins, "The guy looked a little cross-eyed to me."

"He was. They called it stereoblindness. It actually helped his ability to produce a three-dimensional world on flat canvass."

Debartolo's voice raises, "Whatdya' mean?"

The blond couple turns again to see Rene cover one of Debartolo's eyes with the napkin. "Like when art teachers instruct their students to close one eye in order to flatten what they see." Rene waits for the couple to turn back around. "Where?" Possessed, Rene prods Debartolo, "Where is it now?"

Debartolo's fingers motion for compensation. Rene takes out a thick envelope and slides it across the pew. Debartolo tucks the money into his shallow pant's pocket and lights up with the irony, "In the same city that Hitler stashed all the Nazi stolen art."

"Linz, Austria?"

"Yep. I saw it at a private gambling club. It's called the Spielbank Casino. I saw it when they opened their safe to pay me."

"Linz? You're sure?" Rene eyes narrow, "The Bormann brothers, Joseph and Leopold?"

"They have that and your last Blue Mauritius Stamp."

Rene stands. "Not for long."

"Mr. Sorrell," Debartolo eases him back down, "Stay in cushy Manhattan. These guys are dangerous. They have no compunction about shooting people and dumping them in the Danube. Front me the money, I'll buy the stamp." Debartolo titters to himself, "It's not like I don't know what you're going to do with it anyway."

Rene scowls. "The stamp is not all I'm interested in."

"Sir..." Debartolo hesitates, studying Rene's displeasure, "we've been over this. Isabella Gardner was a sweet old widow who built a fifteenth century Venetian palace and realized her dream of bestowing Boston a world class art museum. Only thing is..." his protruding belly bounces as he chortles, "she was naive and reckless enough to protect three hundred million dollars of masterpieces with two marijuana-stoned, college kids, a trombone player and a wannabe rock musician, who moonlighted as night watchmen. The thieves had such free reign inside the museum that they could've ordered in Chinese and stayed all night. After they smashed the frames and cut out the paintings, they had so much time that they were able to make two trips to their car to load up the loot. My kid sister with a toy gun could've cleaned the joint out." Debartolo proudly strokes his stereotypical Florentine moustache, "The two robbers..." he chuckles, "had fake black moustaches, bogus cop uniforms, and no guns. Armed with duct tape, they pulled off the greatest art theft in history."

Rene gets up again. "If the Bormanns have the stolen Rembrandt from the Gardner Museum, *then* they know where Vermeer's The Concert is that was part of the same heist." The Grand Organ elongates the choir's lyrical notes. Rene closes his eyes and accompanies it with an adagio movement of his hand in the air as if a virtuoso, "Vermeer used his brush like a violin bow. And with the impact of that simple implement freed himself and the world from the limitations of imagination." He opens his eyes. "In The Concert, Vermeer mastered the ability to capture one-moment-in-time and make it linger forever. Have you seen the way the delicate young girl in it holds her palm open, seduced to the sentiment of the tempo in her music instructor's lesson?" Rene holds out his palm out as if enfolding a hummingbird. "Can you imagine if no one could ever see that again? The impact of the loss on the art world?"

"Well...." Debartolo drops the pistachio bag of shells in the offering plate, "No none needs to feed a painting to keep it quiet. It's either with some Russian crime lord, billionaire overseas collector, being used as collateral in a cocaine deal for a drug kingpin, stashed in some off shore vault, rolled up in someone's safe, or..." he pushes it dangerously by holding Rene's eyes, "hanging on the wall for the personal pleasure of some reclusive art fanatic. The Statute of Limitations has run, the prosecutor for Boston has granted the thieves full immunity if they return it, and even the Gardner Museum's five million dollar reward hasn't sparked a response in two decades."

Rene makes it clear; "I'll double the reward, ten million, to anyone who throws the painting back over the museum's fence."

"It ain't gonna' happen."

"Then you'll lose out on a lot of money. No matter who gets the reward, if it's returned, you get a ten percent finder's fee." He drills Debartolo's beady eyes, "Find out when the Linz auction is. Do it in twenty-four hours."

"All right, all right." Debartolo puts his arm on Rene's shoulder, "It'll be at your favorite place." Rene moves away from his touch. Debartolo is slighted by the rejection.

"And..." Rene peals off a hundred, "get a shoe shine. It's embarrassing." He can't help but spot Debartolo's pistachio-stained nails. Rene peels off another hundred. "And a manicure too."

"You know," Debartolo looks at his stumpy legs in his shoes, "Johannes Vermeer had short legs just like me. Rene looks at him like he's nuts. Debartolo takes turns shining each foot on the back of the opposite pant leg. "Vermeer's demise was his own doing." Proud of his theory, he waits for Rene's full attention. "The scuncilli..." he grins, "finished only thirty-five paintings and sold half of them to one patron. That's why his name vanished within a few years of his death. With no apprentices, drawings, etchings, or engravings...."

Debartolo burps. "No one heard of him."

"Are you finished?"

Debartolo looks down at his toe-gnarled shoes. "Cleanliness isn't everything." Debartolo burps again. "I'm sorry, it's the nuts." He sees Rene's patience waning and raps it up. "Did you ever see how neat and clean every room was that he painted?" He holds out his stubby hands, "The Sphinx of Delft had to be the most anal painter in Holland. I mean," he checks his pistachio-stained nails and wipes them on his pants, "he lived in a small house and fathered fifteen kids." His voice grows, "Where were all those beds? What else was going on? It's too perfect. He was covering something up."

Rene has had enough. He turns, taking the whole setting in like it's for the last time.

"Mr. Sorrell, I didn't even know you ever went to church."

"I used to." He leaves. "My mother took me here as a child."

"So," Donning his hat, Debartolo follows, "why'd you stop?"

Rene keeps going, "Mind your own business."

Debartolo digs in his pocket and fingers through the cash. His hand comes out with Andre Pope's card. Flaunting it, he holds it out towards Rene. "And your buddy, Andre Pope, what about him?"

Rene briefly turns with a wry smile; "I'll leave that to you."

Tipping his pork-pie hat toward a darling, fifteen-year-old schoolgirl in pigtails, diminutive Pascali Debartolo limps along, trailing after Rene like a little kid. "Did you know that Vermeer got married, moved in and spent his whole life sponging off his mother-in-law?" Rene is out the door and gone as Debartolo shrugs and talks to himself, "This time I got a little surprise for Andre Pope and his trained grizzly bear."

TWENTY-SIX

Tony Stokes leads down the stairs of a dilapidated men's hotel in The Bowery, as a white silk scarf and camel cashmere coat-wearing, recalcitrant Andre Pope takes off his beret and ducks under a wooden sign depicting a lewd, scantily clad, blond college girl advertising Jackin' Jills Flower Shop. As they walk past the row of assorted dehydrated plants in the window of the fake storefront, a gum-cracking, Mississippi white-bread, enthusiastic demimonde in a too-tight cheerleader outfit, hands each of them a string tag, "Attach the string to the level of plant service you want to buy." She gives Andre a head-to-toe assessment and winks, "The orchid is for big spenders."

Tony Stokes opens his beige trench, flashes his old NYPD badge on his belt and waives off the Southern Belle. They enter a closed room at the end of the hall without knocking, and find five-foot-two Pascali Debartolo's caterpillar toes dangling off a massage table. Seeing Stokes' badge, the high-heeled, pony-tailed, topless grad student steps back and blurts, "I'm a licensed therapist."

Stokes points, "Sit down!"

"Don't worry, missy," Andre gentlemanly pats the girl's hand and calms her, "we're leaving in a minute." Andre covers up more of the naked Debartolo than he can afford to see, and leans in close, "Once a mistake, and twice a punishment."

Debartolo looks at the somber face of Tony Stokes. "Helipad twelve, two-thirty sharp." He nods reassurance to the two men, "The stamp will be there."

"You're sure?" Andre insists. "The Blue Mauritius Stamp from Cuba?"

Debartolo nods. He holds out his hand for money.

Leaving, Andre turns, “If...it’s there.”

Stokes takes out a black magic marker, “If it’s not…” he writes on his string tag and attaches it to Debartolo’s big toe, “this is the way you’re gonna’ look in the morgue.”

Debartolo wiggles his toe. It reads, ‘DOA gunshot wound’. Untying it, trying to lighten the mood, Debartolo offers it back, “With the orchid you get the reach-around.”

Stokes follows Andre out.

TWENTY-SEVEN

Thundering overhead, blowing dirt and spouting fumes, a red-striped, navy-blue shuttle helicopter flutters loudly as it lands on the last of the twelve helipad spaces of the landing platform of the Downtown Manhattan Heliport in the East River. A rainbow-spandex-clad, gangly Jamaican bike messenger, with Rastafarian dreadlocks, fans the air as he awaits the pilot's window opening. A hand reaches out with a red security-taped envelope marked RENE SORRELL.

The bike messenger spins by, takes the handoff of the envelope, stuffs it in his backpack, and is off pedaling at top speed. Andre Pope's black Range Rover, with Stokes at the wheel and Andre alongside, takes off after the bike messenger. Artfully slaloming cars and taxis, cutting in front of slow-moving buses, running red lights, dodging and pirouetting pissed pedestrians, the bike messenger flies through Wall Street and Lower Manhattan's Financial District. Approaching a solid red light, the bike messenger dips his goggles scrutinizing the marked NYPD police car waiting for the light. The messenger pulls alongside.

The cops study him. The Jamaican offers a Cheshire smile.

Just as Stokes pulls up in the black Range Rover, a red Ducatti, whose motorcyclist has a black helmet with a dark-smoked visor, edges out of the line of cars. The motorcyclist roars past the stopped cars, grabs the backpack off the bike messenger and full throttles the Ducatti around the corner.

The messenger takes off after the Ducatti -- but it immediately becomes futile. Wheels smoking, the Range Rover cuts out of line. The NYPD squad's lights burst on and its siren wails as the cops go after all of them.

A few blocks later, a two-car police roadblock awaits the motorcyclist on the red Ducatti. The Ducatti's driver drops his knee and screeches to a diverting, sliding stop, swerves up onto the sidewalk, loops a light pole and does a wheelie trying to reverse direction. Halfway up the street, an oncoming unmarked police car speeds around traffic and cuts off the Ducatti. The motorcyclist is trapped. He skids to a stop. Ordered at gunpoint, the motorcyclist removes his helmet. It's some kid.

As Andre Pope's black Range Rover edges up the street, the cops already have the kid spread-eagle on the hood of their car.

The backpack is gone.

TWENTY-EIGHT

Just before midnight, waiting out a fine drizzle, a backpacked Pascali Debartolo is perusing girlie magazines under the awning of an all night Brooklyn newsstand. Losing his patience, the yellow rain-jacketed, balding, Puerto-Rican newsstand owner taps the shoulder of headphone-wearing, beat-humming Pascali Debartolo, "Are you going to buy it or just wrinkle it?" As he waits for an answer, the loud flutter of a shuttle helicopter approaches.

"Huh...?" Debartolo mutters and lifts off one of his IPod earphones beneath the clatter. As the thunder of the helicopter rattles the walls of the newsstand, Debartolo takes out the red security-taped envelope. He slits it open with his long pinky nail. Blowing the paper open, he spits his wad of watermelon gum inside the empty envelope. He crinkles it up and tosses it in the newsstand's garbage.

The Puerto-Rican owner gives him a dirty look. "This ain't your house." The helicopter hovers directly overhead. Holding down his flapping papers, he shouts, "Damn helicopters! I'm sick of 'em."

"What's the big deal?" Debartolo looks up at the helicopter and grins, "All night long we hear the banging clang of steel trash bins being slammed up onto garbage trucks." He shakes the rain off his pork-pie hat, straightens its limp feather and wisecracks, "Nobody complains about that." He looks up at the helicopter and grins. "Why is everybody so sensitive? That's the sound of New York." Closing the magazine, Debartolo puts his headphones back on and bops away without purchasing anything. Humming, he crosses the street.

Barreling behind him, a bus flies by and splashes water.

"Christ!" Debartolo jumps back and still gets soaked. He

looks at his only shoeshine in a year. His shoes are covered with muck. Shaking his hat free of the dirty water, he sees that his orange feather is gone. “Shit! Shit! Shit!” Putting his hat back on, he turns around and looks for his feather.

He only gets a few steps.

Stokes comes up behind him, tips Debartolo’s hat brim over his eyes, and bludgeons him with a blackjack. The little man drops. Debartolo’s feet twitch. Stokes smacks him twice more. This time harder. Stokes relieves Debartolo of his backpack, picks him up by his collar, dead lifts him into an open dumpster and bangs the lid. Stokes opens the backpack. It’s empty. “Son of a bitch!”

Stokes opens the dumpster and slams it shut.

Losing it, he bangs it again and again.

TWENTY-NINE

In the middle of rush hour in Manhattan, Rene's silver Bentley Brooklands speeds into Central Park, pulls up quickly and stops at the top of the grand staircase of Bethesda Terrace. Don Frye monitors the car as Rene rushes out. Rene spins looking all over. Stepping one way, then another, he can't find Saira.

"Hey!" a jogger yells out to get Rene out of his path.

Rene looks at Don Frye and shrugs.

Don Frye points toward the arcade's double-tiered stairwell.

Rene walks over to the entrance and squints down the stairs. At the bottom of the stairs, standing in the shadows of the arcade, he sees Saira. Her back is to him. Alarmed, he calls out, "Saira!" As Rene rushes down two flights of stairs, Saira slowly turns and comes to him with a letter in her hand. "What's wrong? I got here as soon as I could." Apprehensive, Saira avoids his scrutiny. Rene looks at the typed letter in her hands. She withdraws it. He takes her hand. Feeling her trembling, he hugs her and softly asks, "Baby, are you alright?"

She draws a tough breath and nods.

"Don't worry," Rene cups her face in his palm, "whatever it is, I'll make it okay." She closes her eyes, leans on his shoulder and holds onto him as he walks her up the long flights of stairs. As they're walking, a frightened Saira steals a glance at Rene and gauges his reaction. She draws the strength to tell him.

Walking into the heart of the park, Rene guides Saira toward the Angel of the Waters Fountain. Nearby, a Chinese bride and her groom are having their wedding photos taken by the fountain. In a sudden mood swing, it makes Saira twinkle. Waiting on her, Rene asks, "Sweetheart, what were you doing down there in the shadows?"

Saira assesses him again. As they get to the other end of the fountain, Saira sits on the pool's edge and tugs Rene down on the spot next to her, "They've been gone for over twenty-five years and..." Saira studies Rene's eyes, "now they're back."

Rene squints and looks at her clueless. "What...?"

Saira stalls. She looks off, "The tiles, the ceiling tiles in the Bethesda Arcade they're more beautiful than I could ever imagine."

Rene looks at her like she's a little loopy. "Okay..." he takes her hand that holds the letter and delicately asks, "the tiles are back. *What else is*?"

She looks at the patinated, bronze-winged angel floating above the fountain, draws a deep breath and exhales. "All my life I've been alone, and just when I think I've finally learned how to do it, this comes today from Philadelphia in the mail." Rene looks at the one-page, typed letter and reaches for it. Saira holds it back from his grasp, "Promise me nothing will change between us."

"What are you talking about? Of course nothing will change."

Saira holds out the letter. "I have a sister."

"You have a sister...?"

Saira holds his eyes and nods, "And in less than two minutes," Saira passes him the letter, "I've learned more about my background than I've conjured up in a lifetime."

Rene starts reading the letter aloud, *"For years, I was condemned to watch the horror of children in sack cloth, die of illness, injury, hunger, thirst, or exposure to heat or cold. Never visited by a living sole, I existed in a cemetery."*

"Her name is Amanda. She said my mother gave her and I up at the same time. And no name was listed as the father." Saira takes the letter and reads it, "*Fiction is full of children abandoned with birth tokens that act as plot devices to ensure later in life that the special child can be identified. All I got was the sound of isolation. No prince ever came.*" She looks up at Rene and continues to read, "*No one ever found me. I was a secret only to me. I didn't care whether my parents were poor, jobless, ill, or in trouble. It didn't matter. All I knew was how little they loved me, and that I would never forgive them. Never visited once by anyone, I had so much to say but no one to share it with...*" Saira's pauses, "*until I heard about you.*"

Rene puts his hand on Saira's as she takes a deep breath and fights tears. He draws her close. "I know, sweetheart. I know."

She exhales and tells him more. "Amanda said shortly after we were placed in the orphanage, it burnt down, and the children were spread out in several other orphanages."

"And your grandparents, did she say anything about them?"

"Yeah, it was called Partition." Saira goes back to the letter, "*Our mother witnessed our eighty-year old grandparents give up their home in Lahore, load up all their belongings on an ox cart and travel on foot until they dropped on the side of the road and died of exhaustion. The caravan moved on, leaving them to die like hundreds of thousands of others.*" Saira looks up and sums it up, "All in all, they, and another one million, died crossing the newly declared border."

"I never heard of Partition? What was it?"

Saira shakes her head, "It seems no one has." Saira places the letter down on the edge of the fountain. "Partition was the dark side of independence. To India and Punjab, it was the cost of freedom. And to the British and their fading Indian Empire, Partition was cut and run, or else be involved in a bloody civil war that would be impossible to get out of. So in August, 1947, they partitioned British India into two countries based on religion. Pakistan became Islamic. India staying secular. But neither country was prepared to handle the largest migration of people in history. Fifteen million people, who had homes that their families had occupied for decades...for centuries, became politically re-routed refugees forced to take up residence across the new border. The result was total failure. A complete breakdown of law and order. Hundreds of thousands of people died in the riots, were massacred, or just never survived the hardship of the flight to safety." She folds up the letter, "To this day, either in India or Punjab, there is nothing at the border that marks it as the place where millions of people crossed. No plaque. No memorial. No memory to mark the spot where a million people died in search of their new home. Nothing. So..." Saira takes off her glasses and folds them on the letter, "what do Amanda, me, and India all have in common?"

Rene waits on her completion.

She winces, "We come from a history of shame."

"No, sweetheart," Rene kisses her temple, "that's not true. He leans her against his side as they walk away. "We have to meet your sister."

THIRTY

The distant surging baritone of approaching motorcycles pierces a dense, foggy night in West Harlem. Two black-helmeted, leather-jacketed bikers roar under the 12th Avenue Viaduct and pull up on spectacular, muscular, Ecosse Titanium Series, platinum-painted, custom motorcycles with all-titanium frames. As Rene and Don Frye shut down their bikes, a pack of penitentiary-built, felonious bikers in colorful headscarves, standing over a line of nearly identical black Harley Davidson motorcycles, do a slow burn, point, and whisper among themselves. A Fu Manchu-mustached and Asian-tattooed bruiser, that looks like he swallowed a human being whole, struts over.

Rene doesn't move as the group closes in.

The bruiser gets up close. He soul-handshakes Rene and pulls him shoulder close, "Thanks for the word you put in for my daughter. Who woulda' thought a Jersey toll taker's kid would be going to..." his noise lifts in the air as his voice gets snobby, "The School of The Art Institute in Chicago."

Wide-eyed, the rest of the bikers approach to admire the world's most expensive motorcycles. "What she got?" a pink-faced, pony-tailed, muscle-bound, thirty-year-old, in a leather vest boasting ride pins, skulls, and outlaw badges, asks, admiring the lavish, charcoal carbon fiber.

Don Frye rattles it off with smooth modesty, beaming with pride over his birthday present from Rene, "A 220 horsepower, 2150cc polished billet aluminum v-twin engine, and individual brake pads for each of the twelve pistons."

"Shit," the pony-tailed biker toasts it with his can of beer, "that screams you can't afford me."

Rene smiles disarmingly, "But it comes with a free watch."

In black shirts, jeans, and boots, Rene and Don Frye enter the hickory-smoked mood of a New York City roadhouse called Dinosaur Bar-B-Que and wander through an over-crowded, raucous room packed with badass bikers, tough waitresses, and wannabe honky-tonk women barreling about the premises -- wherever you stand, you are in someone's way. The jukebox tune, Cowboy Junkie's *Thirty Summers*, wafts over the racket. A plus-sized waitress, in black tights and a sleeveless shirt, holding a tray of North Carolina styled ribs, chicken wings, and booze over her shoulders, points Don Frye to their time-honored table alongside a giant mural of freakish pigs, twisted hogs, farcical steers, and carnivorous dinosaurs playing poker.

While Don Frye secures their table, Rene goes straight to the back. He enters a washroom that encourages graffiti. Every inch of the walls is covered in spray-painted initials, esoteric poetry, marker-penned bad jokes, obscene political statements, and despairing romantic words of wisdom. Rene ignores the walls' advice and goes straight to the unblemished, white metal condom machine screwed to the wall. His fingers run up the sides, around, over and under the seventy-five cent machine and come up bare. Mystified, he just stares at it. After a moment, he digs in his pocket and puts three quarters in. Only a condom comes out. He throws it on the floor.

As Rene weaves back through the crowd, his eyes linger on a table with a father, mother, and five kids. The kids are paused as the father is offered the choice of three spices for his ribs. They study him as he chooses the hottest, a little bottle called Devil's Duel, and shakes it all over his ribs. He bites into one. "Wow!" he puckers up and kisses the mother, "That's spicy." The kids all crack up.

When Rene gets to the table, Don Frye is on his third corn bread. Rene razzes him, "Come up for air."

Don Frye opens his pants, "My jeans must've shrunk." Rene sits down, noticeably quiet. Don Frye stops eating, "Well, was it there?"

Rene shakes his head no.

"Debartolo's usually reliable."

Muttering to himself, Rene looks back at the family.

Don Frye scrutinizes Rene, "What?"

Rene's hands go out, "I've been single my whole life. I don't know how to do family?"

A pipsqueak waitress, in a rolled up t-shirt exposing wiry biceps, slaps down their slabs of well-done ribs, fries, and coleslaw.

"Don't worry." Don Frye shrugs and digs in, "I'll just have to marry the sister."

Children's laughter draws Rene to study the perfect family for clues to happiness. Preoccupied, his back is to Don Frye, "It's not like Debartolo. He left me specific instructions where it would be. He knows how important this to me." Rene turns back with a grim look, "I got a bad feeling about this."

"Hey." Don Frye points that Rene should get started on his plate. "Then we need to come up with a new game plan on getting that last stamp." When the kids laugh again, Rene turns to watch. Don Frye motions Rene back from staring at them and holds his attention, "When we going to Linz?"

Rene breaks his slab of ribs apart, rips the off meat with his teeth and answers deadpan, "After I meet your future ex-wife."

THIRTY-ONE

The sun peaks from behind fast-moving, menacing clouds and shines off the Flying Silver B adorning the hood of the Bentley. Roommate's faces fill the street-front windows of a third-story, Lower East Side, red brick walkup as they watch Don Frye load Saira's overnight bags in the Bentley's trunk. All eyes are on Rene. His grey hair swept back in a lusty autumn wind, dressed in a charcoal suit covering a matching cashmere turtleneck, Rene is holding the door, waiting for Saira. "Okay…." Tookie elbows the crimped redhead in pajamas next to her and alerts the others. "This is the first time she's leaving him, the kiss will say it all." The girls press their noses close to the window. The redhead's coffee mug nicks the pane.

Rene diverts his attention pretending not to see.

"It's only overnight," the spiked-blonde, in a too-tight t-shirt and sprayed-on blue jeans, dismisses her, "it means nothing."

The redhead shakes her head no and points, "Look." The wind blows away Rene's pocket square. He effortlessly substitutes it with his gloves, fingers up, in the same pocket. "Oh my God," the redhead titillates. "Mr. Bentley is so smooth. He knows how play it."

Uh-uh," the athletic, spiked-blonde disagrees. "He saw us. He's gonna' clutch and just give her a peck."

Seeing Saira walk out the door, the apartment's self-anointed master, Tookie, extends her arms, "Watch."

Rene's hand reaches out for Saira as she approaches. As Saira comes to the door, Rene hugs her and whispers something in Saira's ear. The girls all lean forward as Saira looks into his eyes.

Rene draws her close and kisses her with an indulgent, slow kiss, lingering enough as if to make him immortal.

"Ahhhhh," Tookie screams, "He's hooked." Her long ebony fingers motion the spiked-blonde and redhead to come up with it. They both cough up five-dollar bills.

Just before the Bentley takes off, Rene's window goes down. His fingers trickle a waive goodbye to the girls.

Cuddled up in the back seat, Rene holds Saira dearly as the Bentley soundlessly drives over the highway. Inhaling the fragrance of her forehead, his fingers stroke the fine, dark hair along her temple. As Saira's fingers move from his other hand, Rene's fingers search them out. He whispers, "You okay, Saira?"

She nods. Reveling under the warm kindness of his touch, Saira snuggles closer and studies Rene as he looks at his watch and then up at the darkening skies. Inch-by-inch she scrutinizes Rene's face for proof. She finds inexplicable sanctuary in the seasoned grey of his hair. His furrowed brow innocently frames his face, struggling to love her more selflessly. His doleful, heavy-hearted eyes belie all her attempts to undermine what is true. His safe, boyish smile soothes her and weakens her resistance. She knows. Her mind echoes with the sacred way her name flows so sweetly over his lips. Persuadable, she revels under the adoration on his face. His unguarded devotion is unimpeachable. Yet, the more his love is freely given, the more she questions it. And more importantly, herself. Her deep-seated melancholy exists without a definitive cause. It nags at her, questioning whether she deserves the wonderful honor he is bestowing upon her. Her mind whispers, *"What if I should disappoint him like the disappointment I must've been to my parents?"*

The pitter-patter of raindrops pings the roof. Don Frye turns back from the wheel, "Are you sure you have to go?"

Saira sighs, "Positive."

"She's incorrigible," Rene assures Don Frye, and then looks at Saira lovingly. "I already tried my best to circumvent her plans. But Mr. Kim..."

Saira interrupts him, "You called Freddy?"

He avoids her stare.

Saira puts her hands out in frustration.

"It's just that I knew how important your first meeting with your sister was to you. So, I reached out to him. All he would tell me was that they have several anxious bidders and it was crucial that you authenticate certain Chinese Ceramics before they leave Los Angeles for Christie's next auction." Rene holds her scrutiny and shrugs, "Only you can do it?"

Saira nods and pushes it, paying him back, "You have a valuable fiancée." Protecting her independence, Saira waits for an apology.

"Sweetheart," Rene acquiesces, "I'm sorry."

Saira shuffles through the items in her purse, checking her tickets and itinerary, "It's not Mr. Kim's fault. The Getty Museum has come under a lot of scrutiny for the provenance of what they're acquiring. Since I interned with them, they specifically asked for me."

"Who wouldn't?" Don Frye adds, looking back in the rear view mirror. "Saira, I'm just to blame as much as he is. I got him going when we heard you had to leave. Those items you're going to validate are the Emperor's famous terra-cotta soldiers, right?

"Does everyone know?"

"That's what we do," Don Frye smiles playfully. "They're the soldiers, right?"

Surprised, Saira nods at Don Frye's impetuous gaze in the rear mirror, "Why?"

Don Frye cocks his head, "I'm superstitious. The First Chinese Emperor...? The one that built The Great Wall?"

Saira nods, "Qin Shi Huang."

"Yeah. That's the one. The one who burned all the books and buried all the Chinese scholars alive. The fanatic who ate mercury every night with his food, because he was told it would make him immortal." Don Frye pulls up at the JFK Airport terminal. "Well," he turns around, "those statues are not like the typical blue plate with a dragon on it, or a celadon bowl. Those ceramic soldiers were buried in the Emperor's mausoleum," he holds out his hands, "his grave...and put there to serve a dead person's soul forever." Don Frye searches Saira out in his rear view mirror.

She gives him a riveting stare.

He holds her gaze. "Some things are better left buried."

Saira is strangely silent.

Rene goes over it once more to be sure. "And what time is your flight back?"

"Like I said, first thing in the morning." Saira dons her navy-blue, Parisian straw hat and poses for Rene's approval. He flashes the perfect sign. She takes his hand, "Don't worry, I'll have plenty of time to make our lunch with Amanda."

"And if you're late," Rene asks, "how will I recognize her?"

Saira pauses checking her hair and makeup in the Bentley's vanity mirror. She stares quietly in the mirror and whimsically smiles, "You'll know her when you see her."

After watching Saira disappear through the terminal gate, Don Frye starts up the Bentley and pulls away. After the first bend around the terminal, he suddenly stops and pulls back to the curb. He turns to Rene, "Was she carrying the smaller bag too?"

Before Rene can answer, Don Frye's out of the car and checking the trunk. He holds up a leather tote. Rene takes off running with it. Scanning the packed terminal for Saira's blue hat, he can't spot her. Checking each ticket counter, Rene rushes over to the line queuing up for security clearance. She's not there. Keeping his eyes on the women's washroom door, he seeks assistance from a ticket agent. "Saira DuFour, did she already check in?"

"Sir, we're not allowed to give out that information."

"We just got engaged. Forgive me," he shrugs innocently, "I'm overprotective." Rene holds up Saira's tote bag. "She needs this."

The agent checks her computer. "I'm sorry, sir. She's already checked in and on her way to the boarding gate."

Rene tries to call Saira's cell phone.

He feels a vibration in the leather bag. He opens it and sees Saira's phone. He shakes his head, tucks the tote under his arm and walks back to the car.

THIRTY-TWO

Dressed in a emerald-striped, navy-blue suit, a lime-green polka-dotted tie, a green silk pocket square, and a pair of square emeralds linking each cuff of his shirt, Rene enters the cavernous Main Concourse of Grand Central Station. The dizzying comings and goings of the bustling crowd make him uncomfortable. As he walks toward the center of the concourse, he stares up at the four-faced clock on a tower high above the information booth. It's noon. He looks for Saira. He waits under the clock. In a moment, he smiles. He spots her at the front of the Oyster Bar.

Rene comes up behind Saira. A breathtaking Saira.

Her brunette hair is down, not up. Her glasses replaced by chic sunglasses. Standing in four-inch heels, her back to him, Saira is in a skin-tight, scoop back, black tank dress. Approaching unnoticed, Rene runs his hand up her bare back. He whispers in her ear as he nibbles it, "Saira, you look so hot I have to have you right now."

She turns. "It's Amanda, not Saira." While Rene's face slowly transforms from lust, Amanda lights up seeing him for the first time. Leaning in, she sweetly kisses his cheek. "But..." feeling where his lips touched her ear, she smiles, "thank you very much." She takes off her dark Chanel sunglasses revealing sparkling, indigo-blue eyes. Amanda tussles her hair and looks around, "Where's my sister?"

"I...." All emotion is sucked out of Rene's pale expression. He stares in shock at Saira's identical twin sister. "I thought you were..."

"Her...?" Amanda coos, interrupting him, "Don't worry." Her manicured hand touches his and holds it, "I'm very flattered. "

Rene pulls away from her hand. He's somewhere else as they enter the world famous Oyster Bar. His eyes hang on the vaulted ceiling's suspended herringbone-laid tiles.

Amanda notices. "They're beautiful aren't they?" Amanda takes his arm and draws him close as they walk, "It's called timbrel vaulting. The tiles are able to float in heaven because of a quick drying cement that the architect invented to form a thin skin covering it. And because the skin is as fine as a tambourine, it sticks…" Amanda's eyes affix to his, "instantly." She hangs on him.

"God," he looks back at the tiles and mutters, "they both notice the same things."

Amanda gives him a searching, honeyed-smile, "What?"

He avoids her stare, "Nothing."

Amanda revels in the crowd's attention as she holds Rene.

They're escorted to a table surrounded by the great hall's central seating. As Rene digests the horde of people and continuous buzz of floating conversation, Amanda sits down. Still standing, Rene is uncomfortable with his seat placement and hovers over Amanda. "Would you mind if...if we switched seats?"

Studying him, Amanda complies.

Scurrying by, a waiter, accidentally bumps Rene's elbow. Rene is unnerved by the closeness and invasive touch. As soon as Rene sits down, a waiter offers him a menu. Rene waves him away and barks, "I don't need it."

Amanda looks at him with question.

Rene makes light, "I never read a menu." He looks down and sees that his shirt cuffs are not perfectly sticking out of his jackets' sleeves. He adjusts them. He puts on a perfunctory smile, "You know what, would you excuse me for a moment."

As Rene threads through the crowded dinning room, he moves out of the way of people that stand too close to him. He looks at his watch. Twelve-thirty. He looks for Saira. No sign. He checks his phone. No message. His finger tugs at his shirt collar. At the rear of the restaurant, he finds the men's room. The door is locked. It's occupied. He paces for a minute, and tries the door across from it. Out of Order. He returns to the locked washroom and knocks. No answer. Rene goes back out into the concourse. He's confronted with mass confusion. Charges of frantic commuters pass on each side of him. He dodges between luggage carts and baby buggies. Turning back too quickly to look at the clock above the information booth, his elbow bumps the chest of a gruff stockbroker carrying a briefcase and a small desk lamp. "Excuse me," Rene speed utters and keeps going.

The stockbroker adjusts his glasses. "Asshole."

Rene heads toward a marble and brass pagoda. He opens the door inside it and hurries down the spiral staircase to the lower level. He goes into the first washroom he sees. His eyes trail his reflection as he walks by the mirror.

He turns back.

Rene looks at himself again. He makes his mirror face. He adjusts the knot of his tie. Runs a hand through his hair. Holds out both cuffs of his shirt to make sure they are the same length. His hand moves frenetically adjusting one cuff. His eyes focus on the folds of his pocket square. His hand pinches the points to fluff it exact. As his head turns left to inspect it...his eye ticks.

His jaw jiggers.

A corpulent, beehive-haired, black woman, in an ambulatory tent of a nurse's uniform, enters the washroom. She sees Rene starring at himself in the mirror and starts to raise her hand with objection, but retreats seeing the fanatical look on his face.

Rene's stare locks on his image. A sardonic smile starts in the corner of his mouth. Releasing an involuntary, high-pitched chortle, Rene shakes his head. His head keeps shaking like a bobble-head puppy mounted on a car's dash. He tries to hold out his cufflinks evenly in the mirror. His eyes rivet on the diamond-encased, matching emerald cufflinks. A twitter elongates into a fluttering, high-pitched laugh. He rips one of his emerald cufflinks out and stomps it.

He stops and stares at his mirrored-image.

"She's got a twin." He stomps on the cufflink relentlessly, "An identical twin!"

He pushes into a stall and holds his arms out against its walls. Holding his breath, pushing against the metal walls, he can't stop it. His hands go to his head to contain it. His foot kicks the stall closed. It back flaps. Rene slams it shut.

From inside the washroom stall, Rene implodes with a primal scream. Pulling his hair, he screams again. This time louder.

A wiry, African American, grey-haired railway policewoman comes into the washroom with her hand on her pepper spray.

Rene comes out of the stall. His expression is calm. His appearance and attire perfect. He smiles at the policewoman, "When you gotta' go, you gotta go."

The policewoman follows closely behind him as he walks out, "Next time you gotta' go, use the right washroom or..."

Rene's hand goes up, cutting her off. He walks out.

Rene sits back down perfectly composed. Amanda points at his loose, cufflinkless cuff. Before she speaks, Rene calmly offers, "It fell in the toilet."

THIRTY-THREE

The throaty, angry roar of a polished aluminum Bugatti Veyron Pur Sang flies across the highway as an amused Amanda scrutinizes Rene shift the super car's gears. Looking at the car's tight interior, she teases, "Where would we have put her?"

Rene darts Amanda a hard look, then returns to the road as he pushes it harder, "Saira must've missed her flight." He banks the Bugatti's diamond-cut-finish wheels into a screeching ninety mile per hour turn. "We'll hear from her soon." He gives up a perfunctory smile; "I hope this hasn't been too disappointing for you?"

Amanda puts her hand on his arm, "Not at all."

He moves away from her touch as he holds the turn tighter.

"Wow," Amanda grips the door handle steadying her in the tight-gripping racing seat, "this is a rush." As Rene bears down into a straightaway, Amanda feels the seat's supple leather, running her finger across the Hermes embossed logo, and purposefully mocks him, "I didn't know Hermes made cars."

Rene looks to see if she's serious, and then laughs. He tries to control himself, stops, and then laughs again enjoying her.

"So..." Amanda looks at him oozing heat, "what's it called?"

"A Bugatti," Rene says looking straight ahead. "A Bugatti Veyron Pur Sang. It's named after the famous French race car driver, Pierre Veyron."

"Pur Sang...?" Amanda asks, "Pure Bred?" Rene nods. She takes off her sunglasses and drills him with her haunting blue eyes,

"Just like it's master."

Rene changes the subject. "Where'd the blue eyes come from? The French side of the family?"

Amanda nods. "And Saira? Does she look like me?"

Rene stares in piqued astonishment. His eyes turn away, not accepting it all, "Yeah."

"So…." Amanda's finger draws an imaginary square frame around her face, "What do you think?"

"You're beautiful," he says dispassionately. He lights up, "Just like your sister."

"A Bugatti, huh. So, what's this baby got under the hood?"

Rene reads it off matter-a-factly, "A thousand and one horsepower, sixteen cylinders, two V-8's, and four turbochargers."

"How fast will it go?"

Rene is amused. "One third the speed of sound at sea level." Amanda looks confused. Rene makes it easy, "Two hundred fifty-four miles per hour."

Amanda leans close and dares him, "Show me."

After checking out the highway ahead of him, Rene looks in the rear view mirror for police. He stomps on it. The Bugatti roars as he cranks the speedometer to approaching one hundred and fifty.

"Is that as fast as it'll go?"

Rene pushes it harder. He slams it out of sixth gear and into seventh. The sonic boom of the exhaust screams like a Raptor jet diving into ground attack as the speedometer goes over two hundred.

Amanda defies him again, "Is that as fast as it will go?" Rene gives it a little more. Amanda revels in it. "I love fast cars and fast men." Rene guns it more. Seventh gear is approaching red line. Amanda leans back in the seat and holds on, "Don't stop."

"Sure." Rene pushes it to the max. The speedometer hits two

hundred forty. Amused, he casually turns, "But at top speed the tires will only last for fifteen minutes." He looks at her coolly, "That's okay because the fuel runs out in twelve." Rene's eyes dart to the shimmering blue glass windows of a soaring new high-rise. The Bugatti backfires and bellows into a lower gear as he slows down. He checks that Amanda's seat belt is fastened, "Here's where the fun comes in. From two hundred forty miles per hour it will stop in less than ten seconds." He grips the wheel, slams on the brakes and does a controlled sliding stop down the highway ramp. Thrust back in her seat, Amanda clamps her door handle in sheer aroused terror. Her breath is stolen. She loves it. As Amanda exhales with exhilaration, Rene's eyes size up the blue-mirrored high-rise's unfinished top floors.

"Look!" Amanda points at a packed street fair accompanying a carnival. "Oh my God, look at that carousel. It's unbelievable."

"I don't like crowds."

"Please..." Amanda's palm turns his face towards her, "for me?" Rene arcs the cruising Bugatti towards the festival. As he turns, his sleeve dangles loosely. Amanda tucks his cufflinkless cuff back inside his coat sleeve, "You're pretty causal about losing a diamond and emerald cufflink."

Rene gives her nothing.

"So..." Amanda sizes him up, "you're rich, huh?"

Rene shuts off the Bugatti. Their pulse throbbing, Rene looks straightforward, sitting there in silence staring at the throng of people. Then, he turns with a wary look, "How did you find her?"

Amanda smirks; cracks open her door and motions Rene out.

Rene comes around and helps her out. Exiting, she bends giving him a view of her décolletage. Amanda takes his hand, "The guy I was dating was Muslim. So..." she smiles, "it all depends on the guy. Mohammed, I told I was Arabic." As they walk, Amanda takes hold of Rene's arm, "The Indian ones, I tell I'm Indian." Amanda sparkles, "and so on with the French, Italian, Greek, and Jewish." So...." She draws him tighter against her breasts, "What are you?"

Rene looks straight ahead. "Taken."

As they approach the corner, Rene's walk slows. He stops. He turns to Amanda before crossing the street to the carnival. His tone is emphatic, "*How* did you find her?"

"Well," Amanda shrugs, "my unique ethnic look wasn't quite enough for Mo's family. They wanted to know more about my background, and...they wanted me to convert. Mohamed Abueida," she laments, "my gorgeous MIT Laureate, almost fiancé, was one of those computer nuts that could hunt down anything. He spent months tracking and cross-referencing my last name with all Punjab's remaining orphanage records. Then he came across an orphan with the same last name and exact birth date. Once he found that," Amanda snaps her fingers, "it took seconds to locate Saira DuFour in New York."

As Amanda walks ahead of him, Rene scrutinizes her. Her shoulders thrown back, her stride is long, brazen, almost over confident. All of her weight balanced on the ball of her foot, it's as if her footprints form a single line.

Entering the crowded street fair, Rene uncomfortably moves out of the way of contact with any slower moving people. A loud-talking, baby-strapped, frizzy-haired tourist is in his way. She's on her phone and is oblivious to everything else. He gives her a contemptible look and navigates around her. Rene checks his phone again. Nothing. The multitude of close-quartered, freewheeling public becomes too much for him. Rene goes for an opening. He guides Amanda over to a concession stand. "Would you like anything?"

Preoccupied with the carousel, Amanda shakes her head no.

At the concession stand, a line forms behind Rene because he spends so much time choosing from the limited choices of beverages. The unseasoned temp-kid behind the counter keeps shifting back-and-forth, bouncing on his untied gym shoes, trying to hurry Rene. Rene eventually points at a Royal Crown Cola, "I'll have that." Seeing the crowd behind Rene, an old-time carnival barker, in an oversized top hat and double-knit poly coat with sequin trim, and a mouthful of teeth that resemble a bent fork stuck in cement, enters the booth to help out. The barker hands Rene a blue can of pop. Staring at the simian-shaped barker's unwashed hands, Rene holds out the can, "What am I supposed to drink this out of?"

"We've had a run on crystal," the barker wisecracks and moves to the next in line.

Rene takes out his initialed white handkerchief and wipes the can's lid. Standing behind Amanda, he takes a sip of soda and inspects her from top-to-bottom. "So, what does an Amanda do?"

Turning on cue, Amanda assumes a more dominant stance. Her response is delivered subtly, like a spider to a fly, "I'm getting my doctorate in Psychopathology."

"Well..." Rene kids, "I'll know not to mess with you." He plays it low-key, testing her, "What are you writing your thesis on?"

"The Denied Self." Amanda studies Rene's expression and puts him in her cross-hairs, "Our shadow is our best enemy," she smiles sardonically, "because it makes us aware of our dark side. The ignored brother or sister within us. They call it enantiodromia."

Rene shakes his head as his gaze darts back from the soaring blue-windowed, high-rise in the distance, "Enantio...what?"

"It's a fancy word," Amanda breaks it down into syllables, "en-an-tio-dro-mia." She enjoys driving it home seeing Rene's skepticism. "It means sooner or later everything runs into its opposite. Like the holier-than-thou preacher that gets caught in a motel with a hooker." Her French-manicured hands extend like a balance scale, "It's the law of equilibrium in the natural world. If we resist our dark side, enantiodromia occurs," she raises a perfectly arched eyebrow, "sometimes with cataclysmic results."

The eerie music of Pink Martini's *Que Sera Sera* draws Amanda closer to the spinning antique carousel on loan from the City of Binghamton. Decorated with hand-painted Gay 90's scenes on its running board and crown, the carousel is enclosed within a circular wooden pavilion. Above it, a plaque requires a child to drop one piece of litter found on the street into a garbage can in order to ride free. Amanda looks on the ground, picks up a candy wrapper and throws it in the trash barrel nearby. Consumed, floating with the music, she stares as elaborately carved and hand-painted wooden horses jump up-and-down, galloping three abreast, spinning by to the music.

Rene shakes his head punctuating her reverie. "I don't understand the fascination only to go round and round in circles."

Amanda turns, "It's more than that." The carousel has been around for a thousand years. Carousel means little war," she jousts him in his side with her pointer finger, "and it originated as a cavalry exercise played by my Arabian ancestors preparing them for combat as they wielded their swords on horseback at mock enemies."

Rene squints at the carousel, uncomfortable with its creepy, repeating, singsong organ melody.

"But..." Amanda sneaks up and kisses his cheek, "they kept the training *secret* within castle walls so no one else could find out."

The carousel slows to a stop.

Amanda flirtatiously pulls Rene up on the ride. He looks around and shakes his head, convinced the crowd is studying he and Amanda. As the music trumpets louder, she coaxes, "No one sees us." Amanda boosts herself onto a horse and pats the one next to her, "Saddle up."

Two identically dressed and coiffed, dark-haired, twin boys hop on the ride and get into a miniature chariot next to them. Rene stares transfixed at them. The music starts and the carousel slowly gathers speed. Rene jumps off. As the horses bound up-and-down, Amanda points at the twin boys next to her, "Aren't they adorable?"

Rene is strangely silent.

Holding on the pole with one hand, standing up in the saddle, Amanda comes around reveling in it all. Suggestively driving up and down with the horse, her head arched back with ecstasy, her trickling fingers beckon Rene. "Enantiodromia..." Amanda taunts him, "what you bar at the front door, sneaks around to the back."

The little boys' parents cricket-call out their names each time they come around. While the boys' eyes go wide, their shrieks of joy are drowned out by the building fortissimo of the music. All Rene sees is a twisted masquerade of contorted expressions.

As the carousel twirls, so does Rene's mind. The monotonous melody becomes freakish. The spinning lights and seesaw of the horses are dizzying. Rene draws a heavy breath. The air seems disturbingly still. His jaw clamps. His neck reddening, Rene loosens his tie and unbuttons his shirt collar. As the song amplifies and the trumpets reach crescendo, Rene looks at the twisted twins' opened, gaping mouths and then at the horses' contrived, aberrant expression. Time slows down. The music, spinning horses, Amanda, and the twins all become one blur.

It's all too much for him. Unsteady, he pulls away. Rene's eye's shutter and close. The whole of it triggers a flashback.

Pouncing into the present unbidden, Rene is a five-year-old boy frozen at the threshold of a child's bedroom. He hears his name being called over and over again. It harmonizes with the carousel's haunting theme. Numb, Rene is in a bubble floating, terrified, peering in the bedroom. He's back there in time, splitting into two, somewhere between a child left abandoned and a man tortured.

The carousel slows and the discordant pianissimo of the Wurlitzer organ's bizarre tune stops. Rene's nose wrinkles as his upper lip lifts. He bats his eyelids shaking it off. As he walks, steadying himself, Rene puts the cold aluminum of the Royal Crown Cola against his forehead. He passes a carnival fun mirror. It distorts his appearance. Avoiding it, he shifts left, then right. He stops dead. In mounting quiet fury, he stares and witnesses Rene Sorrell twist at the middle into two identical fiendish images.

He throws his can of pop at the mirror. It shatters.

"Hey!" The top-hatted carny rushes over. "Whatha' hell's wrong with you!" He tries to grab Rene. Rene sidesteps, pushing the crusty old-timer away. His hat toppling as he trips himself up and falls to the ground, the carny blows his whistle and shouts, "Hey, Rube!" Seeing others coming, he moves on Rene.

Rene digs in his pocket, throws a wad of cash in the carnival barker's lap, and keeps going. The carny looks at the thick stack of hundred dollar bills and waives the others off.

THIRTY-FOUR

The last amber-serrated edge of the sun disappears as the Bugatti slowly purrs up Madison Avenue entering Manhattan's posh Upper East Side. Storefronts sparkle as Amanda's head turns with the splendor of one-after-another, not-to-be-outdone, window-trimmed designer store. Rene's oblivious. Out of touch with Saira, he's strangely quiet. He stops at a red light. In the early night's gloaming, Rene's eyes hang on handholding couples sitting outside under a trendy restaurant's sky blue umbrellas. Lasciviously dressed women artfully engage their attentive dates. Rene's eyes close. Time relinquishes its right over him. A lifetime of limitless travels and easily fulfilled desires fuse and flash before him. All the world's countries and the best of their cities spin like the carousel -- in his mind, Saira trumps them all. A quiet calm ebbs and flows over him. Rene knows it; the past of his world is in flight. His eyes open to a raven-haired beauty as she laughs and kisses the older man with her.

The light turns green. The taxi behind him honks.

Amanda presses lightly on Rene's arm. He gives the Bugatti gas and with his shift into first gear, moves from her touch. He turns left onto 71st Street and stops in front of his five-story, limestone townhouse. He sits with the engine running.

Concerned about Saira, Rene stares at his watch.

"Wow!" Amanda gawks out the window, "*This* is where you live? In the heart of New York, a half a block from all those shops?"

Rene nods.

Amanda's finger counts in the air. "Five floors all for you?"

She turns back, "You live here all by yourself?"

Rene's slow to answer. The question is invasive and bothers him. He shakes his head. "My brother..." he half-smiles, "my best friend has his own floor."

Amanda doesn't see any lights on. "Is he home tonight?'

"No," comes out as if to a child, "he's-with-a-lady-friend."

Amanda grabs the Bugatti's door handle. Feeling a vibration in his pocket, Rene stops Amanda. He pulls out Saira's phone. On it is a message. Rene holds the phone, unsure of what to do.

"Is that my sister?" Amanda asks excitedly.

Rene doesn't answer. Amanda studies him as he hesitates whether to open the phone. His eyes squint, and then his finger taps the message screen. It's from Saira. The text reads: 'Security problem at the airport. Missed my plane. Since I forgot my cell phone, I didn't have your number memorized. Don't worry. Will be on next flight.'

"Well?" Amanda pushes, "What did she say?"

Rene holds up a finger, "One second." Rene taps the phone's screen again. The text's sending number is dialed.

"Hello?" An elderly man at the other end answers and asks, "Is this Rene?"

"Yes." Rene switches the phone to the ear furthest from Amanda. "To whom am I speaking to, please?"

"I'm Farhod Armand. I am the curator of the Getty Museum in Los Angeles. Sir," his Middle Eastern accent, while crisp, is professional and disarming, "Ms. DuFour called from the airport and asked me to text her phone, which she said you have, and let you know she missed her flight. She's assuredly safe and on the way now."

"Thank you very much, Mr. Armand."

"Ms. DuFour said she would be back late tonight, not to worry, and requests that her sister please stay and wait for her."

"Thank you, sir. It's very kind of you."

Rene disconnects. He lingers smelling Saira's phone. Seeing Amanda hanging on his response, he holds up the white IPod, "This is Saira's phone. She forgot it." He tucks the phone in his pocket. "She missed her flight. Some security problem at the airport. She'll be in tonight and is anxious to meet you."

Amanda stares at Rene waiting for more.

His hands folded in his lap, Rene gives her nothing.

Amanda flips down the Bugatti's visor's mirror. She glosses her lips making sure Rene is now waiting on her. "Well..." her eyes dart at the townhouse, "I didn't plan on staying the night." She flips up the visor, hiding her smile, "Alright," her torchy-blue eyes focus their magic on Rene, "I'll have to go out and buy a few things." She touches his arm. "Can you leave me a key, I'd love to shower before dinner."

THIRTY-FIVE

Before the Madison Avenue stores close, Amanda flits from one designer store to another. It's like she's traveled with nothing. Her arms looped with bags, she's armed with makeup, black lace underwear, Manolo high-heeled pumps, and a slinky black dress.

Letting herself in with a key, Amanda spins with delight as she enters Rene's townhouse. She rushes into the main floor's drawing room and sits in one sumptuous chair after another. Lying back on the couch, kicking her heels off, she relaxes back as her eyes go wide with the display of opulence.

As she ascends the staircase, she touches the paintings adorning the walls. She stops on the second floor. Choosing the closest bedroom, she tosses her shopping bags onto an antique, canopied, four-poster bed, and starts to undress.

In less than three ounces of flimsy cotton, a braless, hair flowing, high-stepping, glistening Amanda runs on the treadmill in a white muscle t-shirt, and shorts barely covering her buttocks. She stops for a second, grabs a carton of milk, takes a slug, and continues running to the primal beat of Buddha Bar pounding in her earphones.

Amidst white orchid plants on porcelain Chinese temple stands, and a dozen flickering vanilla candles, Amanda arches her naked silhouette under the cascading rainforest spray within a ten-foot, glass enclosed, black marble shower.

Standing in five-inch, red patten, spiked-heels, and black lace underwear struggling to contain her sumptuous body, Amanda stretches over a scalloped, marble pedestal sink putting on the finishing touches of her dark-shadowed eyeliner and mascara. She bats her indigo-blue eyes in the mirror. They squeak sexuality.

A skin-tight, unapologetically plunging V-neck, black chiffon dress slides over Amanda's athletic body. She shakes her hair out, hikes up the form-fitting sleeves, and scoops her breasts higher. She puckers for the mirror and spins on her heels.

THIRTY-SIX

As the Bugatti cruises down Park Avenue, Amanda detours Rene's choice of restaurant with a flirty tug on his sleeve, "Rene, I hope it's alright with you, I've always wanted to see the Buddha Bar." Amanda shrugs disarmingly, "I have all their music." Seeing Rene's recalcitrance, she presses; "Please..." her cutest pout belies her words, "it's the last thing I'll ask for."

Exhausts barrel down as the Bugatti does a fast U-turn and changes direction. Pulling into Manhattan's Meat Packing District, Rene squints at the obscene panoply of characters lined up in front of Buddha Bar. Ill-dressed tourists, wearing their hats with their brims on backward, fan the air polluted by the close-packed, smoking, aloof Euro trash. B & T, suburbanites that have to take a bridge or tunnel to get into Manhattan, side-step so as not to be associated with the balding, desperate old men in ill-fitting suits.

Rene hates it immediately.

Amanda winks. "You can get us in."

Rene pulls the Bugatti up in front. Everyone turns to stare. Both of them dressed in complementary black, the moment they get out, they're waived inside.

The dark, sybaritic aura of electric Asian décor and hypnotizing music beckons them down a barely-lit hallway flanked by sinister, lifelike Asian figures that look like they're shooting poison darts. Tugging Rene's hand, Amanda leads him into a wickedly dark, two-tiered, windowless room with huge jellyfish tanks, and a DJ spinning raucous music over a wooden dance floor. On center stage, towering over the crammed, red-lit space is a three-story, black-lacquered Buddha. Spread out all over the room, hovels of seating areas are packed with sordid party hunters profiling with pursed lips.

As soon as Rene and Amanda are seated, drinks and a fusion of Asian and French appetizers are served. With a ravenous appetite, Amanda tries everything. Just as Rene takes a bite of egg roll, the DJ cranks the music to amp up the crowd. Rene grimaces, extending his jaw, "I think my fillings are getting shaken loose."

"Oh come on," Amanda squeezes his arm, "it's not that bad."

"I can't even hear myself chew."

"You don't need to," Amanda stands and takes both his hands. "Let's dance."

"I don't like to dance."

Confident of her will, Amanda tugs him, "Come on, Rene."

He won't get up.

"Okay…." Amanda pulls the red paper umbrella out of her drink and gulps the last of her Black Buddha. The sugar jolt starts her heart to a hundred and twenty beats. "You won't mind if I do," she bats her dark-highlighted, steely-blue eyes, "will you?" Without giving Rene a chance to answer, she heads for the dance floor.

Rene takes out Saira's phone. He touches the screen and illuminates it. No Saira. Rene checks the time. It's eight o'clock.

While Rene's eyes search for the exit, Amanda pit stops at the bar. The bartenders are two hot chicks. A blonde and brunette. Amanda squeezes into the bar. "Hit me, girls." The girls treat her to another Black Buddha. As she drinks it, a couple of neophyte civil lawyers, with matching parted-haircuts, are down the bar studying her. The drumbeat and cymbals of Le Mani's *1st Class Dandy* thumps over the room's speakers. Slightly buzzed, Amanda gyrates along with it and broadcasts it to her gracious attending bartenders; "Hey girls," her head shakes refuting it, "I know you heard this story before." Her hand's black-polished nails wave idle-talk circles in the air as she mocks herself with a raspier voice, "The story about meeting the man of your dreams and living a happy life ever after. Blah, blah,

blah." She leans over the bar bunching up her breasts sky high for the benefit of the gaping lawyers, "But…." Amanda gloats back at Rene, "*This man* is something really different."

As the beat pulses, she takes another hit of her Black Buddha, looks back at Rene, and goes after the cuter of the two lawyers. Before he can utter a word, Amanda takes him by his necktie and tugs him to the dance floor. Tousling her wild dark hair, hiking her already too-short dress up higher over her thighs, Amanda puts on a show for Rene. A feral creature whose rhythms are primal, Amanda usurps the dance floor. While the lawyer is stiffly motionless, Amanda's hips and shoulders move in perfect fluidity with the music. Though she's dancing with someone else, Amanda's eyes drill Rene. Her lifelong regimen of weight training and unbridled vanity was made for this moment -- like rippling waves on the sea, every fibrous band and tissue of her body moves in effortless synchronization.

The song plays out. Glowing, her pulse speeding, her nostrils flaring, Amanda comes up behind Rene and leans her steamy chest against his back, "I like dancing for you." Amanda sits. Her hair dangling over one eye, her fingertips at her lips, she stares at him.

Rene tries unsuccessfully to finish eating. "Well," he puts his fork down, "The Denied Self?" He smiles summing up her performance, "I guess that's something you don't have to worry about."

Amanda snatches his pocket square and pats her steamy breasts, "I don't deny myself anything."

"Amanda," Rene feigns clearing his throat, "would you like anything else? Desert?"

"I love ice cream..." Amanda stuffs his pocket square back, lingering in her touch, "as much as sex." Staring into him, she delivers it with a slithery, hot whisper, "If it's sweet, slow to defrost, and not good for me…I love it on my tongue."

Rene holds up his hand for the waiter.

As they're served a cocktail glass of hazelnut gelato large-enough-for-two, Amanda zeroes in on Rene. "Now…" she digs in for a spoonful of gelato, "it's my turn. So, what does a Rene Sorrell do?"

Before he can answer, Amanda has the spoon before his mouth.

Rene swallows the gelato. Seeing Amanda's waiting on him, he leans back, "They've good hazelnut."

She folds her arms, "You didn't answer my question."

Rene aligns the points of his red pocket square and smiles, "I'm only good at one thing at a time. I can't eat and be psychoanalyzed at the same time."

Amanda goes to feed him again.

"Okay," Rene puts his hands up in surrender. He sighs, stalls, and then answers, "I collect."

"You're *a collector?"* Her illusions a bit tarnished, she stares at him waiting for more. "Like what...?" Snickering, her tone is mockingly sarcastic, *"Baseball cards?"*

"Exactly."

Suspending a spoonful before her mouth, she doubts him.

"There's a lot of money in it."

"Baseball cards?"

Poker-faced, Rene nods.

"That's how you pay for all those paintings?" Amanda zeroes in searching for credence, "Which is your favorite?"

"I don't have one," he laughs at himself. "Half of them aren't real. I couldn't even tell you which ones are." He shrugs, "I've got a hot decorator who puts all that stuff up on the walls."

Amanda likes his slipperiness. She stands, takes his hand, and looks at him with sexual promise, "Aren't you going to show me your house before Saira comes home?"

Before Rene realizes it, Amanda has got him out the door.

Back in the Bugatti, Amanda enjoys Rene scrutinizing himself in the mirror as he runs a hand through his hair. She smiles,

"Card collector...? *You're* a real card, do you know that?"

Looking at her with controlled charm, Rene separates his thumb and forefinger two-and-a-half-inches, "It's only this big."

At first, Amanda is caught off guard. Then she cracks up.

Rene shrugs, "It's the truth."

Amanda gives him a bewitching smile and cuddles closer. "We'll work with it."

"I'm serious." Rene draws it out. "The Honus Wagner card is the rarest baseball card in the world." The Sorrell magnetism is on. "That little scrap of colored paper is the Holy Grail of baseball cards." His eyes twinkle, "Once upon a time," Rene sticks the key in, flares up the ignition and roars down the street, "in 1910, baseball cards didn't come with bubble gum, they had to fit..." he grins and holds his fingers up a few inches apart, "on the back of a cigarette pack."

Amanda likes the bedtime story. She leans back in the cushy leather and drops her hand on his knee.

Rene doesn't move from it.

In seconds, he flies through a row of solid green lights leading to the highway. Back in his domain of speed, he's spellbinding. "So... the son of a German immigrant, Honus Wagner, drops out of school at twelve to help his father work in the Pittsburg coal mines. But," Rene's eyes dart down to Amanda's hand in his lap, "that wasn't what destiny had in store." While he hits the highway, he continues, "With his windswept hair parted down the middle, baseball called him the Flying Dutchman. He was an amazing hitter, electrifying base runner, and a flawless fielder." He feels Amanda's hand move higher as he continues. "He was ranked second in baseball only to Babe Ruth, but many considered him to be baseball's greatest all-around player."

Amanda's cool blue eyes want more.

"In the early 1900's, it was no different than now, the tobacco industry tried to control everything. Even baseball." Rene looks at her evocatively, "But some people just won't play along."

Amanda gives him her best beguiling smile.

Rene gets sidetracked looking up ahead at a towering blue-tinted high-rise. "Want to see the best view of Manhattan?"

Amanda squeezes his thigh. "I'd love to." Pouting adorably, she holds her other hand out, "But what about the Flying Dutchman?"

"Well, the American Tobacco Company had a monopoly on the market and thought they could get what they wanted just because they were rich, powerful, and so commanding," his eyes dart from the road to her, "because they had no competition." Rene smiles, "With utter disregard for the rules, they did whatever they wanted."

Amanda's eyes go wild-eyed, "Like what?"

"Without his consent, they put Honus Wagner's Pittsburg Pirate picture on their cigarette packs and started distributing them.

"So, what did the Flying Dutchman do?"

"The powers that be, tried to court him, offer him more money," he slowly turns to her, "*seduce him* any way they could."

"And..." Amanda licks her glossy lips in anticipation and stares evocatively at the lesson Rene is offering, "did he succumb?"

"The Flying Dutchman surprised them."

"Oh yeah...." Amanda inches her hand higher. "How?"

"He refused to allow them to continue to distribute their product with his image on it. He didn't want children to buy cigarettes just to get his card."

Amanda leans in sensuously, "Is there a moral to the story?"

"Yeah. The devil can cite scripture for his own purpose."

"Or...." Amanda volleys back. "The best laid plans of mice and men go awry."

Rene suddenly downshifts, careening off the highway. "Before Saira gets here I want to show you something." He heads the car straight for the high-rise with the blue-tinted windows. It's Friday night along the New Jersey shoreline, and Rene quietly lulls the Bugatti up to the back gate of a Gold Coast skyscraper rising seventy-five stories above the shimmering black of the Hudson River. Rene's eyes pinpoint the faint light coming from the security guard's trailer a few hundred yards away. Shutting off the car's engine, he just stares, watching the vinyl-sided trailer.

Studying Rene, trying to figure out why he's waiting, Amanda's unbridled curiosity carries on. "How did you two meet?"

Rene doesn't turn around. "What...?"

"How did you meet Saira?"

Turning, Rene stares at her, transfixed. "Over a fraud."

Dead silence.

Amanda crosses her legs hiking up her dress over her thighs, "Excuse me?"

Turning back to watch the trailer, Rene's back is to her. "She wanted something that was worthless. I rescued her."

Amanda squints, "How did you know it was a fraud?"

Rene turns to Amanda, effusing his practiced charm, "One is never satisfied with a portrait of a person that one knows."

"But, who, who are you talking about?"

Rene opens his door without answering. He waves her out as he shuts the door quietly. Looking behind him, monitoring the security guard's trailer's door, Rene comes around the Bugatti and helps Amanda out. He closes the door, quietly letting it click shut. He takes Amanda's arm and angles her towards an exterior construction elevator. Taking his driving gloves out of his pocket, Rene puts them on and holds up a sagging, rusting chain allowing he and Amanda to slip past the unmonitored back gate. He stops at the exposed steel door of the construction cage and turns, "Are you afraid of heights?"

Amanda shakes her head. "So, what's Saira like?"

Rene opens the elevator's sliding door and guides her in. As he pushes the button for the top floor, a bare bulb goes on the exposed ceiling of the cage. Rene reaches up with his gloved-hand, unscrews the bulb and casually watches the floors whiz by.

"What? You own this building?"

Rene points to the adjacent twin tower being put up, "I try not to buy anything when there's more than one of them."

The winds pick up. The exposed iron cage shimmies as it shoots up the swaying chute. Amanda peeks down and flinches as if frightened. Rene puts his arm around her. The corners of her mouth turn upward. She hides her satisfaction.

Rene takes a deep breath and stares at the twinkling lights punctuating the pitch black of the Hudson River. "What's Saira like?" he repeats as the elevator grinds higher. As the distinctive shapes of humanity get smaller, his eyes strive to stare past the endless dark of the horizon. "She's my glimpse of eternity." Waiting for more, Amanda nestles under Rene's arm and draws him closer as the elevator's cage rocks in its ascent. He lights up, "Each moment I'm with her, I feel I'm starting all over."

Inches from his face, Amanda stares into his distant eyes, "What do you want to change?"

The cage cranks to the top and grinds to a stop on the unfinished seventy-fifth floor. A carpet of sparkling lights spreads before them. Rene doesn't get out. Unbuttoning his suit coat, he kneels. Resting his forearms on his knees, he stares at the world below. "Nothing now."

The wind rattles the stopped cage. Afraid to look down, Amanda anxiously slides the gate open, "Can we get on solid ground?"

"Absolutely. I'm sorry." Rene rises, takes her arm and steps onto the cement roof of the building. The wind howls, blowing a fine-grained powder from the floor into the air. Amanda coughs. Rene stops, "You okay?" She nods. Rene's mood mercurially changes as he walks arm-in-arm across the roof with Amanda hugging his side. He looks at her protectively, "Are you cold?"

Amanda nestles closer.

As Rene is taking off his suit coat, his red pocket square is snatched and stolen by the breeze. He studies it blow east over the edge down toward the Hudson River. Rene drapes his coat around Amanda. "Okay," Rene holds her tighter, "now close your eyes and hold on tight." He walks her toward the end of the roof. As they get within feet of the edge, Rene tells her, "Alright, open them."

Amanda's eyes go wide seeing the majesty that the glittering shorelines of New York City and the State of New Jersey have to offer. "Wow! It's magnificent."

"Picture perfect, isn't it?"

"Yes," Amanda purrs, holding him tighter. She steps closer for a look at the Hudson, "The water is so beautiful."

"Not just water. The Hudson River, the ethereal fluid that flows like blood in the veins of New York City."

"Come on," he guides Amanda further across the roof, "I want to show you something." He points north, just over the river. "That's Saira's wedding present."

"What is?"

Getting closer to the edge, he takes Amanda's hand and points it at the spire of a thousand-foot skyscraper of mythical proportions, "There. See the lights of the two-story penthouse being constructed at the top of that building? It's being designed specifically for Saira. That's where your sister and I will be able to go for riverside strolls and our children will play in the lush greenery of the parks."

"Look," she points down the river at a 106-foot, triple-sailed, wooden boat that looks like an eighteenth century Dutch sailing ship, "look at that old time sailboat."

"No...it's not just a sailboat." He smiles and shakes his head, "It's *a constant reminder*."

"What do you mean?"

Rene walks closer to the lip of the roof and puts his arm around Amanda, "The famous folk singer Pete Seeger, a life long fan of the

Hudson River, was worried about our city's environmental trespasses. An admirer of the great ships that once sailed the waters of Hudson, he got the idea of recreating a classic sloop that," Rene steals a look at her, "would help forever remind everybody about the plight of the river." He points at the sloop, "It's called Clearwater. It's carried thousands of environmentalists from all over the world."

Mesmerized, Amanda walks closer.

"So," Rene eases Amanda even closer. Inches from the edge, "what do you think of Saira's present? It'll be our riverfront paradise."

"Heaven's not that far away," Amanda looks at him with her sultry laser focus, "it's right before your eyes." Dropping his coat off her shoulders, Amanda kisses him fully on his mouth.

Rene jerks away from her and wipes his lips with his hand, "What's wrong with you! I'm engaged to your sister."

"So?" Amanda rebukes him, "An engagement is a testing ground for marriage."

"No, it's a betrothal. A promise." Rene gets behind Amanda. He stares coolly at the sloop Clearwater. "Look," his left hand points, "it's turning." As Amanda turns, Rene, with one fluid movement, pushes her off the roof.

Rene takes a deep breath of the Hudson's cool air and exhales. Turning, he scoops up his coat, flicks off the construction dust, and throws his coat over his shoulder as he walks back to the elevator.

THIRTY-SEVEN

The hydraulic spoiler of the Bugatti flares to full height as a blue fireball of flames shoots out of its nine-inch exhaust. Thundering across the highway, the red stream of the Bugatti's taillights spiking the black of the asphalt like tracer bullets, Rene blows by everything in sight. As the tachometer redlines, Rene shifts fifth gear into six, rocketing the car past two hundred miles per hour. His eyes gaping wide, Rene slams it down into seventh gear, pushing the Bugatti to the max. He squints at the fuel gage. He's running on empty. He smiles and presses it further. Cranking the stereo's twelve speakers to ear splitting level, competing with the Bugatti's supersonic boom, he blasts The Animals' *Don't Let Me Be Understood.*

Flicking fingers of his left hand, then right hand, Rene paddle shifts the Bugatti at breakneck speeds through a slalom course of honking tractor-trailers. His eye ticks. His jaw juts. He shakes it off, his sardonic wit grinning in the mirror as the song's reprise resounds, *"Baby, do you understand me now. Sometimes I feel a little mad."* His hands leave the wheel. The Bugatti veers onto the asphalt kicking up a cloud cover of gravel. Enjoying the loss of control, he grabs the wheel again and paddle shifts from left-to-right with the lyrics, *"Don't you know that no one alive can always be an angel. When things go wrong I seem to be bad. I'm just a soul whose intentions are good. Oh Lord...please don't let me be misunderstood."*

Red oscillating lights explode on as a New Jersey State Trooper patrol car fishtails onto the toll way and races after the Bugatti. It's siren blares as it tries to pursue the Bugatti. It's futile, the trooper feels like his squad car's traveling in slow motion. The Bugatti's taillights become microscopic red specs. The trooper radios ahead. The Bugatti's four turbos full vent as the car vaporizes by the next exit.

Waiting a mile ahead is another state trooper's car. It takes off barreling well before Rene gets close to it. Just as the Bugatti catches up to it, the trooper's car swerves at Rene. The Bugatti dodges it like a whip snap and darts ahead. Seeing the cement dividers of the tollbooths up ahead, Rene stomps on the brakes. Screeching, the Bugatti bites asphalt. Trying to stop alongside Rene, fishtailing across lanes, the trooper's car lays a swerving rubber patch of smoking tread a hundred yards past the Bugatti and buries into a grass embankment.

Twenty seconds later, the first state trooper pulls up alongside Rene. A featureless, swollen-faced, six-foot-four, Polish state trooper with ham-hock hands, jerks the door open and yanks Rene out by his collar, "Big shot, in a fancy, fast car, huh?" The trooper throws Rene over the side of his car, presses him down and brags, "You can't outrun Motorola." Slapping a handcuff on Rene's wrist, the trooper turns to the receiver attached to the epaulet on his shoulder, "Sergeant, I got him. Send a cage car." Trying to catch his breath, the bug-eyed trooper grunts, "You know why we're stopping you, right?"

Rene tilts his head matter-a-factly, "Speeding?"

"Nah...speeding is for motorists." He grins and leans in, "You broke the sound barrier." The trooper laughs at his own humor. He immediately starts frisking Rene. As he pulls out a huge wad of hundreds out of Rene's pocket, the trooper moans with obscene pleasure," Ooooh." He lights up, "You know how in all our urban cities..." by force of habit, the trooper looks around and mockingly whispers, "Blacks and Latinos complain about the filthy rich getting a different kind of justice?" He slams the second cuff on Rene's wrist. "Well, you're gonna' be our poster boy of equality."

Another New Jersey State Trooper's car screeches up. This one is unmarked. A greying, African American, spit-polished, uniformed-sergeant, with yellow slash patches boasting thirty years of service on his sleeve, militarily marches over like the hangar is still in his coat. The arresting trooper spins Rene around and holds out the thick knot of cash he seized.

The sergeant eyeballs the choking stack of hundreds.

Rene shrugs, "Toll money."

As a line of stopped cars honk at a stalled tollbooth, a two-fingered whistle turns the three men around. "Hey, Pete!" the Fu Manchu-mustached and Asian-tattooed, Falstaffian Jersey toll taker, whose daughter Rene helped get into school, waddles over.

"What's up, Ritchie?" The sergeant quips, eyeing the line of cars at Ritchie's tollbooth. "Someone give you a slug for a nickel?"

"Him. This same guy," the toll taker, Ritchie, points at Rene, "he was here just last week." He snubs his fat thumb at the Bugatti, "driving that same foreign piece of crap." Ritchie goes over to the Bugatti, opens the door and looks inside, "Yep. Same thing. His gas pedal got stuck. Nothing he could do about it. He had to have it towed. Then, he came over and apologized for tying up traffic. Guy was a real gentleman."

Cocking his head, squinting, the sergeant folds his arms with incredulity.

"The same thing must've happened tonight." Ritchie turns to Rene and holds his eyes, "Right?"

Rene nods, "Exactly."

"Are you kidding me?" The trooper butts in and tries to push Ritchie back -- it's like trying to move a buffalo. He points at Rene, "He's goin' to jail."

The sergeant motions Ritchie over to his unmarked car. As they walk, a domino chorus of honking horns at the toll booth turns Ritchie's head back. "Screw 'em."

Crooking his size-eighteen neck, the Polish trooper scrutinizes his sergeant and Ritchie talk in hushed tones. As Ritchie's hands go out, the sergeant shakes his head no. Ritchie tugs the sergeant closer and whispers. The sergeant looks at Rene, head-to-toe, sizing him up. He turns to Ritchie and holds his eyes. Ritchie winces a shrug.

The trooper shakes his head seeing Ritchie waddle back with a half-buried smile. He tries to read his sergeant's inscrutable stare, "Gas pedal stuck up my ass, right?"

The sergeant goes over to Rene, uncuffs him and leans in

close. "Not his ass, yours. And you must have a horseshoe there." As Rene brushes off and buttons his suit, the sergeant holds onto his arm, "Mr. Sorrell, I'm not going to ever see you again unless it's some old lady honking at you for going under the speed limit. Understood?"

"Perfectly." Rene nods at Ritchie as the toll taker heads back to his booth.

THIRTY-EIGHT

Quickly pulling on and tying a black velvet robe over his pajamas, his breath strained, Andre Pope rushes to the front double-doors of his seventy-seventh floor, duplex penthouse atop the Time Warner Center. As he opens the door, his blue-veined hand covers his mouth, "Oh my God. Are you alright?"

Her face colorless, her hair streaked with plaster, her eyes tearing and on the verge of going into shock, Saira DuFour stands before him trembling in a torn, muddied cocktail dress.

Cradling her, Andre draws her into his home, "Sit down. Sit down." Taking his cashmere topcoat out of the hall closet, he wraps it around her for warmth and guides her to the drawing room couch. "What happened? Is Rene alright?" Sitting down with her, he holds Saira as she tremors. Andre cups her soiled hands, "Saira, talk to me."

Saira sits motionless. Drawing heavy, stilted breaths, her eyes close. As her head drops, her shaking hands cover the top of it as she bites her lip, fighting sobbing.

Andre gets on his knees before her, "You're scaring me Saira, what happened?"

Drawing a breath, Saira lifts her head. "He tried to kill me…" she shakes her head, "well, not me, I mean my sister."

"What! Who did?" he hangs on her words. "Your sister? What do you mean?"

Saira stands, avoiding his stare. Confronted with the penthouses' 360 degree view of New York, she spins not knowing where to go. She walks to the floor-to-ceiling windows and stares out at the Hudson River. She winces and steps back from the height of the drop. "I did a horrible thing."

"What? What've you done?" Andre stands, tilting his head to find Saira's face. His words stick to her, "Is Rene alright?"

"Yes." She turns. "Except for pushing me off the roof of a seventy-five story building."

"What?" Andre shakes his head, looking at her like she's out of her mind, "What are you talking about?"

"He tried to kill me. I mean someone he thought was a human being. Amanda."

"Saira," Andre's hands go out, "you're making no sense." He goes to her and escorts her back to the couch. "Who is Amanda?"

Saira sits down. Putting her glasses on, she pins back her plaster-smeared hair into a ponytail. Her shaking hands futilely try to seam the ripped fabric of her dress together. Seeing Andre is waiting on her, she takes a deep breath. Stalling, she realigns her bent glasses, "It all went so fast. I...." Shaking her head, she looks down at her scraped shoes, "I...I was afraid to trust it. It all felt so out of control." Saira slides out of Andre's coat, "Rene created another reality. So...." Condemning herself, she shrugs, "So did I."

Andre leans in. His tone is severe, "What-did-you-do?"

Saira turns from his drilling stare. "Andre, please try...." Her head drops again as she starts to sob. Her hand covers her mouth trying to gain control again. "Please try to understand." She clutches his hands begging for understanding, "I lost the taste of myself." Shaking her head, she tries to repress it all back. She swallows and sniffles, "Everything was so perfect." She shrugs into herself like a little girl, "I...I didn't know how to accept it." Her hands clutch at the fabric of Andre's robe, kneading it, drawing him protectively closer, "To just be happy. I never lived that simply." Saira can't hold her head up. Taking off her glasses, she caves onto Andre's chest.

Andre's hand enfolds her head, soothing her. "It's okay. Saira, it's okay. *Now...*" his tone remains impatient, "tell me what you did."

Wiping the smudge of tearing eye shadow off Andre's robe, Saira raises her head. "I wanted to see how Rene was...or would be with someone else."

He squints at Saira, "And...?"

"Well, Andre..." Saira winces, "you know how Rene collects everything?" Her head shakes, "I...I didn't want to just be another possession. So...." Defeated, she exhales, looking away from Andre's eyes anticipating his response, "So, I created another one of me."

"You-did-what?"

"I wrote myself a fictional letter claiming it was from the sister separated from me in an orphanage in Punjab." Saira shakes her head trying to undo it, "A twin sister."

Andre's head drops. His hand runs through his long white hair. "*Saira DuFour....*" he tries to speak, but can't. He exhales. "Saira, Saira," his hands go out in utter frustration, "you're engaged to the man. You've traveled with him. Been at his house." His stare holds on to her, "Didn't you ever look around?" His eyes go gelid, "Rene only has *one* of everything."

Ashamed, Saira turns away.

Andre stands. He takes her hand and walks her over to a nineteenth century credenza. He opens it up and pours her a cognac. His tongs pause at the container of ice. Saira nods. Pinching a few cubes, Andre drops them into the amber liquid. He stiffens the drink with more cognac, "You're going to need this." He sets the drink down on a desk whose sides have undulating lines of carved-mahogany. As Saira sits, Andre turns on a Art Nouveau lamp. Leaning over her, he cups her face in the soft light. "My child," wetting his handkerchief, he tenderly wipes the ash from her face, "he loves you so much."

"Who...?" Biting her lip, she turns away, "Who am I?"

"No," he comforts her, "don't say that. You don't mean that." His fingertips catch a tear on her dirt-smudged cheek. "Saira DuFour," Andre waits for her full attention, "Take it from a connoisseur.

You're a masterpiece."

Saira shakes her head with doubting exasperation.

"What do you mean he pushed you off a roof?"

Saira's hand mimics it, moving effortlessly over the desk's edge and downward. "Just like that. Without a care. And," she snaps her fingers, "Amanda was gone."

"Rene pushed you off a roof?" His hands go out in repudiation. "How are you here?"

"The high-rise's blue window panes were still being installed. You couldn't see it, but, on the side facing the Hudson, the top installation wasn't completed. There was a yellow honeycomb of protective netting three floors down. That stopped my fall."

"Rene pushed you? He purposely pushed you off the roof?"

"No. Not me. Amanda."

"And you convinced him you were this woman, Amanda?"

"Obviously." She takes the drink, shakes up the ice and gets the semblance of an ironic, strained half-smile, "When you have no history, you're not limited to what you make up." Taking a strong gulp, Saira continues, "It was easy to be convincing. Nobody knew it better than me. The isolated life of an outcast."

Andre sits on the edge of the desk. Looking at the floor, exhaling, he folds his arms. Saira hesitates. Andre waves for more.

"So..." Saira elaborates, "I set up a test date."

"To do what?"

Stalling, Saira looks at the desk and picks up a twelve-inch, ivory figurine of a naked woman lying prone on a strip of rosewood.

Andre removes it from her hand, "For what purpose?"

Saira grimaces saying it, "To test my mate's loyalty."

"*What loyalty*?" Andre's voice raises. His hand covers his

forehead with the pain of it all. "What loyalty, you were engaged?"

Again, Saira picks up the ivory figurine. "What is this?"

Andre takes it from her. "How-did-you-do-it?"

Saira cocks her head, "Drama club in high school." Seeing Andre is not pleased, she continues, "My job at Christie's was a perfect cover. I knew I was going out of town to Los Angeles for only a day. So, when Rene took me to the airport, I purposely left my phone in his car. That way I knew I was free to juggle my time schedule and flight plans without him reaching me. I got to LA, did what I had to at the Getty Museum and caught the early plane back to New York just like I was supposed to. Except..." she devilishly shrugs, "I told a white lie and called my contact at The Getty and told him that I missed my plane. I told him that I forgot my phone, and that, since I didn't have it, I didn't know my fiancé, Rene Sorrell's, number by heart." Saira shrugs, "The part about not knowing the number was true."

Andre nods, "I have so many locker combinations, bank codes, and pin numbers, I don't have anybody's number memorized."

"Then, I asked the man at The Getty to text my phone and let my fiancé know I missed my flight." She nods, "I knew Rene would look at my phone and see the text."

"Then?"

"Then...I created Amanda."

"And Rene didn't know? You fooled him?"

She nods. "With a few years of psychoanalysis under my belt, blue contacts and dressed up like my roommates when they go out bar-hopping...." Taking off her glasses, she perks up her posture, pulls out her pony tail, dips her head and thrusts it back, surprising Andre with a primal shake of her hair. Her hand on her hip, defying him with her sudden self-possession, a different Saira owns the moment, "You'd be surprised what a person's id can accomplish."

Andre leans back trying to take it all in. Staring at her scraped, dirty shoes, his head shakes as he exhales with frustration.

"I enjoyed it until I got pushed off the roof."

"And fell three floors into the netting?"

"And swayed in the dark, creaking in the breeze, convinced I was going die, until I clawed my way back into the building."

"My God." Andre covers his mouth.

"That's how close it was for her. I mean me."

Andre's look of disapproval defies Saira. "So…" he squints, "is Amanda you?"

Caught off guard, Saira is silent. She struggles to answer.

"If not, you need to say goodbye to her."

Lost, Saira's eyes return to the evocative ivory statue.

Andre picks it up. "It's called a Doctor's Lady. In China, the recognized standard of propriety didn't permit a Chinese woman to disrobe before a man doctor. In order to meet this restriction, the Chinese doctor always carried what was known as a medical doll as a diagnostic figure." He holds the ivory statue out to her, "The doctor passed it to the patient with a request." Andre's eyes search Saira's, "Point to where it hurts."

Saira stares at the statue. She starts to point at the head and stops. Her eyes close. "Everywhere."

Andre is tortured. His head drops, "Saira, Saira, Saira."

Saira covers her face with shame.

Exhaling, raising his head, Andre places the statue in her lap. He sits next to Saira, puts an arm around her, easing her head on his shoulder. Staring out at the black of the windows, Andre can't suppress it any longer. Exhaling deeply, he bares a long held secret, "I was hoping I'd never have to revisit this moment again."

Saira cranks her head up, "What does that mean?"

Andre stands. He goes over to a velvet, antique Empire chair and pushes it closer, facing Saira. He sits and takes a deep breath.

"When Rene was just a child, he had a traumatic experience."

"I know," Saira interrupts, "Don Frye told me about his parents dying when he was nine."

Holding her stare, Andre shakes his head solemnly. "That's not what I'm talking about."

"What do you mean? There's something else?"

Andre slowly nods. He sits with his hands over his mouth deciding whether to tell her. He hedges, "Besides being business partners, Rene's parents were my closest friends. Like I told you before, I spent a lot of time at their house." He bites his tongue, as his face turns expressionless. He sighs, "There was this one Thanksgiving. Rene was five." His tongue scurries in his mouth, buying time. His words come out slowly, painfully, "Everyone was at the dinner table, except Rene. His mother kept calling him." Andre avoids Saira's invasive stare. "After a while of no answer, we all went to look for him." He turns to Saira, "He was in the doorway of his baby brother's room."

"He had a brother? No one told me that?"

"He was born when Rene was four and a half."

"And…." Holding her breath, Saira is afraid to ask. "What happened?"

Andre's eyes close and then open, "The child was dead."

Saira's hand covers her mouth.

Andre shakes his head with consternation, "The doctors couldn't figure it out. They thought..." he shakes his head denying it, "they thought it might be asphyxiation."

"Like suffocation? What are you saying?"

Andre walks across the room to the windows overlooking Central Park's blackness, "I'd rather not say anything. Maybe I should keep my mouth shut."

"But, you're inferring…you're suggesting Rene had something to do with it. You are…." Saira puts the ivory statue back down.

Her hands go out, "Aren't you?"

Andre sighs deeply. He takes awhile to answer. "No. No, I'm not. There was no medical proof." He looks away, "After the child's death, that's when Rene's father started drinking."

"Rene was standing in the door alone?"

"Not alone. His childhood friend, Don Frye, was there too. Both boys were frozen. Traumatized."

"What about the autopsy? What caused the baby's death?"

"The results were inconclusive. The medical examiner eventually labeled it Sudden Infant Death Syndrome. He posited it could've been some type of genetic flaw."

"Genetic flaw? Did Rene have it?"

Andre shakes his head no. "His parents submitted him for a battery of tests." Andre turns his back to Saira as he stares out at the blackness; it hides the contortion in his face. "Rene was found to be…" his head cocks, "medically dissimilar to the child."

"Dissimilar? What do you mean dissimilar?"

Moving to the credenza, Andre dodges Saira's scrutiny. He pours himself a cognac. After downing the glass, Andre turns, "Rene was…" hesitating, he delivers it matter-a-factly, "Rene was quite healthy, except for some neurological imaging."

"What does that mean?"

"They detected some physiological markers," he shrugs, "electrochemical synapses in his brain. It suggested an abnormality in the hypothalamic-pituitary-adrenal axis possibly causing chemical imbalances. Something like low cortisol."

"Before or after the child's death?"

Andre picks up the Doctor's Lady and runs his fingers over the polished ivory as if he's trying to know the pain himself. "He was only tested after. The doctors were unable to determine if it was genetic or as a result of the trauma splitting."

"Trauma splitting?"

"Rene's brain exhibited a borderline pathology they felt was caused by a child's coping strategies being overwhelmed in response to stress. They believed Rene's system went into permanent alert as if the danger might return at any moment." Andre pours himself another drink. "Have you ever witnessed Rene's obsession with speed?"

Saira nods.

"It's the moth to the flame. Like an automobile driven at maximum speed, the brain is pushed flat-out past its limits. The overwhelmed child ignores the trauma by splitting off the experiences and not integrating them into his personality or daily life." Andre shrugs, "He creates another reality and goes to it during traumatic events."

Saira gets it all too well. "A fantasy reality?"

"Exactly." Andre nods. "The doctors explained that quite often once this defense mechanism has been internalized, it's recycled later in life whenever the adult experiences triggers or stimuli that replicated the original challenge."

"So, splitting is an attempt to protect oneself?"

Andre hands her back the ivory Doctor's Lady. "You understand..." his look penetrates her defenses, "don't you?"

Saira holds the statue fragilely, intimately examining it. Grasping it, she nods.

"In his own way," Andre shrugs, "he protected you."

"What?" Saira stares in disbelief. "What are you saying?"

"Saira, your source of happiness hasn't been touched. It's more secure now. Nothing can harm you." Andre shrugs. "In his own way, Rene loved you more."

She gives him back the ivory statue, "I'm his *one and only*?"

Andre relinquishes a nod.

Saira folds her arms, "You two are exactly alike."

"You've seen the oil painting of Rene as a child. You can see it in his eyes. Like of all of us children, he thought his parents would be there forever. With their sudden death, Rene split at nine, breaking into two pieces mentally. Half of him had a life as a child; the other half dividing into an adult."

"Where does that leave me? Which half do I get?"

Andre's eyes narrow, "Rene could ask you the same question."

Saira's voice is emotional, defenseless, "That's not fair."

"Forgive me, I'm sorry." Andre takes her hands in his. He searches her face. "They say the same look that's stamped in a child's eyes remains with her as an adult and is an indication of who she is." Andre hands her back the ivory Doctor's Lady. "Tell me about Saira as a child. What was in her eyes?"

Exposed, Saira holds the ivory statue to her lips. "Fear."

"Aren't you reliving it? Doing it again?"

Saira has no words for him.

Andre smiles, "And you also, my dearest, "you're just like him." He stares into her soul. "A tender moment shared between you and Amanda meant the disappearance of one into the other." He cups her face, "In blocking love to yourself you prevent the healthy expression of love from others. And defeat the joy of your own life." He closes his eyes and relives his past. They open, exposing his pain. "Take it from someone who knows. Sabotage is an addiction. Three lives have suffered for it because of me."

"Three?" She shakes her head in confusion. "Who?"

His eyes shift away, "Not now, Saira. This isn't about me."

"How do you know so much about Rene's condition?"

Andre sighs. "Once upon a time, I was family."

"What do I do, Andre?"

"Tell me about being happy." His hands fold under his chin,

"When do you remember being happy?"

At first she shrugs. Saira eyes go distant. Memories spin in her eyes. Cupping the ivory statue, she surrenders a sense of calm. "Los Cabos, Mexico." Her eyes twinkle, "Painting Rene's toenails while he slept. Horseback riding in the rain forest." She nearly laughs, "When he walked out in a pilot's hat on the plane to Paris. Picnicking in the French countryside. Waking up with him and watching the glass house tincture orange." Holding herself, her eyes flutter. Saira sighs and gauges Andre's reaction as she speaks, "Seeing him kneel and cry at my bedside. Telling Tookie about him. Discovering about him from Don Frye." Saira cocks her head, "Dancing with a real Maharaja..." she pauses, illuminating as she evaluates it all, "and missing my fiancé." Saira grins at Andre. "Dressing up like the Punjabi princess and conspiring with Rene to outbid everybody at the auction." She enfolds the Doctor's Lady to her heart, "Listening to him. Hearing his voice...." She accedes, acknowledging it just for herself, "Having him teach and mentor me. I guess..." she shrugs, drawing a deep breath, "just having him totally there -- always accountable." Torn, she looks up in torment, "Feeling so loved."

Andre smiles. "Go home, Saira. Go home to your fiancé."

"How do I? I feel like a ghost. It feels like another life."

"Let it go. You may have needed that passing. While there is breath in your body go home to him." Cupping her face, he kisses her forehead, "You were the real Saira with Rene."

THIRTY-NINE

Steam pours out of the marble and glass rain forest shower behind Saira as she stands before the washroom's full-length mirror. Standing on her tiptoes in a towel, she pivots on the marble floor, staring at herself. She spots a bruise on her thigh and covers it with makeup. As she turns back, she winces. Raising the towel higher, she feels another bruise on her hip. Lifting her arms, she examines her elbows. Running her hand over her forearm, a scrape on her knuckle catches her eye. She puts a Band-Aid on it. She stretches her neck side-to-side loosening its stiffness. Saira's eyes catch something in the mirror. A flake of plaster is lodged in the strands of her hair. She combs it out and twists looking for a hint of anything else. Turning back, she faces herself. She squints with focus.

Saira moves closer to the mirror and stares into it.

Her voice says it barely audibly, "Saira DuFour." She folds her hands under her chin and says her name louder, trying to discover what she hears, "Saira DuFour." In Punjabi, Saira asks herself what should she do, "Tuhanu ki karna chaida hai?"

A double-knock on the closed washroom door startles her out of her towel. She quickly picks up a robe and spins toward the door.

"Saira." Rene's voice booms, "It's me. Who you talking to?"

Saira steals one more glimpse of herself and goes to open the door. Two steps later, she stops and rushes back to the mirror.

The doorknob rattles.

"Since when do we lock doors?"

"One second, Rene." Saira leans into the mirror and gasps. Her fingers rush to her eyes and take out the blue contacts. She flushes them down the toilet and rushes to reach the door.

The second she unlocks it; Rene sweeps her off her feet. Lifting her off the ground, he spins her around, "I missed you so much." He cradles her into his shoulder as he draws in the nectar of her scent, "Mmm." He inhales the crook of her neck, "I can't live without that smell." Letting her down, he cups her face and kisses her lips. "Thank God you're back safe."

She tickles his side. "I was only gone for a day."

Rene pokes fun, "Who were you talking to in here?"

"I was having a talk with myself."

"In Punjabi?" He cracks himself up.

"I was anxious to see you." She shrugs, "I was nervous."

He takes her hands in his and sits down with her on his lap. "Tell me everything. How did it go?" He kisses her from the back of her neck forward. Like two children playing in a sandbox, he soaks her up. He finger-waves rivulets of wet hair off the side of her face. "Did you play nice with the other kids?"

"Well, Los Angeles is…." Saira looks over Rene's shoulder and nearly goes into cardiac arrest. Right behind him, next to the shower, she sees her dirty shoes and tattered dress. She hugs Rene closer. "Well, Los Angeles is…" she quickly extemporizes, "palm trees, profilers, and posers. Who'd want to live in a place where the only cultural advantage is movie billboards." Anxious, Saira stands. "My taxi driver never even heard of the Getty Museum." Her arms keeping Rene in the same-seated position, she slips out of her robe, swiftly pushing it with her foot on top of her dress and shoes.

Rene kisses her bare shoulder, "That's more like it."

Saira guides him to the door, "Wait for me in bed. Give me a minute." As Rene goes into the bedroom, Saira closes the door. She scoops up her shoes and dress, bundles them together, and spins looking for a place to put them. Nowhere. She starts to wrap them up in a towel and then changes her mind. Her eyes scour the room. She goes to the window, opens it and shoves the dress and shoes out. Saira looks back in the mirror one last time trying to find herself. Smoothing her hair, she spots a scratch on her forehead under the tuft of a wave. As she covers it with makeup, she holds out her hand. It shakes. Drawing a deep breath, Saira walks out of the washroom in her robe. She strides across the bedroom to turn the overhead spots off.

Arms-crossed, relishing watching her, Rene is shirtless and in jeans, leaning against the bed's headboard. "Sweetheart, could you leave the lights on. I want to watch you walk."

Saira dims them, "Is that okay."

"Sure." Rene pats the bed next to him.

After a few steps, Saira turns back and lowers the lights a caliber more. She looks to see if Rene minds.

Puzzled, he's waiting on her. "Well...?" His hands go out, "Aren't you going to ask me?"

Saira stares at him, spinning in her mind a host of defensive scenarios. Then it hits her. "Oh my God! My sister! I...I've been rushing so much, I'm spun out." She shakes her head with her senselessness, "Missing the plane. The jet lag and all." Keeping a distance, sitting at the foot of the bed, she takes off Rene's shoes and socks, and rubs his feet. "What happened?"

He's silent. He just stares at her as she stares back at him.

"Well?" Seeing the look change on his face, she freezes.

Rene moves next to her. "Saira," he pauses as he gathers her hands in his, "You know I'm going to be with you forever." Hanging on his every expression, Saira stares at him not knowing what he's going to say. Rene cradles her in his arms, sheltering her from what he's about to tell her.

Saira pulls free, "What? What is it?" Her chest heaving, her face inches from his, she holds her breath, "Rene, tell me."

"In all my life..." Rene holds his palm before her, "I could count the promises I've made myself on one hand. "Saira…." Emotional, he swallows. He cradles her face in his hands, "I swear, all the days I've got left, I'll spend loving you." His finger twirls in the air, "Spinning the world at your feet…making up for everything."

Numb, she waits on him.

Rene's eyes close and flutter open. He shakes his head. "There is no sister."

Just then, scampering in the room, whining as he slips across the floor's wooden planks, the bloodhound puppy, Beauregard, does a beeline for Saira. Howling, he immediately starts to sniff and plant a hundred lizard-quick licks on her bare toes.

Bizarrely, Saira almost laughs as her face loses all its color.

Rene separates Beauregard from Saira, and calms him down with a few pats. "I guess he missed you as much as I did." Still whining, Bo is not happy until Rene lifts him up in bed with them. The puppy cuddles up and is instantly quiet.

"Rene, what are you saying? What do you mean there's no sister? But," her head shakes denying the disappointment, "you read the letter. She went into detail about..."

"Baby," Rene interrupts, cupping her cheek. He delivers it gently, "She wasn't who she said she was. She was a fraud."

"A fraud?"

"A gold-digger who tracked us down on the Internet. I found her out…" his eyes turn cold, "and sent her on her way."

Saira stares at Rene's face searching for acknowledgement of what happened. He gives her nothing more. Still seeing in her mind's eye what happened to her, her head drops reliving the details. How the chilling wind off the Hudson swayed her, banging her side against the high-rise empty window frame. Surprisingly, Saira still pushes it, "What was she like?" She raises her head, "Did she look like me?"

He says it matter-a-factly, "Mixed. East Indian. Physically attractive. But…" he stares at her with adoration, "no one is like you."

Saira eyes close. Tears of fright fight the tears of the possibility of hope. She peeks at Rene Sorrell. She sees the exaltation of a man that truly loves her. "So, I guess..." Saira sighs and shrugs, "it's back to being only me in the world."

Rene cups her face, "No. No. No. Don't be disappointed. Please." His shaking head banishes her perceived fate. "Remember when we were in Mexico and you kept asking me why I collected things that were one-of-a-kind?"

Saira nods, drinking in the devotion in his face.

"In the past..." Rene nods in full contrition, "I was defined by my possessions. The finest Ming vase, the most sought after Faberge egg, the consummate jade necklace, whatever. When I possessed what everyone else couldn't, it was like..." his eyes close with the truth of it, "being able to touch the work of God." His eyes open, appealing to her, "But Saira," he takes her fingers and kisses them, "with you, and the love we share, it transcends it all. I couldn't care if there is one God or many Gods." Just then, the brindle puppy whines to be held. "It's all about..." Rene scoops Bo up under one arm, "whether you feel you belong or are abandoned." His other hand takes Saira's and holds it over his heart, "I belong to you. And you belong to me."

Rene takes a pillow and sets it on the floor. "Bo," he leans into the puppy's face, "now it's time for you to learn to share." He puts the puppy on the pillow. It whines for a moment, lies down and buries his nose in the pillow. Rene draws Saira to him and teases, "He's just like me. He loses all discipline when Don Frye's not around." Pulling off the belt of Saira's robe, Rene runs his hands inside it. As his hand grazes up her thigh and over her hip, Saira winces with pain.

Rene sits up, "What's wrong? Did I hurt you?"

"No. Not all," she diminishes it. "I was a total klutz this trip. Rushing, disorientated," she rubs her hipbone, "I tripped and banged it on the plane." Making fun of herself, she holds out her hand with the Band Aid over her knuckles.

Rene kisses her hand, "Poor baby." He opens her robe and proceeds to her hip. He kisses it and everything around it.

Saira lays back. “I’ll have to forget my phone more often.”

“Oh,” Rene lifts his head, “gear up for Austria. We’re leaving Sunday night.”

“What now?” She questions the pursuit of yet another possession. “Don’t tell me this is about the last Blue Mauritius Stamp?”

“That and…” his voice comes out muffled and then gets distinctly purposeful and lucid, “and there’s something else I have to do.”

FORTY

As a hazy afternoon sun sets, Don Frye, driving the Bentley Brooklands with Saira in the seat next to him, pulls up in front of her red brick Lower East Side apartment building. He turns off the motor and eases up the country western tune on the radio. "I'm gonna' just take it easy out here." He smiles patience, "Take your time packing."

Avoiding his gaze, Saira looks up at her building, "I think I'd like to catch up with my roommates and spend the night here."

"Of course." He starts to get out to open her door.

Saira's hand stops him, "Not just yet."

"Sure, partner." Don Frye notices Saira's not looking him straight in the eyes. Her head slightly tilted, she seems unsettled. He reaches over and envelops her hands in his, "Is there something wrong?" His palm goes to his forehead as he blows off a gust of frustration, "Damn, sometimes I can be a stump of wood." He sighs, tilts his Stetson back, and turns fully towards her, "Rene told me."

Saira scours his eyes for a scintilla of something more.

He nods sympathy.

"Everything?"

"Yeah. She was a con-artist."

"I still wish I could've been there. What kind of person would do that? Make something like that up? Did he say…." diverting from his stare, Saira manufactures lint to brush off her pants. "Did Rene tell you what happened to her?"

"She was a fraud and he rode her out of town."

Saira is silent. As she looks at her feet, it sneaks out, "I'm afraid."

Babying her, he dotes on her, "About what?"

Saira shrugs, quickly trying to make light of it.

"Darlin'..." he lowers the music, "at times we all are. Don't you worry about anything." He smiles reassurance, "You know how everyone wants someone to get them as much as they do themselves. He does. Rene gets you that way. All your life he'll protect you."

Saira searches for validation. "Are you sure? You swear?"

He runs his hand through his thick stock of black hair, "When I was a little kid, before we moved in with Rene's parents, we lived in Alabama. And..." he shivers from the memory and then laughs at himself, "and...I was afraid there were witches in the hills. Every time it got real cold and the wind howled..." he leans in and imparts it hushed, like a secret, "I could hear 'em calling my name."

Getting the birth of a smile, Saira squints at him wondering where it's all going.

Don Frye holds up a finger. "Later when my folks moved to New York to work for Rene's father, every year for the Jewish Holidays, Rene's grandfather would come from France and drag us along to the synagogue. The first year, the Manhattan Synagogue was so overcrowded that they held the services in St. Patrick's Cathedral."

"Really?"

"St. Patrick's offered its cathedral for the overflow of holiday worshippers. The night we went, the whole cathedral was packed with Jews. There were no crosses on the stage, just a podium with a gold Jewish star on it and old bearded men in funny robes sitting behind it. So, late, at the close of the night, when this old lady takes the stage and starts singing real loud in Hebrew over the sound system, her shrill, harsh sounding words scared me." Embarrassed, he covers his mouth with hand, "It sounded like the witches in the hills."

Fighting laughing, she squints to see if he's telling the truth.

He nods he is. "I was scared, and when I started to bolt, Rene held me." He smiles with the memory, "He made me stay."

"Why?"

"As everybody was filing out, the old bearded Jews on stage blew out the candles. We watched the smoke waft across the cathedral," Don Frye's fingers move from right-to-left, "and as it did, workmen came and moved the podium with the Jewish star out and replaced it with one with a cross."

"And?"

"Rene said at that moment the cathedral was the most powerful because it didn't know what it was -- a synagogue or a church. He pointed at the drifting smoke above us and said it was God's breath blowing on us. That God was sending a message he was watching over us..." he smiles, "and that nothing would ever hurt us."

Saira lights up, "You really love him, don't you?"

"He has an itch and I scratch." He puts an arm around her, "Up until now, we're all each other had. Now, we've got you."

Saira throws her arms around him, tilting his Stetson as she hugs him, "That means we're both lucky."

He adjusts his hat, "You think I'm the one watching out for him." He shakes his head, "He's the one that protects me."

"What's going on you two?" Tookie calls out teasingly as she comes out of the store below their apartment and sees them hugging. Her hair in shimmering Nubian knots, wearing overalls with red suspenders over a t-shirt, and eating out of a Cracker Jack box, she prances around to the driver's side and offers the box to Don Frye, "Care for a nibble?"

"Don Frye," Saira interjects, orchestrating with her hand, "this is my roommate. The one and only Tookie."

"Ma'am," He tips his hat and waves off the Cracker Jacks. "We never really ate that in the South."

"Why?"

"You know, the name and all."

Tookie finally figures it out and coughs a snicker. "So...." Eyeing him, making it clear she's flirting and assessing his broncobuster authenticity, Tookie leans in close with her elbows on his window, "You a real cowboy?"

"Darlin'," he smiles, "I got cowboy boots older than you."

"I'd like to see them."

"Tookie…." Saira motions with a tilt of her head that it's time to go. Saira clutches Don Frye's cheek and pecks him, "Thank you."

Tookie drops the Cracker Jacks in Don Frye's lap, "Cheerio."

Tookie hooks Saira's arm as they walk back to their door. "So," she peeks back as Don Frye watches them safely get to their door, "when are we having a pizza party sleepover at Mr. Bentley's?"

Saira pulls Tookie tight, "Tookie, I feel I'm under a spell."

"That's what it's like when you love someone."

Saira stops at their doorstop. She turns and looks down the block. "Let's get some coffee." As they walk, Saira's silent.

Tookie scrutinizes her but waits to say anything.

Sitting in the corner of the coffee shop, next to a fireplace, Tookie and Saira sip their Carmel Macchiatos. Aware of Tookie's critical eye, Saira stalls and preempts the conversation. She smiles, teasing Tookie, "Since when do you eat Cracker Jacks?"

Tookie shrugs devilishly.

"He said he didn't even really like them." She shakes her head at Tookie's boldness; "You dropped them right in his lap."

"You know…." Tookie raises an eyebrow. "The box always comes with a surprise in it."

Saira squints at Tookie trying to figure out her game. Then, it comes to her. "No, tell me you didn't?"

"One of my royalty cards had my phone number on it."

"You're shameless." Saira smiles as her hand waves for more, "Are the cards finished? I'm so excited for you. Let's see them?"

Tookie lays out her Royalty Cards. Printed from wood blocks and hand-painted in brilliant hues, Tookie's cards are modeled after real people. Her fingers spread out the Queen Margot as the Queen of Roses; Luis XIV as the King of Orchids; the bearded, red-caped Flemish Duc de Sully as the Jack of Hearts; and the sixteen-year-old, pale-skinned Christina of Denmark, as the Duchess of Fleurs-de-lis.

"Tookie, you're so talented." Saira puts the king and queen cards next to each other. "They're exquisite." Her eyes narrow at the royal pair, "They're a perfect match."

"What's your favorite?"

Saira picks up the oversized card with Christina of Denmark, posed, full-faced, with her hands resting on the bodice of a black velvet mourning dress outlined with mink. Saira holds it up to the light of the fireplace and examines it. "I like her demure smile and her elegant hands." Seeing Tookie's look, she hands it back to Tookie, "You going to read my fortune now?"

As Tookie puts the card down, she stares into Saira's eyes.

"What?" Saira flinches superstitiously.

"She just narrowly escaped. Henry VIII fell in love with her just from seeing her portrait. After beheading Anne Boleyn, he wanted Christina to be his next wife after the death of Jane Seymour. The young Duchess is noted for sarcastically saying, "If I was two people, one of my heads should be at the King of England's disposal."

Saira slips the Christina of Denmark card back in the deck.

"Is there anything you want to tell a sister?"

"It's complicated," Saira shakes her head and surrenders, "but I love him. So, Madame Fortune Teller," exhaling, Saira leans back, crosses her arms and feigns a smile, "what's the answer?"

"He loves you? And you love him?"

Resting her head on her palm, Saira nods.

"Then..." Tookie packs up the deck of cards, "don't let yourself get in the way."

FORTY-ONE

It's Sunday morning. There's a pounding on the gates of Rene's front door. Don Frye, bare-chested, in cowboy boots, white boxer shorts, and holding a nickel-plated, ten-inch-barreled, Israeli Desert Eagle revolver at his side, goes cautiously to the town house's front door. In the foyer, he slides a small oil painting to the left, checks the security monitor on the wall, and grins. He tucks the gun in an armoire, swipes the system's red-lit, biometric scanner with his pointer finger, and unlocks the patinated art deco gates. "Mornin', partner." He swings the red door open for Andre Pope. A sweeping handshake tugs Andre in, "It feels like old times."

"I just wanted…" Andre's soft hands go out, "I'm sorry to come by without..." He catches himself, "God…" he shakes his head, "I don't even have his number."

"It's okay." Don Frye puts an arm around him and gives him a welcoming hug. "How long has it been, partner?"

Andre looks up at Don Frye and smiles painfully, "Since you were a little kid."

Both grown men look at each for a lifetime moment.

Andre spins taking in the house that he came to every holiday. The house it all started. His eyes consume the dramatic foyer's soaring ceiling and the hall's forty-five foot wide palatial sweep of marble. An untouchable, inviolate, hallowed cocoon within which every wall has a masterpiece. A one man, unparalleled museum designed around a home. Andre's eyes flash upward. He reminisces the nights he spent there dining and laughing. Like pearls, he speed recounts each of them over. His face gets emotional. He hides it from Don Frye by turning to the five-story, winding, brass-railed staircase. "It's so much more beautiful than I remember. Whew," taking out a white handkerchief, he blots his nose, "it's quite cold out there."

Don Frye helps Andre off with his cashmere camel topcoat, takes his gloves and scarf, and turns away, giving Andre his moment. "Have you eaten yet? Would you like some hot tea?"

His face hidden, Andre nods, "Tea would be perfect."

"You got it." He hangs Andre's coat up in the closet. "It'll be served in the conservatory over the garden. It's beautiful this time of the year." Don Frye looks back, "You know the way, don't you?"

Andre turns toward the elevator. "I believe I still do."

"I'll go get the man." Don Frye bolts up stairs two at a time; "I assume that's why you're here."

Andre stops at the foyer mirror and tightens the knot of his paisley bow tie, making the ends identical in length. He holds his image in the mirror as he stares at himself in the Sorrell house. He tames his wind-swept, long white hair. He holds the hand out before him. It trembles. He quickly hides his cold hands in his brown, three-piece suit's vest pockets, and moves to the masterpieces lining the stairwell's marble walls. He walks over to one and straightens it out.

Rene, hair messed up, and in a white t-shirt, sweat pants, and white socks, stands two flights above. "Andre…?" His hands go out not understanding why he's there.

Andre shrugs self-consciously.

Rene starts down the stairs, "What are you doing here?"

Andre looks at his feet and exhales. His languished smile looks up at the winding walls, "Is she here?"

"Saira?" Rene squints a hard look at Andre. "No. Why?"

"Not Saira." Uncomfortable, Andre turns away. "Rene," he shrugs, "I woke up this morning and..." his hands rub the stiff chill in his chest, "and realized...I'm getting old." Andre turns back. His smile turns melancholy, "Alone…like the rest of the last decade and the one before that and the one before that." He exhales. "You're so blessed to have her."

"And you came here to tell me that?"

As Don Frye comes across the second floor landing with a platter of teacups, Rene holds up a hand stopping him.

Rene waits on Andre.

One of the reasons Andre's there comes out. Thirty years of rivalry shares life's secret, "Don't ever, ever let her go. For any reason. But…." Andre smiles cryptically, "But that's not why I'm here." Turning to face Rene, he implores the eyes of his lifelong competitor, "Can I see *her* before it's too late?"

Don Frye's eyes dart to Rene's. Andre stares at both of them, waiting for a reprieve. Reading Rene's eyes, Don Frye nods at Rene. Rene shakes his head imperceptibly no. Don Frye drills Rene's eyes. Rene is immobile and then acquiesces.

Don Frye walks by Rene, "I'm proud of you." He heads up the stairs; "I guess you two aesthetes are having tea in Rene's study."

Step-by-step, Rene and Andre walk silently to the third floor. Slightly out of breath, Andre holds the railing, while Rene walks briskly along the wall. A lifetime of memories, questions, disillusionments, disappointments, and sorrows swirl as they ascend. As they get to the third floor, Rene turns at the door. "How did you know?"

"I've known a lifetime of Sorrells. I knew your grandfather, may his soul rest in peace. And once upon a time I was a best friend to your father and mother. We were like family." He puts his arm on Rene's shoulder, "She was the candle," he emotionally sighs. "Us three males just reflected her light."

Rene moves into the room.

Don Frye comes out of the study; "I'll leave you two alone." At the stairs, he turns back with a grin, "Don't make me come back up here and separate you two."

In seconds, Andre stops in his tracks. He stares, mesmerized by the painting before him. His sigh releases a lifetime of torment. Tears come to his eyes. He closes them. His fingers cover his tears.

Vermeer's Girl with a Pearl Earring holds court.

Teacups in their laps, the two men sit shoulder-to-shoulder, cross-legged on the parquet floor, staring up at her.

"My God…." Andre breaks the silence. His hand covers his mouth in awe. "Her glow is numinous," he loosens his tie and opens his collar, "like from some otherworldly source. It's…." Andre flushes as he stares at the seventeen-and-a-half-inch by fifteen-and-three-eighths-inch luminous oil. Overheated, he slips off his suit coat, "It's like she's been looking over her shoulder waiting for us forever."

Enjoying his moment, Rene steals a glance at Andre.

Andre feels it. "Only a father could paint that."

"Maria, right? It was his daughter?"

Andre nods. "Has to be." His titter lightens the mood. "He had enough of them. What was it, eleven girls, four boys?"

"I always told myself it was Maria. He had no money for models, and what little he did have, he splurged on the finest, most expensive paint."

Andre stares at the cornflower-blue turban, "Lapis lazuli."

"He refused to use anything else. He mixed it with lead white, ground it and created a pigment that was the brightest blue."

"A stereomicroscope…?" Andre challenges. "Infrared radiographic photography to prove the underpainting?"

"Of course. State-of-the-art authentication. I did it myself."

"What about the pearl?" Andre volleys, testing Rene.

"A glass sphere filled with a preparation made of wax and the silvery scales of a river fish called an ablette. Vermeer used a fan-shaped badger brush to blend it in with the adjacent areas of color. "

"Right," Andre nods with authority. "Then it was varnished

to look real. No pearl was that size. Certainly not one Vermeer could afford." Andre's hands go out in submission. "But how? How did you get it? What about The Hague's Mauritshuis Museum? A Dutch collector named Des Tombes bequeathed it to them. They claim…"

"Yeah, sure." Rene's laugh interrupts. "Unfortunately the alleged invoice, which was given to the Mauritshuis with it in 1944, has disappeared without a trace." He turns to Andre, "A museum's most important painting and they lose the provenance? Sure."

"But the world's foremost art historians all swore..."

"Right," Rene cuts him off. "Like eight-three-year-old Abraham Bredius, the one they called The Pope in all the art circles? In the Burlington Magazine, the art bible of the times, he misidentified as authentic the most famously forged Vermeer in history."

"How, Rene? How did you get it?"

"Well, it wasn't even titled The Girl with a Pearl Earring until 1950. That accounts for much of the confusion with the real genuine one. "You see," he points up at his muse, "way before then, she started out as a miscellaneous tronie left in Vermeer's kitchen. " Now, it's Rene's turn. He volleys back. "Guess where she was before then?"

"Where?"

"Well, where she wasn't was The Hague's Mauritshuis. The painting they maintain…." He scoffs, his tone hitting the absurd, "The one they maintain is *authentic* has a signature whose paint layers are so abraded that it can't even be analyzed." Rene directs Andre's attention to the upper left-hand corner of his painting.

Andre stands and looks closer. "I see it! The light-toned I.V. monogram inserted in the Meer signature. How…" Andre pushes, "how did you get it?"

"During World War II, do you remember hearing about the operatic insanity of Hitler's desire to amass a private art collection to rival the rest of the world's?"

"When the Nazis looted the masterpieces of Europe."

"The ill-conceived Fuhrer-Museum."

Andre is silent. His mind races. "No...?" Smiling, he shakes his head no. He sets his tea on the floor. "Hans Van Meergen?"

Rene nods and gloats childlike with his coup.

"The master Dutch forger who beat his treason charge for collaborating with the enemy by claiming he was bartering with the Germans as a patriot reclaiming Dutch treasures? He sold his forged Vermeer to Nazi Field Marshal Goering in return for two hundred original Dutch paintings that the Germans seized invading Holland."

Rene smiles. "One of the two hundred Dutch paintings was an unrecognized tronie. During the trial, Hans Van Meergen was so busy painting his way out of jail, by proving his defense that he was a heroic forger and not a traitor, that he didn't assess a degenerated, overpainted, tiny tronie that he got back in trade. Pascali Debartolo helped get it for me from someone that Hans Van Meergen had sold it to raising money for his legal defense fund." Rene looks up at the Vermeer, "When I first got her she was so overpainted that she was nearly unrecognizable. But when I removed the old varnish with cotton swabs and solvent, the original fresh and delicate use of color was more apparent." Rene's eyes sparkle, "That's when I saw a small reflection near the left corner of her mouth. Two pink dots were there. After that, I found his signature."

"So...the painting in the Mauritshuis?"

"It's a seventeenth century Dutch painting all right." Rene smiles, "Hans Van Meergen's. The world's best forger solved the biggest problem first."

"Getting the oil paints to harden thoroughly?"

Rene sets his tea down. "It took him four years to work out the technique to make a painting look old. He got around a natural process that took centuries, by mixing resin instead of oil." Rene grins, "Then he purchased inexpensive seventeenth century paintings and removed most of the picture with pumice and water. Being careful not to remove all traces of the complex centuries old cracks."

"So...?" Enjoying it all, Andre folds his arms, "The Hague's

Mauritshuis has another critically acclaimed Van Meergen fake?"

"Yep." Rene shrugs, "But after two hundred and twenty years of Vermeer obscurity and all that the little country had to fend off... the French-Dutch War, English-Dutch War, and the Nazi Invasion; and then the embarrassment of so many erroneously authenticated masterpieces being pulled from their museum's walls...." He smirks, "It got a bit confusing for them."

The Girl with a Pearl Earring draws Andre closer.

"Andre..." Rene reiterates Pascali Debartolo's theory, "did you ever notice anything unusual about the stability and orderliness in all of Vermeer's interior scenes?"

Andre peers down at Rene; the second reason he's there pops up. "I've heard it said..." he tries reading Rene's eyes, "that it may have been indicative of some conflict tormenting his personal life." Silent, Rene gives him nothing. "Well, you got to give it to him." He searches Rene's eyes, "at least he didn't let life pierce his armor."

An interminable moment of silence. It's like they're back, both bidding on the same object. Rene bottoms his tea and stands, "Thanks for the visit."

Andre struggles for a smile, "I guess I better be going before I wear out my welcome."

Standing, Rene shakes Andre's hand but doesn't let go. "My Vermeer?"

Andre nods. "A family secret."

Rene lets go of his grasp and walks Andre to the elevator.

The elevator doors open to Pink Martini's *Never on Sunday* playing over the elevator's speakers. It helps that the melancholy words are sung in Greek, it leaves so much more to the imagination. Side-by-side, in the elevator's tight, leather-upholstered, Tudor chamber, the two men are completely silent. As the elevator slowly churns downward, they steal looks at each other, trying to know the secrets of thirty years of unfamiliarity.

Struggling, they try using the other as a lens to their own life.

Three floors seem like an eternity. They've never been alone together this long. The close-quartered scent of Andre's cologne propels Rene back to his childhood. Their stillness and the fanciful float of the music erases a lost irretrievable generation. Andre stares at the reflection of two near indistinguishable men in the elevator's polished brass door. So many similarities, he thinks to himself. Listening to Andre's stilted breathing is too much for Rene. He looks down. The first floor door releases the elevator's grasp upon them.

Rene walks Andre to the front door.

"So..." Andre turns and looks up the flights of the fanciful home, "Saira, The Girl with a Pearl Earring...." He locks Rene's eyes. "What more could you want?"

Rene guides Andre to the front door. He cavalierly smiles, "See you in Linz?"

FORTY-TWO

Stretching its ultra long-range capability, competing with the speed of sound, Rene's white Bombardier slices a luminous sky as the jet cruises over the endless black of the Atlantic. Inside, a state-of-the-art noise cancellation system ensures a hushed ride as Rene and Saira finish a late night meal in the stateroom near the plane's aft. Don Frye strides out of the cockpit and before he can get back to them, Rene has him made. Rene's head tilts bridling Don Frye because of Saira.

Saira spots it. "What? I want to hear too."

Catching Don Frye's look, Rene subtly shakes his head no.

Saira takes off her glasses and folds them on the table. She pushes a Chinese takeout box away and waits for Rene's attention. "Am I part of the family or not?"

Rene motions for Don Frye to sit. "What's up?" Rene tries making light of it, "We running out of fuel?"

"Want to know why Pascali Debartolo never showed up?" Don Frye winces anticipating Saira's reaction, "They found him in a Brooklyn dumpster."

Hiding his wrath, his clenched fist covering his mouth, Rene looks away. "And?"

"He's in the morgue now."

Saira interjects, "Who's Pascali Debartolo?"

Rene's eyes drill the floor, "Do they know who did it?"

Don Frye shakes his head. He checks out the Chinese take-out boxes of food. "Remember the warning Debartolo gave you?"

Rene sticks an egg roll in Don Frye's mouth to shut him up.

Clearly bothered, Saira persists, "Who is he?"

"Someone who worked for me."

Saira tries to read Rene's blank face. "Doing what?"

"Providing information."

Don Frye mutters, "Not anymore. Unless there's a priceless antiquity in a Brooklyn dumpster."

Rene shoots Don Frye an irritated look.

Saira prods, "What do you mean information?"

Rene takes a cocktail napkin out of the pocket of his black, cashmere coat. He shows the sketch on it to Saira. She sees a sepia crayon drawing of a long-haired, soft-capped Rembrandt. "Pascali Debartolo secretly sketched this after seeing it in someone's safe."

"Okay. So, why did it have to be so secretive?"

Rene folds the sketch back up, "It's stolen."

A somber Don Frye adds, "Very stolen."

"What does that have to do with us? I thought we were going to Linz, Austria to bid on the last remaining Blue Mauritius stamp?"

Just then, the brindle puppy, Bo, comes out of the cockpit sniffing for Don Frye. Amused, Don Frye cocks his head at Rene, "Looks like we got two bloodhounds."

Rene tucks the Rembrandt sketch back in his coat pocket. "Our information was that the same people that have the stamp also have the stolen Rembrandt."

"So, let's see if I've got this right." Saira turns to Don Frye for confirmation and then stays locked on Rene, "The person that gave you this inside information about where we are going… " she searches both their faces, "was murdered?"

Rene gives up a slight nod.

"Rene," Saira leans back, "what exactly are we getting into?" Rene doesn't answer. He calmly takes the cloth napkin from his lap and places it on the table. Frustrated, Saira shifts in her seat waiting. She gets no answer. She appeals to Don Frye, "Make him."

Don Frye looks at Rene. They both can't help but laugh. Dropping his head, shaking it with relinquished amusement, Rene pushes his plate away. Folding his hands in front of his mouth, thinking, buying time, he shoots Don Frye an exasperated look. Don Frye's moustache lifts a corner smile, "How do you expect her to learn?"

Rene cocks his head, and runs it down to Saira, "Twenty years ago, while Bostonians were celebrating St. Patrick's Day, a poorly-guarded Venetian-style museum there, The Isabella Gardner Museum, was robbed. Two hundred million dollars in masterpieces were taken. They've never been recovered. Regardless of the multi-million dollar rewards offered, no investigation until now has ever turned up a trace of the priceless paintings." Rene's eyes turn vengeful, "Smashing the masterpieces out of their frames, leaving shards of glass and canvass behind, the thieves not only ripped out Rembrandt's self portrait, but also Johannes Vermeer's masterpiece The Concert."

"Who would want to steal such instantly recognizable paintings? How could they ever expect to sell them?"

"That's the catch, darlin'," Don Frye offers. "Ninety-percent of stolen art is gone forever. It's never intended for public offering." He lifts the puppy up by folds of loose skin and drops him in his lap, "Paintings like those go to sheiks, drug lords, recluses..." his eyes dart at Rene, "or billionaires who would never let them surface."

She zeroes in on Rene, "You want the Vermeer, don't you?"

Rene scowls at Don Frye, "See what you've done." He makes it clear to Saira; "I only want it in one place -- back at the Gardner Museum where everyone can enjoy it."

"And whoever took it, are they the ones that killed your employee, Pascali Debartolo? What do you want to happen to them?"

Silent, Rene is expressionless. He picks up a lemon and a paring knife. He spins the lemon and skillfully skins it. His expression turns acerbic as he sucks the lemon's juice. "Not the finder's fee."

A static click resonates over the plane's sound system. "Mr. Sorrell, excuse me…." the co-pilot requests over the plane's speakers, "It's advisable that you and Ms. DuFour please try to complete dinner. We've got weather coming up as we approach the continent."

Don Frye picks up the intercom. "What's up?" He listens for a few seconds and responds, "I'll be up front shortly." Don Frye hesitates standing. His look questions Rene's eyes.

"Go ahead, Mr. Blabbermouth," Rene impatiently waves him on, "you already told her everything else."

Don Frye points at Rene's wedding ring finger and smiles, "For better or worse." He turns to Saira and tries to disarm her, "Saira, the police don't know who's responsible for the death of Pascali Debartolo, but here's whom he warned us about." He unzips the brown leather valise at his feet. As he does, Saira notices it's packed high with row-after-row of strapped, hundred-dollar bills. Moving around the cash, Don Frye pulls out a picture. "This is where the Bormann brothers have set up shop. It's called the Linz Castle and it's nestled on a hill overlooking the Danube." He lays out photos of a Gothic, nineteenth century, vermeil-painted, brick chateau, with a six foot cement statue of Jesus blessing those that enter its wrought iron gates; "It's the coach house behind the castle's landmark Alter Dom," his head cocks, "the Old Cathedral." He smirks, "It's now a private casino. You can gamble and confess without getting out of the saddle."

Rene barely fights the pleasure of an ironic smile, "Every year, two cities are chosen to be European Capitals of Culture. This year, they're Vilnius, the capital of Lithuania, and…" he sniggers, "Linz. But Linz," Rene enjoys pronouncing it with a strong Germanic accent, "Linz isn't a fairytale town like Salzburg. In Austria," he grins, "Linz has a bit of a dark side."

"How so?" Saira asks.

"Well, the idea of making Linz a Capital of Culture, is far from a new one."

"Why is that?"

"Someone else had the same idea seventy years ago. Now, his dream is being fulfilled. In Linz," Rene sneers, "there's no way getting away from *the H-word*."

"H-word, what's that?"

"Hitler. It's Hitler's birthplace."

Don Frye jumps in. "Hitler had the idea before anyone else. It was the city of the Fuhrer's youth. Hitler's fantasy town. The last photograph of Hitler before his suicide in his bunker, showed him crouched down studying a mock up of his architectural plans to make his childhood city of Linz the site of the world's greatest Aryan achievement." He smirks with ridicule, "The Fuhrer Museum."

"I'm afraid I haven't heard of it." Saira shakes her head, "The Fuhrer Museum?"

"It was to become Hitler's Nazi Smithsonian." Don Frye makes a mocking jerk-off movement with his hand. "He had delusional plans to make it outshine the Louvre in Paris and the Hermitage of St. Petersburg. Fortunately, due to the successful Allied Forces, all that Hitler ever accomplished building was a rickety bridge over the Danube." Don Frye unfolds a colored map and points at a 700-foot-wide green river. "That's the Danube, it's about the size of our East River in Manhattan."

"Gentlemen," Saira shrugs, "maybe it's a gaping hole in my education, but we didn't study this in art school." Her hands go out, "How did this all come about?"

Rene fills in the historical background, "After occupying France, Holland, Belgium, Italy, Czechoslovakia, Poland," Rene rolls his hand, "almost all of Europe. While the Jews were being sent to death camps, the Nazis confiscated the art the people left behind. They confiscated artworks everywhere. From prominent Jewish collectors, dealers, and families," he holds her eyes, "like the Rothschilds. Tens of thousands of paintings were Aryanized."

"Aryanized?"

"Stolen from their owners," Don Frye quips.

Rene continues, "Then in 1943, when Hitler ran into the brutal reality that he had lost the war, his hysteria manifested itself in a wholesale evacuation of all the Nazi's art repositories and he had them sent to Austria to be hidden underground. In the dead of winter, as several feet of snow blanketed the country, Nazi convoys dragged their precious cargo as they climbed the unassailable Austrian Alps. The destination ended up being subterranean vaults dug inside the fourteenth century salt mines of the mountain. In 1945, when the Allied troops prevailed and the U.S. Army arrived in Austria, our American soldiers found thousands of the precious paintings, sculptures, and gold that had been hidden there."

"And now?" Saira prods.

"Now, the Bormann brothers, with a little help from their home town, Linz, are fulfilling the brutal megalomania of Hitler's dream. Europe's latest Capital of Culture will be displaying Hitler's blueprints and the art he planned to hang in his Fuhrer Museum."

"No way." Saira contests it all, "You can't be serious?"

Rene's face turns ominous. "The Bormann's auction, the one we're attending, I believe will have some of the stolen art."

Saira thinks for a few seconds. "What about the rest of it? Where did all the other stolen art end up?"

"Well, a few heirs of the original owners have been successful in court trying to reclaim their family's possessions. Very few. As far as the rest," Rene shows his clear contempt, "the museums all across Europe were glad to take it in with open hands."

"And the Bormanns?" Saira seeks, "Who are they?"

Don Frye takes out two faded photos. The squat, crew-cutted men look like matching milk cans. Giant heads on two legs. Fifty years of being too short is stuck on their pasty, Napoleon-complexed faces. "After the bombing of Austria by Allied Forces, U.S. military personnel were stationed in the city and many of the servicemen took home brides from Linz. Their children, the Bormann brothers, immigrated back to Austria after doing a few too many stints in American prisons. They picked up where Hitler's art curator's left off."

Rene picks up the twin's pictures. "They're not uneducated and they know their art. Their grandfather was Karl Bormann, director of Herman Goering's art collection. Now, besides being thieves," Rene shrugs off the absurdity of it, "they run a very exclusive, private gambling casino as a front for their illegal activity."

"And…." trying to take it all in, Saira looks at the picture of the Linz Castle and picks up the map of the Danube. "What exactly was Pascali Debartolo's warning?"

Distant thunder rumbles as faraway lightning crackles. Needle rain hits the windows. "Well," Don Frye looks at Rene, "I'm needed up front." He takes an egg roll and smiles, "She's all yours."

"Rene," Saira reiterates, "what was the warning?"

Rene stands. "That the Bormann's have no compunction about shooting people," he grins as he points at the river on the map, "and dumping them in the Danube."

"That's funny to you." Saira drills him with her stare. "And you're going to do business with him? Let's not go."

"Saira," his look conveys that he's unshakable, "I have too."

The seat belt warning dings as the ambient overhead lighting flickers in the storm. Rene eases Saira up, escorts her back up front to the oversized leather seats and buckles her up. He pulls a purple, RS-monogrammed, cashmere blanket over her and tucks it up to her neck. "We'll be fine, Saira. I promise," he gets lost looking out at the blackness of the storm, "this is the last stamp."

"And the Vermeer?" She holds his eyes, "If it's there?"

Thunder crackles as Rene settles back and closes his eyes, giving up a vengeful, roguish grin, "It won't be for long."

Saira stares once again evaluating Rene as he drifts off to sleep. As his fingers find hers, his expression changes to that of peaceful child. Struggling to stay open, fluttering under the hushed drone of the engines, her eyes close too.

FORTY-THREE

The illuminated industrial complex of Linz sits like a giant black tarantula with its legs spread over the dark expanse of the Danube as the city shimmers in a sea of lights. The Bombardier screeches down and does its magic. The plane's carbon brakes and anti-skid system bite wet asphalt as the glistening jet comes to a stop in less than three thousand feet. A port side door, at the front of the cabin, electronically drops airstairs. Don Frye comes out first. He checks the private runway back-and-forth and smiles seeing a waiting black Bentley's exhaust steaming in the rain. Holding an umbrella, Don Frye waves Rene and Saira out.

The steady patter of the rain is punctuated by flashes of lightning fissuring across the sky and replicating on the expanse of the black water. Saira takes in Europe's most celebrated river. "Wow!"

Rene holds Saira as he hurries toward the waiting Bentley. "Contrary, to the name of the famous waltz, it's not blue."

Don Frye leans in to Saira, "Beautiful, isn't it?"

"What...?" Rene murmurs. He shifts his laser-lock focus from the castle at the top of the hill and darts his eyes at Don Frye, "What did you say?"

Don Frye whispers in Saira's ear, "I forgot to warn you, he's in Sorrell focus."

Saira's look questions him.

"Competitive mode."

Saira pulls her gaze away from the lure of the Danube and

teases Rene about the Bentley, "You've got one everywhere?"

Don Frye puts and arm around them both, "Our friends at Crewe, England see to it that we're kept comfortable." Holding the sedan's back door, he makes sure that Rene and Saira are in safely. He opens the driver's door and taps the twenty-one-year-old, navy-suited, blond-haired chauffeur on the shoulder, "You're done, sonny." He passes him a rubber-banded wad of cash, "Go have a Zipfer beer."

The young chauffeur fingers through the thousand dollars. "Tausend Dank!"

Don Frye gets in the driver's seat and grabs the kid's arm as he's leaving. "You're as good as they say you are?"

The kid gives up a cocky smile.

Don Frye adjusts the seat further back and revs the rpm's. "This isn't like driving an Opel on the track." He holds the kid's eyes. "You know what we expect you to do?"

"Ich kann das aus dem Effeff."

"Excuse me?"

"I can do it standing on my head."

Don Frye flashes another rubber-banded wad. "We'll see." Keeping an eye on the rear and side mirrors, Don Frye keeps his brown valise on the seat close to him, shifts the car into gear and gets it moving quickly. The Bentley whizzes by a seemingly idyllic city nestled on the Danube. Boasting Medieval and Baroque architecture, dim, narrow alleyways display cherry-hued timber framing drawing the speeding Bentley through a labyrinth of identical brick houses with green-sloped roofs. As Saira stares out the rain-soaked window, Don Frye notices her fascination, "Don't be fooled by the scenery. This is a dangerous town."

Pushing Don Frye's shoulder to let up, Rene tries to ease Saira, "Touch-and-go. That's all we're here for. Touch-and-go."

Saira laments, "No bed and breakfast?"

"Not this trip." His eyes narrow, "That's for everyone else."

"Everyone else? Who else is coming?"

Passing through the old quarter of the town, Rene stares out the soaked window, "All the other losing bidders."

The Bentley slows down as they enter the expansive, grey cobblestone street of the business district. Don Frye points at the balcony of the old town hall, "That's the balcony where Hitler gave his famous rant after seizing Austria in 1938."

Rene stares up ahead. A mile up, atop a hill, behind the well-preserved town gate, sits Linz Castle. Rene taps Don Frye's shoulder, "Here is good."

Don Frye pulls the car over to the median strip of the Baroque main square's broad thoroughfare. The Bentley sits under the shadowed anonymity of a low hanging tree's branches dripping in a steady stream of rain. Moving his valise onto his lap, Don Frye repositions the rear and side mirrors to watch behind them.

Rene looks at his watch and stares up ahead at the tracks that ascend the hill. "We're right on time, let's hope it is."

Spooked, Saira asks, "What is?"

Don Frye turns the speed of the windshield wipers up. The windshield clears to reveal a canary-yellow tram with four cars approaching the business district's Urfahr Section. "The only way up is on foot or by tram. Every twenty minutes the tram climbs up to the top of the hill. That's how we're going."

Rene checks the valise on the seat, "And everyone knows it."

Saira flinches seeing Don Frye reposition the butt of a gun in his shoulder holster. "Are there Nazis still here?"

Don Frye and Rene lock eyes in the rear view mirror. They both crack up. "Sweetheart, sweetheart," Rene puts an arm around Saira soothing her. "No, there aren't." He double-kisses her cheek, "But there still are bad guys. And everyone at this auction is coming with a satchel full of cash."

The yellow tram clangs its bell pulling into the station.

"We got a train to catch," Don Frye interrupts. The Bentley takes off, its rear wheels spitting circles of rain. Don Frye speed slaloms past the lazy traffic. The only car going three times the speed limit, it pulls into the Urfahr Station just as the tram does. The Bentley does a skidding, full-reversing turn and backs up to the platform, nearly overlapping the rails. With one hand on his holster and another on the brown valise, Don Frye gets out quickly. Checking the platform, Don Frye stops in his tracks. Up ahead, a tall, lean man in a black hooded-sweatshirt is kneeling behind a ten-speed on the bike stand. Don Frye's hand goes up keeping Rene and Saira in the car.

The hooded-biker stands up as his bike unlocks. Taking the bike lock, he tucks it into a backpack. His hand lingers in the backpack and then tucks something in his jacket.

Don Frye's hand slips inside his coat.

The hooded-man mounts the bike and pedals towards them.

Stepping back, Don Frye positions himself so that he blocks the passenger windows of the Bentley. As the hooded-biker pedals towards them, Rene pushes Saira's head down. Lifting the valise up chest high, Don Frye pulls a black 9mm. Beretta out of his coat.

As the bike picks up speed, Don Frye cocks the Beretta.

The biker's hand goes into his jacket. A gust of wind blows the bicyclist's hood back. It's just a tow-haired school kid. He pedals down the hill as he takes out his IPod.

Don Frye opens the door and hurries Rene and Saira out.

Rene teases Saira, "Still want to stay for breakfast?"

"No."

They board the tram. Inside the steamy windows of the cable car, recorded music of Linz's greatest composer, Anton Bruckner's 7th Symphony plays over the sound system. As the tram jerks upward, Saira squints through the rain at the initials on the western front gate to the Old Cathedral, "Look." She points at the bronze Latin letters, A.E.I.O.U., emblazoned on the gate, "What's with the vowels?"

Don Frye answers her, "The last Austrian Emperor to be crowned by the Pope in Rome, Frederic III, resided there in that castle and engraved his motto on the gate."

"It stands for," Rene sneers, "Austria Will Outlive Any Other Power On Earth."

Don Frye's eyes scan the tram's compartments trailing behind them. Everyone stays seated. The trolley listlessly climbs upward to the adagio of Anton Bruckner's symphony. Overhanging trees sweep the tin roof with wet branches to the strokes of the violins. A limp branch bangs the window. Saira jolts. Hiding his smile, Rene puts his arm around her. Brakes squeak as the tram grinds down. The Linz tram platform stands fully lit against the drizzly night. Halogen lights smoke and hiss in the rain. Machine gun carrying, black-capped guards stand on the platform. As Don Frye, Rene, and Saira exit, the guards angle their gun barrels pointing the way.

A soaked red carpet leads to Linz's Spielbank Casino.

Passing two monolithic guards at the opened, gilded-iron gates, Saira stares up at the statue of Jesus as they enter the casino.

Don Frye's head tilts to Rene as an overhead surveillance camera turns on them. An outwardly austere, six-foot-five, stone-faced overseer in a meticulous dark suit and tie, holds out his manicured hand, "Passports please." The man scowls at Don Frye's jeans, lack of jacket and tie. He points at the sign mandating the casino's dress code. His large hand holds out to stop Don Frye's admittance. The man makes the mistake of touching Don Frye's chest.

Don Frye's moustache lifts, "If you're not more careful," he twists the man's wrist dropping him to his knees, "you're gonna be buyin' one glove for Christmas."

As a phalanx of guards close in, five-foot high and near five-foot wide, Joseph Bormann pushes through the crowd. "Dummkophs!" sharkskin-suited Joseph Bormann shouts as he points at the valise Don Frye's carrying and shoves back the guards. "They're not here to gamble. They're my guests for the auction tonight."

Rene makes the introductions.

After Joseph Bormann's clammy hand shakes Rene's, Rene takes out a handkerchief and wipes his hand. Joseph notices. He extends his stubby-fingered hand towards the back of the casino, "Care to join the competition in the smoking room."

Don Frye fights smiling, "We don't smoke."

Rene steps forward. "I want to be the first to see it."

"Of course, Mr. Sorrell, I anticipated you would." Joseph Bormann simpers, "The little Jew engraver. If he only knew what his incompetence was worth." Joseph spits his gum out at a brass spittoon. It misses. Pointing at the six-foot-five overseer to pick it up the gum, Joseph waves Rene into the casino. Inside, gilded-sconces light the three-story Gothic casino's pale walls, while ten-foot, double-tiered crystal chandeliers grace the vaulted ceilings. Discreet locals, and bourgeois Euros, intermix with anonymous distinguished gentlemen wagering on a scant half-dozen tables devoted to gambling on the main floor. As they pass the tables, Joseph points at Rene, "Only you."

Rene pulls Saira close, pretends to just kiss her and whispers, "Don't leave Don Frye's side." Saira holds onto him. Rene smiles, "I'll be right back."

Joseph waves Rene on, "We only have a few minutes."

As Rene follows Joseph Bormann through the casino, Rene audits out loud the stolen Holocaust art on the walls, "Picasso. Degas. Gauguin. Monet. Renoir."

Joseph turns sideways. "Paintings don't have memory."

Rene shoots him a disdainful look. "People do."

"What's that supposed to mean?" Joseph clearly knows what he means, but challenges him anyway, "What's fair?" He looks up at the paintings, "Just as it may have been wrong for the Nazis to take property off Jewish people, it's just as wrong, without a proper proof of provenance, to take it away from all the world's museums displaying it for the benefit of the public."

"You're not a museum."

Shrugging, Joseph boasts with a grin, "We don't put the real ones on the walls anyway."

Rene turns a second time to scrutinize a post-Impressionistic Baroque work of art with contrasting themes. An erotic, white cast of cupid stands in front of the canvas of an artificial oil painting. Rene cocks his head and scoffs, "That supposed to be Cezanne's Still Life with Cupid."

"No one knows it's not. Except maybe you."

Rene looks back again at the bogus Cezanne, "Passion and plunder, the absurdity of life and Nazi Germany."

"The Jews made it so easy." He leers at the sheer foolishness of it, "They were required to register all their possessions." He sneers, "So the Nazis made a shopping list and knew just what to take."

A gnarled, crooked-shouldered Leopold Bormann, in a near matching sharkskin suit, joins them. "Ready to see the real thing?"

Rene glares at the Bormanns as they stand in front of him. Seeing the pasty milk can twins together repulses him.

Joseph Bormann waves, " Follow me."

Rene checks Saira and Don Frye. As they're served beer mugs with the hot spice Gluhwein and jellied Linz tarts, Don Frye lifts his finger up to his mouth feigning gagging.

Leopold Bormann withdraws a thick-linked, gold key chain out of his pocket and unlocks the black iron basement door. He looks around, waves over a guard to stand at the door, and tugs Rene's sleeve. "Maybe both things you want to see are here."

Rene follows the Bormanns down a poorly lit wooden stairway into the underground of the seventeenth century coach house. Though the stairway sways, Rene refuses to touch the railing.

Leopold notices. "Ever been in a real life dungeon?"

Wobbling side-by-side like giant geese, the cube-shaped Bormanns take up nearly the whole corridor as they wind around its turns. Leopold calls back in a high-pitched demonic voice, "The passageways served to muffle the tortured victim's screams."

They enter a surviving torture chamber.

Rene eyes scan the rusted chains and iron cuffs hanging from the planked-walls. He spins walking by a wooden head crusher, knee splitter, and thumbscrew. Rene stops in his tracks. Before him is a steel chair with two thousand thick spikes covering the back, armrests, leg-rests, and footrests. Leather gags, straps, and steel bars, are attached to keep the victim securely in the chair.

"It's called the Judas Chair." Joseph interjects. "Try it out. Seven centuries ago, this was all built by a fat, red-haired troll, the Archbishop of Cologne, in order to collect custom fees for ships trying to transport down our beautiful river." He belly chortles, "The Church liked to get paid too."

Splicing his words right after his twin, Leopold Bormann states the bill of fare, "Fifteen million takes the stamp."

Rene backs up looking at the Chair of Torture. He bumps the wall. An axe falls.

Leopold laughs, "The Archbishop kept his victims here until their debt was paid." He turns his back on Rene and kneels before a small, cast iron, turn-of-the-century safe. Graphically painted in lurid red, its ball feet sit on a wooden dolly. Leopold wipes his fingers on his shirt, spins the black dial several times and starts the combination.

"Fifteen million…?" Rene angles closer for a better look at the old cast iron safe. He buries his grin.

Joseph blocks Rene's view of Leopold calibrating the safe's combination, "You know how it works, Sorrell." He puts a fleshy arm around Rene moving him further away, "We're qualifying buyers."

"I thought it was an auction."

"Not for you," Leopold winks. "For fifteen million you get the stamp right now."

"And the others?"

Leopold cranks the handle and opens the safe revealing its engraved bolt work. "They're spending the night." His squat, fat block of hippo flesh turns, "You are joining the other guests in my chateau next door, aren't you?"

Rene steps closer and motions for the stamp.

Leopold takes it out with a tweezers and carefully passes it to Rene. Rene walks it over to the chain mail-covered, cracked light fixture on the wall. He turns the blue stamp back-and-forth. He takes out a gold Dunhill lighter, and with a flick of his thumb, snaps its cap open and lights its butane flame.

"Hey!" Joseph bowling ball shoves him, knocking the lighter to the ground.

Leopold grabs a nine-inch, serrated knife off the table, "What the hell are you trying to do?"

"Relax." Rene picks up the lighter and holds it and the stamp well apart. "It's too dark in here. I need to get a better look." His thumb trick-snaps the lighter on again.

"Be careful, Sorrell," Leopold wedges in close with the knife. "Everything in here is old wood."

Rotating the stamp to the blue flame, Rene squints. He snaps the lighter shut. He smells the Blue Mauritius stamp and smiles.

Joseph chortles, "Does it smell like fifteen million?"

Rene hands back the stamp and waves for more.

The Bormanns block the antique safe with wall-to-wall Austrian flesh. Leopold hikes up his belt, "Debartolo told you, huh?"

Joseph sneers, "We knew he would."

Rene holds out his hand.

The Bormanns slowly turn to each other. Leopold nods to Joseph. Joseph shakes his head no, then squints. "All right," he glares a smile at Rene. "It'll cost you a million to see it."

"Put it on my bill."

Joseph's fat hand goes inside the safe and tweezers out Rembrandt's tiny, stamp-sized, self-portrait. He shows it to Rene. Rene snatches it. His eyes pinpoint, "Where's the Vermeer?"

"We…" Joseph looks at Leopold and they coyly finish the sentence in unison, "we don't know what you're talking about."

Rene scrutinizes the Rembrandt. "I brought your fifteen million. You can have it if the Vermeer is returned to where it belongs."

Leopold takes the Rembrandt. "It's gone."

"How much for the Rembrandt?"

"It's already sold." Joseph rubs it in, "It's leaving tonight," he looks at his diamond Rolex, "as soon as we get back upstairs."

"I'll pay more."

Joseph tucks the Rembrandt inside a glassine envelope and slides it into his maroon, lizard skin wallet. Leopold slams the safe, "The Sheikh already did."

"What's the magic number?"

"The magic number?" Leopold starts the sentence, "Life or death..." and Joseph finishes it, "if we don't deliver."

The Bormanns wave Rene to follow them out.

Rene sidesteps and studies the safe's dimensions.

Joseph's fat fingers flick, "Let's go."

Coming around the last twisting wooden corridor, Rene stops and looks up at the wooden stairway leading to the casino. "The real Holocaust art? Is any of it here?"

Leopold claws his itchy armpit. "We're not that stupid." Joseph adds, "We've got salt mines Hitler never even heard about."

FORTY-FOUR

With a hundred dollars in five-dollar chips before her, Saira is seated alone at the roulette table on the Spielbank Casino's crystal, chandelier-lit main floor. Watching her from across the room, huddled in a corner next to a marble pillar, Rene and Don Frye are talking in hushed tones. As a tuxedoed-waiter walks by with a tray of drinks, Don Frye stops talking. Waiting for the waiter to pass, Don Frye whispers to Rene, "Perlite? Vermiculite lined?"

Rene shakes his head. "No protection at all. It's a hundred-and-fifty-year-old, cast iron relic sitting on a wooden dolly."

"So much for its fire and impact rating." Don Frye grins, "That's the difference between fireproof and fire tested."

Elegantly dressed in a hip, black silk suit, a close-coiffed, incisively-mustached and triangular-goateed, shadowy-skinned, young Arabic man, whose black diamond pupils float in triple-white-eyes, nods at Saira as he sits down across from her. Everything about him, his manner, style, and modern attire, is in direct contrast to the four, kaffiyeh-wearing bodyguards standing behind him. As the roulette wheel is spun, the young man puts a purple one hundred thousand dollar chip on top of Saira's five-dollar bet on number four.

Saira looks up at the line of bodyguards. The young man sees it. He looks back at them and mocks them with a scary face.

Saira can't help but snicker.

"My babysitters," he shrugs and trickles a self-effacing laugh.

As the wheel slows down, the ivory ball jumps onto number

four. A bodyguard excitedly utters encouragement, “Arba’a!”

The ball rolls out to the next number. Saira smiles a shrug.

The young man speaks in Arabic and asks Saira her name, “Shismak?”

Don Frye elbows Rene as the Bormann brothers approach the young Arabic man. His triple-ringed hand rises instructing his bodyguards to let them in.

“Your majesty,” the Bormanns both try to bow. They’re too stout to bend. Joseph withdraws the lizard wallet with the glassine envelope holding the stamp-sized Rembrandt and gives it to the young man. He doesn’t even look at the it. He passes it to one of the bodyguards and returns his attention to Saira. He awaits her response.

“Sheikh Rashid,” Leopold Bormann presses, “aren’t you even going to...”

The young man’s eyes turn stern. He dismisses both Bormanns with a look. He returns his attention to Saira. As Saira places her next bet, she uses her other hand, the one with her engagement ring. The Sheikh notices and smiles, “Ayounak helween.” He sees Saira doesn’t understand. He shakes his head, “Terrref Arabic?”

“Sorry. I don’t speak Arabic. Your...” she tries to be proper, “Your Majesty.”

“You’re not Arabic?” he says doubting her with a squint.

Saira holds up a pinch, “One-fourth. My father was French Moroccan.”

Pleased, he bows his head to her. “I’m older than you think,” he smiles, making fun of his attempt to convince her. His head cocks, “It’s my twenty-first birthday.”

Saira keeps her ring hand on the table and nods respectfully, “Happy birthday.”

He nods and sighs. “Here,” he glances at his guards, “I’m the fourth son of one of the ruling families of Dubai.” Rashid shrugs, “Back home, I’m the baby.”

Saira looks across the room at Rene. He's enjoying the attention she's getting.

Sheikh Rashid leans closer, "Ayounak helween. It means your eyes are very pretty." He makes it clear he's looking at her ring. "I've never seen a stone like it. It's magnificent. But your one-fourth Arabic sparkles much brighter."

"Thank you." Saira sees Rene's focus on the bodyguard that received the stamp-sized Rembrandt. She subtly probes the Sheikh, "Are you a collector?"

"Not really." Sheikh Rashid enjoys pushing the mystique and gives up a little, "My birthday assignment was to bring something back home." He stares into her, "Can I tell my father it was you?"

A crystal bell tinkles! "Meine Dammen und Herren," the six-foot-five, stone-faced overseer announces in a guttural voice, "Ladies and Gentlemen, the casino is closed."

"What!" A chair tips over across the room. Everybody turns to see several of the casino guards drag a protesting, over-intoxicated, losing local out by his collar.

The Bormanns wave the Sheikh and Rene to follow them.

As the Sheikh's bodyguards pick up his chips, Sheikh Rashid follows Saira out. "Habibity," he leans in close and bets it all, "I would run away to the mountains with you right now."

Saira coyly responds, "They have mountains in Dubai?"

Sheikh Rashid shrugs adorably, "Any mountains."

FORTY-FIVE

Two ten-foot, eighteenth century, elaborately carved, wooden choir stalls, peppered with grotesques and grimacing cherubs, sit on the high altar of Linz's Alter Dom Cathedral. It's the fitting backdrop for the mixed bag of auction invitees seated on its benches. Sporting a pink fleur-de-lis tie, inside a vested, black sport coat over grey flannel pants, Rene is visibly uncomfortable sandwiched between a Vodka slinging, weed-patch-haired, Chechen underworld thug losing the battle to sit up sober, and an unshaven, no-necked, pie-faced Kazakh oil magnate. To Rene's left, a chronically sanitary, tiny Dutch pornographer is alongside a sausage eating, wild-eyed Wall Street hedge-funder dodging Interpol arrest warrants. In the corner seat, a partially paralyzed, blind-in-one-eye, hirsute-chested German arms manufacturer sits in front of a pretentious Albanian Mafioso resembling a skinned, tattooed weasel. In the high-backed second row, a hearing-aid-wearing Swiss banker slouches amongst ferocious-faced men that if left alone in a room would eat each other. At the last minute, Andre Pope comes in. His pearly hands lifted high, he squeezes in the only open seat on the top row, just behind Rene.

On stage, standing barely above a gold pulpit, are the Bormann brothers. Boasting of Baroque excess, the white-stucco cathedral's nave, with its gilded, barrel-vaulted ceilings, and pink columns separating an abundance of chalky marble statues, is scantily attended by the sparsely seated guests accompanying the bidders. Saira and Don Frye sit amongst only a couple dozen other scattered people. Alone, slouched in the last row, NYPD-suspended cop, Tony Stokes enjoys studying his incongruous employer, Andre Pope.

Sheik Rashid and his bodyguards are nowhere to be seen.

Leopold Bormann stretches up to the microphone on the podium, looks up at the cathedral's windows and then directs his remarks to his blue-ribbon panel, "Looking up at the scenes in the stained glass windows you'll undoubtedly notice how beautiful they are, yet they don't chronicle the unique history of our town. We've been bombed, burned down, and struck by lightning," he smiles, "but we're still here. Wolfgang Mozart may have been baptized in Salzburg's Cathedral; and Ludwig van Beethoven may have discovered the totality of his deafness in Vienna's St. Stephens' Cathedral when he saw the birds flying out of the bell tower and couldn't hear the bells; but here in Linz…" Leopold points up at the organ above the pulpit, "while the world famous composer, Anton Bruckner, played the organ, Adolph Hitler was confirmed -- here in this Alter Dom."

The crowd does nothing. Confused, two people in the nave reluctantly applaud.

Joseph Bormann steps alongside his twin, barely fitting before the width of the podium. "As our city celebrates its European City of Culture Award," his portly hands go out, "instead of shying away from our past we're embracing it."

While most of the bidders in the choir stall smile amusement, the Russians look at each other and implode in laugher. Don Frye sees Rene shake his head as his eyes close.

"You'll notice…." Leopold bumps his brother to the side, monopolizing the mike. "You'll notice that when you go back into the casino tonight, the rare art is down and Adolph Hitler's own architectural plans for making Linz the world's greatest Aryan cultural achievement will be on display."

The tanked-up Chechen gangster burps in total disinterest. "Ni nada!"

"Genug! Who cares, " barks the German arms manufacturer, "Get on with the auction."

Joseph nods to Leopold. Leopold motions armed guards to approach the pulpit. They bring him a silver platter. Joseph hands him a white envelope. Leopold opens the envelope and shakes it into his palm. A blue stamp drops out. He turns to his choir, "Gentlemen," he takes the stamp, licks it and pastes it on the envelope.

The bidders gasp.

Leopold cough-laughs, "Just kidding. I just wanted to get your attention." He takes out another white envelope out of his pocket, tweezers out a blue stamp and holds it in the air with fanfare, "The Blue Mauritius!" He places the stamp on the platter. "In 1847, this was first stamp of the British Empire produced outside of Great Britain." Joseph walks the platter in front of the choir as Leopold continues; "Please inspect the intaglio method of recessed printing giving the two pence stamp its distinct primitive character." He watches the bidders lean in. "And notice the engraver, Joseph Barnard's initials, JB, on the lower right margin of the bust of Queen Victoria."

Andre squeezes out of the back row, goes over to the silver platter and inspects the stamp with a loupe. He smiles his approval.

Saira squints when the stamp gets to Rene. He doesn't even bother to look at it. Don Frye dislodges her scrutiny, "This is all over two words. 'Post Office' versus 'Post Paid'. When you buy a stamp you pay for it and the post office marks it post paid. What's the big deal?" He shrugs, "But back then, half the letters that left the islands in the Indian Ocean had their apology inscribed on them, 'Eaten by Rats'." He grins, "I'd buy that stamp."

"The two words were mixed up in error. Right?"

"Rene says that's just legend." He cocks his head at Rene, "Your fiancé over there is regarded as one of the foremost philatelic scholars in the world. Rene maintains the initial plates were approved by Mauritius and issued that way. He says the exact same Post Office engraving was used by the United States that very same year."

Leopold gets the stamp back. He looks at the two Russians, "From our Eastern European friends, do I hear five million?"

"Da!" the no-neck Kazakh oil magnate raises one hand's spread fingers waking the marinated Chechen gangster from dozing.

"Suka!" The soused Chechen jerks up and insults the Russian's mother, "Ildi k yobani materi!" He holds up six fingers.

Rene casually says, "Seven."

Andre raises his jeweler's loupe and quietly bids, "Eight."

The Swiss banker and Dutch pornographer push it to ten million. Holding up his Albanian blue-eagle-tattooed-forearm, the Mafioso raises it another million.

"Zwolf!" reluctantly retorts the German arms dealer.

Rene stands and says it definitively, "Two million more!"

"Arschloch!" The German retires and walks out to see the Hitler blueprints.

Yawning, the outlaw Wall Street hedge-funder shakes his head and follows him.

Glancing at Rene, Andre raises it a half million more to fourteen and a half.

"Fifteen million." Rene turns to the others and raises his own bid, "Sixteen million." Both his hands go up in the air like a commodity trader, "Seventeen million!"

The choir stall of bidders goes silent trying to figure out what's happening.

The Chechen gangster stands, scowls at the garishness of the Austrian cathedral and walks out reserving a last dirty look for Rene, "Na huya popu garmon'?"

Rene leans over to the Kazahk, "What did he say?"

"He said," the Kazahk's hand waves as he struggles with the translation, "it means…what the fuck does a priest need an accordion for?" He sums it up, "Like a fish needs a bicycle."

Andre Pope stands and gets everyone's attention but Rene's. He waits for it. In the middle of the choir stall, Rene turns and faces Andre. Rene's hard look dissipates. Squinting, shaking his head ever so slightly, Rene mouths the word no.

The two adversaries lock eyes.

Andre quietly delivers it at Rene, "Eighteen million."

The cathedral goes silent.

Rene stares and assesses Andre like he's done dozens of times before. Smiling, Rene bows his head to Andre, offering his palm, signifying the stamp is his.

The Bormanns wait. Joseph asks, "Anyone else?"

"Mr. Pope," Leopold points at Andre, "it's yours."

The crowd reluctantly applauds. As Joseph tweezers the Blue Mauritius stamp back in its envelope, Leopold directs him, "Lock it back up."

Rene's eyes follow the stamp out the door.

Andre stands seeing Rene get up.

Rene tilts his head signaling Don Frye to escort Saira out.

Leopold sees it and motions a guard to follow Don Frye.

As Don Frye is walking Saira out, she leaves his side and goes over to Andre. "Mr. Pope," she shakes his hand, "congratulations." Saira palms Andre's soft cheek and kisses him goodbye. She sneaks him a twinkle, "I hope we'll be seeing you again soon."

Seeing Rene take Saira's hand, Andre stops him, "You're leaving? It's so late. You're not staying the night? I was hoping we could...."

Rene shakes his head and surrenders a smile, "Congratulations, Andre." He leans in close, "Don't pay for it until you get it." Andre bypasses Rene's congratulatory hand and hugs him. Hands at his sides, Rene is stiff as Andre holds on a moment. Suddenly self-conscious, Andre lets go. Rene takes a step away and turns back, "You started all this."

Andre is a bit slow to respond. He squints, "Excuse me?"

Rene holds his eyes. "You know."

Andre falters. His blank stare goes to Saira and then back to

Rene. Defensive, he shakes his head like he doesn't understand.

"My mother." Rene invades Andre's eyes, "She told me."

Andre's breathing gets stilted. It barely escapes, "When?"

"When I was a little boy."

Andre's head shakes, failing to comprehend what's next.

"The Blue Mauritius stamp. You gave it to her as a present for when I was born." Rene steps a bit closer. His eyes flutter with the memory; "She'd take it out, show it to me every year at my birthday," he half-smiles, "and tell me it would be all mine one day. When she... when she was gone," he sighs, "it started me collecting."

"Indeed." Andre closes his eyes, feels the beginning of the shadow of his grey beard, and nods surrender. Stretching his spine, he stands up straighter and rubs his eyes, "I'm getting too old for this." Faltering a bit as he steps forward, Andre hugs Rene, "Goodbye, Rene. I...I...." He shrugs, unable to get out more. "Take care."

Walking out, Saira turns back to look at Andre. His scant smile shows his pain. As the guests file out, Andre walks over to the pulpit. He inquires of Leopold, "When do I get the stamp?"

"Tomorrow, when you pay." Leopold looks over the cathedral and smiles, "When the workers were doing the build-out for our casino they unearthed a crypt of burials beneath it." He looks into Andre's eyes, "Remember, everybody wants to be buried next to a saint. Don't let it happen prematurely. Make sure the money is right."

Outside the cathedral, as Rene and Saira leave, Don Frye meets up with them. Rene looks around, "The guard...?"

Don Frye's thick moustache lifts. He grasps Rene's palm, secretly slipping him back his Dunhill lighter.

Rene lets go of Saira's arm for a second. "Excuse me, darling." He pulls Don Frye aside and whispers, "It's got to last an hour."

FORTY-SIX

The gaming tables of the Spielbank Casino have been cleared away. The magnificent crystal chandeliers all dimmed. Crowning red shades, emblazoned with the single-headed black eagle of the Austrian Coat of Arms, jacket the flickering candles set on white linen-covered tables accommodating the Bormann's overnight guests. As a soft medley of the classical Viennese music of Wagner, Mozart, Bach, Schubert, and Haydn filters through speakers, a babel of harsh accents and languages floats over the room's dozen tables cramped together. Drinking and laughing, the misplaced romantic setting is lost on the remaining raucous, lowbrow crowd. Fountain pen in hand, a meticulously dressed, ascot-wearing Andre Pope sits at a small table all by himself. Chin resting on his palm, he looks at the louche world he exists in and wonders how he misplaced his whole life.

Gnawing on the neck of a lewdly dressed hired-companion, the jet black-haired Albanian Mafioso pauses to flash his incisors as he nods victory to Andre. Andre returns to himself. He closes his eyes flushing the panoply before him. Sighing, he opens his malachite-colored, leather note pad, and writes, trying to unravel it all.

Amused, Tony Stokes stands a ways off studying his employer scribble notes on the peacock-blue paper. He waits a moment. "What're you writing?"

Andre tucks the note pad in his coat. "Well?"

Stokes sits down. "You're not going to believe this."

A waiter comes over with a cardboard-sleeve-covered, green wine bottle. He squints a hard look at Stokes' wrinkled suit and curled shirt collar and places just one glass before Andre. "This is a gift from the Bormanns for tonight's winner."

Focusing on the burgundy, heat-shrink top of the cork, Andre barely notices Leopold and Joseph Bormann wave from across the room. He nods a token thank you at them and returns to studying the bottle. As the waiter takes out a corkscrew, Andre stops him. With the affection of undressing an inamorata, Andre slowly slides the cardboard sleeve down over the bottle's perfect jade glass and lights up seeing the golden V above the crested label. Covering his mouth with a hand, it fails to contain his laugh of ironic delight.

"Boy," Stokes quips, "it doesn't take much to please you."

Andre waves the waiter back. "Two glasses please."

"Now, you're talking my language," Stokes smiles. "You can't drink a Vermeer."

"You're right," Andre rotates the bottle in his hands, "but *it is* a masterpiece. A 1945 Mouton Rothschild. Ten, maybe a dozen, exist." Andre turns the bottle's V towards Stokes and enlightens him, "Bottled at the end of WWII, Baron Rothschild crowned the Mouton Rothschild label with a symbol to celebrate the liberation of France -- the label V for victory. After that, it started a tradition for identifying each of the following vintage labels with an original work of art by famous artists like Miro, Chagall, and Picasso."

"Great," Stokes sarcasically manages. He holds his glass ready to taste it, "As I was saying, I saw Don Frye go down the..."

Holding out the Mouton Rothschild, Andre interrupts him and unravels its history, "It's a story about a father who loved his sons but let them go." He passes the bottle to Stokes and rests his chin on his folded hands, "In the beginning of the nineteenth century, this visionary father, Baron Rothschild, wanting his five sons to succeed on their own and expand his family business across Europe, had his sons sent to different European cities to establish financial institutions." Andre perks his ear taking in the Viennese music. "They played an integral role in developing the Austrian economy. Until the Anschluss."

"Bless you," Stokes wisecracks. "The what?"

"When the Nazis occupied Austria and annexed it to Germany. They forced the sale of all the Rothschild's banking operations. Stripping their palaces of all their art, they held it as extortion donations for exit visas. Even Baron Rothschild was held in prison until a phenomenal ransom of artwork was paid for his release."

Stokes notices a woozy guard stumble his way across the room to the Bormann's table. He raises a finger, pointing it, trying to direct Andre's attention across the room, but Andre is preoccupied carefully detaching the label off the Mouton Rothschild.

Andre glances at the casino's walls laden with the framed-blueprints of Hitler's architectural plans for Linz. "Hitler proclaimed his Third Reich would survive a thousand years." He raises the bottle, "Looks like the Rothschilds' wine lasted longer than he did." Andre slices the label off, licks the back of it, gets up and sticks it on one of the framed-blueprints. Ignoring the Bormann's glare, Andre walks back to his table and uncorks the bottle. After a slight chemical burn off, a garnet-colored wine pours out into the glasses. Andre revolves the dark fluid in his glass and smells it, "Wet-clay-chocolate with a hint of berry fruit and shale." He sips a mouthful and sighs, "Glorious." He pours a glassful for Stokes, "You're tasting greatness."

Stokes takes it down in one gulp and feigns appreciation, "Yeah. Don't you want to know..."

Turning his back to Stokes, Andre searches the corners of the casino for the art removed during the stamp's auction. "After the war, the Rothschild's artworks were governmentally appropriated and placed in museums all over Austria."

Stokes helps himself to more wine. "So, if the Rothschilds were such big shots why didn't they get them back?"

"Austria claimed it was also a victim of the Nazis and allowed no appeal. And..." he shrugs, "a great many of the judges in the Austrian courts were former Nazis."

Stokes takes a gulp of wine as his head turns monitoring the Bormanns hasty exit. "There they go. And they look real pissed."

Preoccupied with the wine, Andre casually asks, "Who?"

"Our hosts."

That gets Andre's attention. He spins around.

Stokes laughs. "Don Frye convinced the guard to show him where the washroom was." He pours another glassful. "Then he came back without the guard. In two seconds Don Frye opened the lock on the basement door and disappeared down the stairs."

"You moron, why didn't you tell me that sooner?"

"I tried to but you kept interrupting me with wine stories."

Staring across the casino, Andre squints at the unlocked iron door. "Don Frye wasn't interested in finding a washroom."

A blaring alarm sounds!

Red plastic balls labeled FEUERALARM on the casino's walls flash and light up. Smoke floods in from the floor vents. Chairs push back and fall over. The evening's guests grab valises and briefcases, and run out. Andre stands frozen. His eyes dart back up at the walls. "There's not just my stamp down there. The art must be down there too." He tugs Stokes up, "Let's go!"

They both head toward the basement door. Andre comes back to the table and grabs the bottle of Mouton Rothschild.

FORTY-SEVEN

Ricocheting off monolithic cement patches of blackness, creating ever-changing shadows on massive walls and ceilings, Don Frye's moving flashlight beam pierces the vast darkness of a disused web of concrete tunnels beneath the Alter Dom. Limited by the bounce of light in front of them, Don Frye leads Rene and Saira through the cold, shadowy, twelve-foot high underground passage. In the background, the blare of a fire alarm deadens with each winding turn.

Accelerating Saira's walk, Rene hustles her forward. Catching her breath, she looks down the tunnel. "How did you know about this? Why are we not taking the tram?"

"The tram's not safe."

As Don Frye's beam shaves angles of light in the darkness, their shadows distort into grotesque images. Saira cringes. "And this is? How do we know someone's not out there waiting for us?"

Don Frye turns, "This hasn't been used for sixty years."

Rene hustles Saira onward quickening the pace to a near run.

Don Frye's flashlight goes out. They are left in pitch black.

Saira gasps and grabs onto Rene.

Don Frye bangs the flashlight against the wall. It goes back on. He checks Saira, "You okay, darlin'?"

She nods and looks around. "What is this?"

"It's where forty thousand prisoners were worked to death."

Don Frye explains, "Working in twenty-four hour shifts in the cold Austrian winter, wearing wooden clogs or going barefoot when the clogs fell apart, the prisoners from the Mauthausen concentration camps were made to dig this tunnel as an underground project for the mass production of Nazi assembly lines of submachine guns and Messerschmitt jet fighters."

"Planes?"

Don Frye nods. "That's why it's so high and wide. Bored into a hill, it was invulnerable to attack." The flashlight goes out again. He smacks it against his palm. Nothing. He smashes the flashlight against the wall.

Lighting crackles illuminating an opening at the end of the tunnel. "There." Rene squints seeing it. "Just up ahead."

Saira grabs onto Rene, "I want to go home."

Their hands skimming alongside the gravelly wall, they head toward the glint of light at the tunnel's end. Don Frye withdraws his Beretta as they approach the opening. They exit a small bunker entrance carved into the side of a hill. A steady rain drips through the thick foliage protecting the entrance. Don Frye looks back at the Alter Dom up the hill. A billowing dark smoke rolls in the sky.

Rene stares at the red plume of fire. "Just in time."

Saira stops Rene, "What about Andre?"

Don Frye looks to Rene; "He's got that cop with him."

"Yeah," Rene assures them. "I'm sure he's okay."

Saira squints at Rene.

As they weave through a patch of Austrian pine draping limbs and soaked bushes, they hear dogs barking in the tunnel. Just outside the trees, beams of light flicker. Don Frye sees the Bentley waiting a hundred yards up ahead alongside the bank of the Danube. Passing Rene the brown valise, Don Frye waves he and Saira on. "Keep going, get to the car." As the bark of the dogs gets closer, Don Frye crouches down behind a tree trunk and trains his gun on the bunker entrance.

Running on a narrow path alongside Rene, Saira asks, "The art in the casino?"

"It was all fake. The only thing inside there now belonged to Adolph Hitler." Rene looks back at the orange plume of fire, "It's going where he is."

Rene whistles. The twenty-one-year-old, blond-haired chauffeur sees them and floors the Bentley. Swerving, slaloming between trees, he speeds the car toward them. Skidding on wet leaves, the chauffeur does an expert donut turn and flings open the door for them. Rene secures Saira in the car and closes the door.

Saira's window goes down. "What're you doing?"

"Stay down." Rene takes off running. The yelping of the dogs gets louder. He meets Don Frye coming up the path toward him. Rene grabs his arm, "Let's go." They sprint toward the Bentley.

Don Frye glances at Rene, "You enjoy this, don't you?"

A shot is fired. It pings the metal of the Bentley's trunk.

In seconds, Rene and Don Frye are inside the Bentley. Don Frye shoves the chauffeur over, stomps on the gas and skids the car down the bank of the Danube. Guards wielding machine guns and snarling Alsatians, rush out of the tunnel. They fire a surge of shots. The Bentley's windshield punctures.

Sheltering Saira, Rene crouches over her body.

In his rear mirror, Don Frye spots the headlights of a black Mercedes pull out of an opening in the forest. He turns to Rene; "We can't let them get near the plane."

They both look at the brown valise.

Rene takes a wad of hundreds out of his pocket. He opens the window and tosses the valise, along with a scattering of the cash, down the bank. Directing the dogs, the guards go after the valise. So does the Mercedes.

Whizzing through the Austrian night at over a hundred miles per hour, the sea of lights along the Danube is a blur. The Bentley flies into the runway of a private airport. Don Frye slides a rubber-banded stack of cash to the chauffeur. "Thanks kid."

"The Bentley?" the kid asks.

"Put it somewhere safe."

Don Frye gets out and opens the door for Rene and Saira. Hustling them on, he watches them run and takes off after them.

The jet's port side door opens.

In minutes, the Bombardier jet screams off the runway. As the jet slices dark-cerulean-blue Austrian sky, Rene, Saira, and Don Frye look down at Linz. Billowing black plumes of rolling smoke dance above the Alter Dom.

FORTY-EIGHT

In an open air conservatory shaded from the morning sun by overhead vines of gardenias, Rene and Don Frye sit across from each other on wrought iron sofas padded with white linen cushions and oversized pillows. Rene's head is down. The New York Times separates them. As clouds shift, the stark light of the Manhattan morning sun streaks through the vines and highlights the headline that reads, CASINO FIRE IN AUSTRIA CLAIMS FOUR.

In agony, Don Frye stares at Rene, "Everyone had plenty of time to get out."

Rene lifts his head. All charm and personality are gone. His expression is numb. "What in God's name was he doing in the basement with the Bormanns?"

"I saw that crooked cop, Tony Stokes, watching me. He must've took him down there." Don Frye shakes his head; "I didn't like the fact that Andre even brought him. For what reason?" He falls back into the folds of his cushion, "I'll bet Stokes is the one responsible for killing Pascali Debartolo. He had it in for him."

Rene pushes the paper further away, "The newspaper said that Andre must've been trying to save the art?" He shakes his head, "He had to know it was fake."

Saira comes onto the rooftop, "Good morning, gentlemen."

Rene folds the paper under a plate of quartered watermelon.

Saira kisses Rene on the lips and Don Frye on the cheek. Fearing something is wrong, she looks back-and-forth at their faces.

"What's up guys?" They're both silent. That heightens her fears immediately. She squints trying to read Rene, "What's wrong?"

Rene eases her down next to him on the sofa. "Saira…." Squinting with anguish, he draws a deep breath and stares into her eyes, "Saira, I'm afraid I have something very distressing to tell you." He sighs anticipating hurting her, "Andre Pope..." Rene corrects himself and is less detached, "Andre died in Linz." His eyes flutter, "In the fire."

Saira gasps. "Oh my God." She shakes her head trying to undo it. "No. No." Standing, backing off, her hands tremble as she covers her mouth. "What? How did…?" She tries to speak, but can't. She starts to cry.

Rene pulls her close, comforting her, "I know sweetheart."

Tears run down her cheeks, "That sweet man. He was so…" she bites her lip trying to stop sobbing, "he was so kind to me."

Don Frye comes over and puts his hand on Saira's shoulder. Saira stands and clings onto him. "Shh, darlin," he gently strokes her head to soothe her. "It's okay. We're here. We love you."

She fights for a breath, "He was my friend."

Don Frye blots her tears with his napkin, "Ours too, Saira." He looks at Rene. "Ours too." He coaxes her down and holds her hands. "When the fire alarm rang," he shakes his head, "Andre didn't leave with the other guests." He looks at the folded paper. "The newspaper said he was trapped when a wall collapsed in the basement."

"The basement? What was down there?"

Don Frye looks to Rene to answer.

Rene picks up the newspaper. "The paper said it was possible he was trying to save the art."

"Art…? You said it was all fake. But Rene…" Saira sniffles and inhales deeply, "he was like you. An expert." Saira looks to Rene for an answer.

Expressionless, he's silent.

She turns back to Don Frye. His eyes drill Rene's.

"Well," Rene cocks his head to the side, "we think he went down in the basement for the Blue Mauritius stamp." He shrugs, "It was all centuries old wood down here."

Don Frye catches Saira's stare and quickly backs up Rene, "And add to that the difficulty of getting fire equipment up that hill."

Saira scrutinizes Rene. "How did you know it was *all wood* in the basement?"

"You know," Rene's eyes dart to Don Frye and return to Saira. "I saw it when the Bormanns took me there to look at the stamp."

"Is that why you didn't examine the stamp at the auction?"

Rene nods.

"Where exactly did they take you?"

"In the basement."

Saira's look waits for more.

Rene adds it nonchalantly, "To a safe."

"Did the stamp burn?"

Uncomfortable, Rene repeats himself, "It was in a safe."

Saira stands and stays on him. "Do you think it burned?"

Rene looks to Don Frye. He offers nothing. Rene sees Saira is locked on him. His face twists almost surrendering a wry smile, "It was an old safe."

"*Did the stamp burn?*"

Rene nods.

"How many stamps are left now?"

"What...?" Rene feels Saira evaluating him like it's for the first time.

Saira's eyes flutter and close. They open to a dizzying roof-top view of Manhattan. She relives what happened on the high-rise over the Hudson River. She shivers remembering Rene's uncaring, cold-blooded push. Short of breath, her eyes close as she feels herself dropping in mid air. She falters a bit. Rene touches her back. Saira flinches from his touch. She feels her whole body tremble. She turns on him, "How many are left?"

Rene's neck jerks. "Now…" his eyes go cold, "just one."

Don Frye gathers up the newspaper. "I'm going to give you two some privacy."

They both watch Don Frye leave.

An interminable silence is broken by the music and sounds of parading street traffic below. Rene is uncomfortable with the way Saira is looking at him. His gut sinks with her next question.

"Rene, why did you throw the briefcase away?" Saira scrutinizes him, "All that money out the window?"

"What do you mean? They were chasing us. Shooting at us."

"Why the handful of cash?"

Rene is silent.

"What was in the briefcase?"

Rene assesses his alternatives. He's never lied to Saira. The vanity of his ego triumphs, he can only choose the truth. "Nothing. We left the money on the plane."

"And you left Andre at the casino...." Saira transforms from tormented despair to tormented rage. "You knew you were going to burn it from the beginning, *didn't you*?"

Rene is silent. He feels himself shrink, split between child and adult.

"You're playing God." Saira's voice elevates, "You can't decide what exists and what doesn't."

Watching her love evaporate, Rene disappears into himself.

Saira feels her world stolen from her. It's the same nightmare all over again. With one fluid movement, she feels herself pushed over the edge, swaying in the dark, convinced she's going to die. Clawing her way back. Her eyes close recalling Andre's soothing voice. How Andre told her she was the real Saira with Rene. She looks at Rene with new eyes. She sees the little boy Andre told her about. The one standing in the doorway of the room of his dead baby brother. Rene's face loses its reality. She has no idea who he really is. What he's capable of. Her eyes burning, Saira takes off her engagement ring and drops it on the table. It clinks on the glass.

She turns and walks out.

Rene is devoid of speech. His tongue cleaved in his mouth.

As she leaves, Rene watches what is most precious to him, his life with Saira, float away. All his possessions pale and become worthless. He picks up the diamond ring. Holds it in his palm. Was it all a dream? He peers out over the skyline of the New York. Desolate, amorphous, high-rise steel and stone blocks punctuate his infinity. Country Western music wafts up from the street parade below him. He hears an invisible troupe of musicians playing Rosanne Cash's *Blue Moon With Heartache.* It draws him to the rooftop's edge. He looks for the procession of floats. They're gone. His eyes search for the musicians defying his alchemy. They're not to be found. Their music taunts him making the purpose and meaning of his life vanish. His ability to create his own reality disappears with it.

Rene's drawn down his marble staircase.

Vermeer's Girl With a Pearl Earring turns away from him. As he passes her, Rene turns back. Vermeer's girl gives him nothing.

"You too?"

Sitting at his desk, amidst a lifetime of his possessions, Rene's world spins. Holding the sides of his head, he tries to focus on something. Diamonds shimmer from across the room. His attention turns to the fireplace mantle. Rene's eyes rivet on the diamond-encrusted, pink Faberge egg defying him with its promise of perpetuity. He gets up and holds it in the palm of his hand. It's gone cold.

He places the egg on his desk and opens it. The invisible troupe's music comes out of the egg. He turns his back to it.

The music won't stop. Roseanne Cash's melancholy words taunt him, "*What would I give to be a diamond in your eyes again. What would I give to bring back those old times. What did I say to make your cold heart beat this way?*"

With the swing of a fireplace poker he smashes the egg. The unendurable music disappears, as does the joy of his life.

FORTY-NINE

Bathed in celestial sunlight, a Bell-Boeing, Tilt Rotor, helicopter flutters over the endless verdant hills of Siena on its way to Tuscany's Val d'Orcia. The bloodhound puppy in his lap, Rene looks out over a landscape written in Renaissance times. The Tuscan dream offers itself to his imagination announcing its untouched place in the order of things. Carefully cultivated and exquisitely proportioned, never-ending, conical hills, painted in the colors of spring, present a landscape chessboard with each tree, bush, road, hill, and ravine manning its post. Thousand year old serpentining Cyprus trees are perfectly spaced G-clefs on a musical staff of dry road and open vistas of ploughed and sewn land. Golden earth and dark-green grass marry flat plains and rolling hills with fortified castles. Rocky crags and rose fields embellishing vineyards, mix with the silver-grey of olive groves. Farmhouses stuck in the fifteenth century, stand in defiance against stylish villas perched on hills overlooking the Orcia Valley.

Wild geese fly over the Tuscan sky. They call to Rene, their harsh cries letting him know he's out of his control zone. He looks once more at the Sienese palette. The symmetry between man and his environment gnaws at Rene. The solitude and empty spaces only serving to heighten his loneliness.

It's been a month since Saira's left.

Wearing a chalk-striped, double-breasted, taupe, wool suit and an open-collared white shirt, with his brown, kidskin leather gloves stuffed in his breast pocket, Rene assuages the puppy as it peers out the window, "Ah, ah, ah. I know what you're thinking Bo," he shakes his head, "you're not ready to go hunting with the big dogs yet." The puppy whines like it knows what he's talking about.

With a three-day beard under his moustache, pilot Don Frye, sporting a russet and blackwatch plaid hunting jacket, takes off his Stetson and runs his hand through his shock of dark hair. "Look at it down there. I thought this was a private membership club." As the helicopter arcs downward toward an 800-year-old estate boasting a renovated stone castle reigning over 4,000 acres devoted to boar hunting, a gaggle of hoteliers, wine makers, apparel merchants, food purveyors, and local hucksters await their arrival. "Those guys are trying to turn it into a theme park."

Rene is somewhere else. He sighs, "I can't imagine my life without her."

Don Frye gently drops the helicopter down on a field of grass. The two men sit there in silence as the blades whoosh down. Wearing white shirts and shiny, brass-belted, khaki pants, the welcoming party of bronzed, smiling hosts of the private hunting club of Castiglion del Bosco streams their way. Rene winces.

"Rene…." Before the greeting party gets to them Don Frye tries to read his old friend, "Is there anything you haven't told me?"

Rene's silent.

Don Frye's finger goes back to the copter's starter button, "You want to leave?"

Rene shakes his head no. As the blades wind down, the rotor clinks and resonates in the glass cockpit. The clink of Sarah's ring hitting the glass table echoes in Rene's mind.

A mounted, khaki-hatted huntsman, Paolo de Vecchi, with a huge, double-barreled shotgun strapped over his back, gallops over first, and greets Rene and Don Frye as they depart the helicopter. "Signore Sorrell, Signore Frye." He sweeps his hat with panache, "Gentleman, welcome to the land of *il cinghiale*. It doesn't get any fresher than shooting your own dinner. Ready for the best tasting boar of your life?"

Rene and Don Frye look at each and find humor in their first greeting. They laugh, and so does huntsman, Paolo de Vecchi. Rene and Don Frye laugh harder.

Paolo de Vecchi gets a little defensive. Beauregard hops down from the copter and goes flat spread out on his belly. The huntsman looks at the pipsqueak bloodhound peeing on their manicured grass. "The boars will wash him down with their black truffles." He squints at Rene's designer outfit, "Ever shot anything?"

"Do a couple of Sports Illustrated swimsuit models count?"

As Paolo de Veechi frowns, Rene and Don Frye laugh again, their laughter just the medicine they need.

As their bags are taken, Rene and Don Frye go to the hunting club's stone castle to register and get the keys to their lodge. The castle exterior, while carefully true to its rustic origin, stands in deep contrast to its interior which has been modernized with every state-of-the-art luxury. White-coated waiters move through the well-heeled crowd, while guests air-kiss, and pick at hors d'oeuvres and hot pizza as they gather to watch soccer on giant plasma TVs.

"Signores," the lodge manager directs Rene and Don Frye to the corner of the room and sits them at a private desk, "your request for privacy has been strictly honored. Your cabin's most valuable amenity is its seclusion. There are no neighbors. Your property is only accessible by private boat, hydroplane, or helicopter."

Don Frye grabs the keys, "That works."

FIFTY

The isolated stretch of the snow-covered mountain range of Nanga Parbat stands in the distant background as a run-down, baggage-topped bus kicks up dust as it tilts into a gravelly turn crossing the desolate Punjab plain. The road is barren for miles. Spaced toothpicks of weathered phone poles, seamed together with sagging telephone lines, are the only sign of civilization. Staring out the window, squeezed in between packed rows of turbaned Pakistani, Indian, and Punjabi men, is a dispirited Saira. Betrayed by her dreams, the make-believe of her life is gone from her eyes.

As the rose-tinted sun sets, crossing the India-Pakistan border, the rickety bus stops at Wagah, the small village that is the checkpoint linking the two countries.

A bag-strapped, self-important, turquoise-turbaned Punjabi college student helps his understated, pregnant Sikh wife carefully up the steps of the bus. Saira slides over to the window to allow the handholding Punjabi couple to sit together.

"Bhala Hove," the wife nods to Saira, thanking her.

Drums beat. Passengers jostle each other to get a better view as the flags of both countries are lowered. Saira studies the crowd, as people from all walks of life, age groups, sects, and races stand to cheer and chant Bharat ki jai and nationalistic slogans. The turbaned college student sneers, "It's called the Ritual of Hate." He analyzes Saira's attire and curious stare, "Are you French?"

Saira falters, and then makes him smile, "Punjabi."

Saira avoids his scrutiny as the full dress ceremony of the

tall, khaki-uniformed, red-plumed Jawans soldiers of the Indian Border Security Force, and the black-suited and black-plumed Pakistani Rangers, each on their own side of the border, a handshake from each other, start their marching drills for the night's closing ceremony. Chests-puffed out, swelled with the pride of their country, legs are lifted to chest-level to show the soles of their shoes to the opponent, and outdo the other by hitting the ground harder.

"Things change," the turbaned student laments. "The Indians aren't kicking as high and stomping as hard." He shrugs, "Relations aren't as bitter as they used to be."

Night falls and the converted school bus continues on its bumpy, lonely ride. The Sikh couple nestles up to each other. Saira tries to close her eyes and sleep, but can't. She opens the purse on her lap. She sighs as she fans through pictures of Rene and her in Mexico. The pregnant Sikh watches Saira linger on the gilded picture of Rene. The bus hits a bump. The gilded picture drops.

The woman picks it up and hands it to Saira, "Tuhada naan ki hai?" (What's your name?)

"Saira. Saira DuFour."

Seeing the pain in Saira's eyes, the young woman puts her hand on Saira's to comfort her and asks, "Tussi kithhon aye?" (What is the sweetest fruit?).

Saira sighs but can't respond.

Studying Saira's eyes, she sees she understands but her emotions prevent her from answering. The woman gives her the answer. "Pyaar" (Love).

Entering the heart of the ancient Punjab region, the emotion changes as the bus approaches the train crossing between Kapurthala and the holy city of the Sikh religion, Amristar. Entering the city, the empty highway metamorphoses into a packed market of urban chaos. Ingress and egress are indistinguishable. Railroad crossing bells clang and rails close, as scores of pedestrians and bicyclists play daredevil with an approaching blue boxcar commuter train. The theatre of everyday life in Punjab borders on absurd as the pastiche of its workforce amalgamates. Hundreds of Punjabis pack into a bottleneck of direction-possessed pilgrims. The bus is surrounded with a medley of every kind of Sikh imaginable. Nearly all of them are colorfully turbaned men going to-and-from work on every imaginable permutation of multiple-wheeled bicycles balancing their wares.

Bicycles, with attached wooden platforms, miraculously counter balance everything from bananas to barrels, from twenty-foot fiberglass pipes to stacks of acetylene torches. Tightly roped, massive bales of cotton, and suitcases of silk and wool, miraculously hang in equipoise over feeble metal frames with spoked-wheels. A burgundy-turbaned, grey-bearded Sikh in a tattered Punjabi Sergeant's military coat, riding on a wooden flatbed pulled by a donkey, stops feet from Saira's open window. The turquoise-turbaned student salutes him and proudly shouts out the window, "Punjab, the defenders of India!" The student turns around to the other passengers daring a response. The mélange of old bearded men offer nothing.

The commuter train's horn blares.

Foolhardy pedestrians and heedless bicyclists make a last second dash across the tracks. Defying them with its horn, the train ignores it all. The ground rumbles as a succession of over-sized blue box cars rattle by on the tracks.

The young Sikh student laments, "Every invasion into India had to trample through Punjab." His voice amplifies, "We were good enough to fight their wars but not deserving enough to benefit from them." He points to the quiet desperation on the bicyclist's faces, "Look at them. Time has stopped for these people. It's the same here as it was in the seventeen hundreds. After decades of hostility and bloodshed, Punjab is still the stepchild of India and Pakistan. We've wasted years resenting our colonial masters, criticizing western countries, and remembering centuries of past glory." He shrugs, "I know a few happy people...maybe. Until we take pride in ourselves we stay trapped." He leans out the window and shouts, "One blood!"

Darkness and a monotonous bouncing stretch of empty road close Saira's eyes. A few hours later whispers of excitement stir a groggy Saira. Sparkling veils of lights twinkle around an illuminated, massive, three-tiered fairy tale castle of gold shimmering on black water. The Golden Temple comes into view. Chanting breaks out amongst the passengers. Saira studies the impassioned faces as tears drop from them. She strains to see the golden shrine.

As a white-bearded, eighty-year-old man behind her leans in and informs her, "That's real gold on the outside of the temple," the bus swerves. Three motorcyclists, all with passengers on the back of their bikes, weave along with the bus.

Saira looks back on the road.

Undisturbed, a short-horned, grey cow calmly occupies the middle of the road and possesses the right of way. All traffic dodges it. The white-bearded man behind Saira, taps her shoulder, "You go to jail for injuring a cow." He laughs as the traffic swerves around it. "They ought to give them license plates or at least reflectors."

In the first morning light, hundreds of Sikhs cross the white marble Causeway to the shore's end where The Golden Temple's gilded, fluted-domes shimmer in the water. Saira leaves her shoes at the entrance. Stepping off stone steps carved with scriptures, she dunks her feet in the shallow sacred water before entering the temple.

An old man waves at Saira.

The white-bearded man from the bus is now bare-chested and holding onto a rope as he dunks his entire body in the holy water of the Pool of Immortality surrounding the temple. Old women pray and weep as they enter the shrine. Saira picks up a white scarf and wraps her head before entering. She kneels and prays before the Granth Sahib, the Sikh holy book.

A lazy morning, with the mist still hanging over the fields, finds Saira in the back of a chauffeured black Toyota on an empty country road. A farmer, standing atop a flatbed, oxen-drawn cart, stops shoveling dung as the shiny car passes. His eyes contemptuously judge its chauffeured, well-dressed passenger.

Saira passes her young driver an address in the old section of Chandigarh. Assessing her in the rear view mirror, the driver excitedly turns, "I hear the high-rise there is going to be the capital's finest. Are you going to live there?"

"No..." Saira's face is expressionless, "I used to."

Passing one indistinguishable desolate farm after another, Saira opens the brown bag next to her. She spreads a napkin carefully over her lap and takes out a sandwich and plastic bottle of warm water. As she unwraps her sandwich, Saira pauses. The sun's glare overheating her; she blots her neck with her hankie. Saira opens the window for a breeze. The gentle wind takes her back to her wicker basket picnic in Paris. Her hand holds up her head as she fights sobbing.

The chauffeur looks in his mirror. "Missy, are you okay?"

Saira's hand holds up, waiving him off.

Several hours later, under the oppressing heat of the midday sun, Saira walks across the construction site of the new, steel high-rise frame built on the location of the burnt down Nawanshar Orphanage. Saira scoops up some of the loose dirt and stares at it in her palm. She withdraws a glass vial and puts some of the dirt into it. She casts the rest to the wind.

As the sun sets, a brilliant, pink sky sees the chauffeured car pull into the small village of Podiala, in the Mohali district. The driver goes back to the trunk, takes out shopping bags, and follows Saira past an unlocked steel gate that leads to a deteriorating, lifetime-ago white-washed, two-story building.

Saira enters the building.

As Saira goes down a tight, shadowy hall, she stops as her eyes hang on a plaque on the wall quoting Mother Theresa. A demure, white-draped and white-turbaned nun, with a fat, round face, comes up behind her and translates the Punjabi to English, "The greatest disease and greatest suffering is to be unwanted, unloved, and uncared for..."

Saira interrupts and finishes translating the Punjabi quote, "To be shunned by everybody. To be just nobody to no one."

"Miss DuFour," the nun's eyes sparkle as she reassesses her, "you have no accent. Do you know the language?"

Saira gives nothing away, "Once upon a time."

The nun stares for a moment and locks arms with Saira. "Well," she guides Saira forward, "our girls are the lucky ones. In most places in the world, a mother can find out the sex of her unborn child, but here in Punjab and India, it's illegal. That's because if she's female, there a good chance she will never be born."

As the nun escorts Saira into the orphanage, she notices Saira draw a deep breath. A dimly lit, paint-peeling, narrow dormitory room that holds a row of eighteen, matching, green-blanketed steel beds, facing another eighteen, identical, green-blanketed beds, confronts Saira. As she walks down the narrow passageway in between the thirty-six teenage girls, sitting on the ends of their beds, barefoot and cross-legged, colorfully wrapped in pastel-hued, cotton shalwaars and long gauze scarves, they light up seeing Saira. Saira goes to one particular reticent girl who is lying face down, afraid to face the visitor. Saira sits next to her and whispers into her ear. The girl turns, takes Saira in, smiles and sits up in amazement. They hug.

The nun pulls Saira aside, "What did you say to her?"

"I told her I used to be just like her."

Saira nods at her young chauffeur. As the nun's well-shaped nose flares with anticipation, the chauffeur opens the shopping bags of presents for the girls. Surrounded by wide-eyed girls, Saira distributes diaries and books, watches and pins, tortoise combs and berets, and cameras with film discs to her attendees.

The group of girls crowd around Saira. Respectful of Saira's personal space, the nun stands in the doorway witnessing Saira's interaction. Occasionally touching Saira's hair and clothes, the girls try different color gauze scarves on her. Several of them laugh and titter as they perform the age-old Indian art of Mehndi by designing intricate, swirling, henna tattoos on Saira's palms. Others do her makeup, hair, and adorn her wrists with brass bangles.

Saira looks at her watch and sighs. She stands and takes it all in. Seeing the girls are all studying her, she smiles courage. It doesn't seem to be enough. She promises, "Ankhon se dur hopar dil se nahi." (You are away from my eyes but not from my heart.)

Clutching their presents, the girls push to get to Saira. One stern look from the nun gets them to all stand in line. Taking turns, they each hug Saira as she leaves. After an elongated hold, the reticent young girl weeps and runs back into the home.

At the door, Saira takes a handkerchief-wrapped item out of her purse. She gives it to the nun, “Put this toward their education.”

As the nun watches Saira leave, she opens the handkerchief. Her eyes go wide seeing the sparkle of the diamond- and turquoise-studded pin that the Maharaja gave Saira.

On the way back to the car, Saira fights weakening. She gets back into the car. It’s all too much for her. She sobs.

FIFTY-ONE

Windows of billowy Tuscan fog surround a bare-chested Rene as he stares himself down in the mirror. Dawn sneaks through at his back. An errant sparkle hits his mirror. He looks down at Saira's diamond ring sitting on the ledge before him. His eyes close. He floats in the memory of the morning he and Saira witnessed his glass house tincture orange. How he laid the diamond ring next to Saira's pillow. How, on a golden-orange bed, the sun consecrated their sweet lovemaking. His eyes open to a wearier Rene. He's torn with what he sees. He lifts his chin up. The skin of his neck seems less taut. He pinches it, evaluating his aging -- his mortality. Fingers to each earlobe, he lifts the skin contemplating cosmetic surgery.

He turns on the hot water, letting its steam fog what he sees.

A towel wipes it all clean. Rene sighs and starts over. Standing straighter, puffing up his chest, affirming his well-toned physique, he lathers his face with gusto. Reaching for the blue, disposable razor provided by the lodge, Rene hesitates. Squinting, his gaze turns to his leather Dobb kit. His hand just over it, he stares at it, hesitating to open its zipper. He smiles. He drops the plastic razor in a glass. Opening up the kit, Rene takes out a straight razor. He flips it open. Sticking his chin out, he holds the blade to his neck. He draws the blade up against the grain. Humming to himself with the advent of the new day, he flinches from the sting of pain. The razor drops to the floor as blood trickles from a cut. Rene immediately stiffens as his eyes widen at the sight of his blood on the white sink. He grabs a towel, wets it, and applies pressure to the wound. Quickly tearing out a bandage, he sighs, seeing it's nothing more than a small nick.

He throws the straight razor in the garbage. He presses a styptic pencil to the wound. The bleeding stops. Rene smiles defiance. Burying his face in a hot washcloth, he turns hearing something.

Pulling a second horse behind him, Don Frye rides up to the front of what was originally built as a nineteenth century stable and has now been renovated into a lavish hunting lodge. With his characteristic Stetson and boots on, and with his shirtsleeves rolled up, and two shotguns strapped over his shoulder, he whistles for Rene. Rene steps out sporting a brown, felt hat, whose brim is turned upside down, a brown, corduroy hunting jacket with leather shoulder patches, a spread collar shirt with a paisley tie, and a vest over corduroy pants tucked into leather boots.

"You gonna' hunt 'em or romance 'em?" Don Frye snatches the felt hat and throws it in the air. "The hat's not you."

Both men turn to the sound of furious, scratching nails. Left behind, the bloodhound puppy is pawing and howling in the window. Rene puts his fingers to his lips, points, and shushes Bo.

Don Frye tugs Rene. He mimics their welcoming huntsman, "Il cinghiale...is waiting." He holds the second horse as Rene puts his foot in the stirrup and mounts. "Paolo was real disappointed hearing you didn't want him or any of his dogs."

Rene takes a handbook out of his coat. As the horses walk down the road, Rene reads it, enjoying educating his buddy, "It says here, dogs will chase a boar up and down a hill. Running up and down hills builds up lactic acid in the muscles diminishing the flavor of the meat and making it tough." He passes the handbook to Don Frye, "A true boar aficionado hunts alone. No guides. No dogs."

Don Frye throws the book away and passes Rene one of the double-barreled shotguns. Rene slides it into his saddle pouch. He withdraws a compact, black, metal crossbow, and quiver of arrows from his saddlebag. Strapping the quiver over his shoulder, Rene squints into the fog. His mood turns serious. He goads his horse.

"You sure you wanna' do this?" Don Frye trots after him entering the dark, piney woods. "Why here? Why boar hunting?" He calls out, "It makes no sense."

Going deeper into the thick of the forest, quickly disappearing in the fog, Rene shouts back, "Man is not a creature of reason."

"Hey!" He catches up with Rene, "Slow down." He bats him with his Stetson, "You're going to get a cowboy speeding ticket."

"What?"

"Breaking the barrier before the chute release."

They both laugh like they've done so many times before.

Rene steals a look at his best friend. A lifetime of comradeship flashes. If only he could be like him -- fit in simpler to life.

Don Frye feels Rene's stare and turns. Rene quickly busies himself with taking an arrow from his quiver and arming his crossbow. Don Frye smiles, "You sure you know how to use that thing?"

As the men ride through the patchy fog, Rene winks cockiness. "You have to be able to look into the eyes of your opponent." Feigning farcical, he dances his eyebrows, "Feel his longing for the stillness of the profound peace of death."

Don Frye guffaws. Studying Rene gearing up the crossbow, he shakes his head, "Boy, if your grandfather could see you now."

"*My grandfather*?"

"Yeah. Remember how on that Thanksgiving he told my father Jews don't hunt."

"Jews don't hunt. He was and didn't." Rene secures the bow on his saddle, "I'm only half. The Irish half loves barbequed ribs."

Don Frye shakes his head. "You're nuts, you know that?"

Rene recalls Amanda's tutorial to him. How, as he watched the street fair's carousel spin, Amanda preached 'that one's shadow was one's best enemy'. He liked that. He understood the power of one's dark side. What it could do. Rene becomes aware of Don Frye's scrutiny. "Nuts…? No." Rene gets wild-eyed. "It's enantiodromia."

"What's that?"

"It's the law of equilibrium. Sooner or later everything seeks out its opposite."

"What're you talking about?"

"Boars are the lowest rung on the conservation status. I like that." He cocks his head, "I'm helping 'em along. Extinction adds to the value of something."

They hear a scurrying through the bushes. Rene nudges his horse. Don Frye's hand stops Rene and points out footprints around matted grass where the boar has foraged for food. "Remember you're not hunting cute little pink pigs from the county fair. They're feral, wild animals. These Italian boars are muscular, fast, smart, thirty-inches tall at the shoulder, four-to-five-feet in length, and three hundred pounds fat from gorging themselves on Tuscan truffles."

Following the footprints, Rene prods his horse to a trot.

"Stay where I can see you." Don Frye rides alongside of him, "Remember what I told you on the plane. Don't try to see the boar. You'll hear him first."

Rene hears a rustle in the grass and kicks his horse into a gallop. He forges deeper into the forest. A dark, hairy, squat form scurries through the trees. Rene lifts his crossbow to his shoulder and fires. His arrow buries itself in a tree trunk.

Don Frye cracks up. "Remember, aim for the shoulder. Hit the vital organs. It's a quick kill. Otherwise you'll just piss him off. And *you don't* want to piss him off."

The two men ride quietly, single file through the forest, listening, watching. Rene eyes scour the forest's dark shadows. Nothing seems to move. The high grass, bushes, and trees close in on him. The stillness disquiets him. Suddenly, a chilly morning wind picks up, rustling the tree's leaves. In the swish he hears the whisper of Saira's voice. Like a siren, it pulls him, beckoning him deeper into the folds of the forest. The fog swirls creating shadows of light in the depth of the trees. In the shadows, he imagines Saira waiting somewhere far away from this verdant world. Waiting forever. A slight rain falls. Mists of rain swirl against his face. The fragrant Cyprus wood's rich, resinous oils dizzy him. Time compresses into six-feet before him. The deeds and misdeeds of his life whirl by. His life seems to balance on whether Saira returns. He imagines the Cyprus as tall sentinels whose supernatural powers and aroma ward off the demons of death. Yet, all the while, the pungent aroma of the forest blankets him with depression. Nothing will take away the wound to his immortality.

Hooves dash across dead leaves lying on flat stones.

Rene's horse flinches as a wild boar bolts from the underbrush. Don Frye kicks his horse after it. The chase is on.

Snorting and grunting, the boar darts right, then left, then right again. In full gallop, Rene and Don Frye pursue it. Don Frye ahead of him, a scurrying click, click, click, click turns Rene back. He sees nothing. All he hears is a dashing click, click, click, click on the rocky ground. Like the devil's toenails running across a blackboard. Jerking his horse's reigns, he turns it around and trails the sound. Rene kicks his horse to a gallop, and then pulls back halting it.

Nothing. Just the swirl of upswept rain fanning dead leaves.

Click, click, click, click.

Rene turns to see a four hundred pound, male boar sixty-feet in front of him. Trapped in a corner of rocks, instead of being hunted, it stops and turns on Rene. Black eyes glowing, the coarse, bristly hair of his shoulder blades rising, the boar scrapes its curling, ten-inch tusks against a rock to sharpen them. His back rises to attack. Snarling, wild-eyed, the primeval beast lowers its head and charges. Slashing through the bushes with its tusks, it comes straight for Rene. Waiting, focusing, Rene takes aim and slowly presses the crossbow's trigger. His arrow hits the back hindquarter of the boar. The boar shrieks a bloodcurdling squeal as its back leg caves from the hit. Grunting, its back rising into a hunch, it stands again and charges. Its black eyes demonic, it's mouth frothing, its head lowered and bobbing, it keeps coming, only faster, more possessed. As Rene reaches back for another arrow, his horse rears. Rene tumbles backward.

As the horse gallops away, the boar heads straight for Rene. Thrashing its sharpened tusks left and right, the beast slashes a swath through the high grass as it closes the ten-feet to Rene. Scampering on the wet ground, Rene stretches for his crossbow and fallen arrow.

The savage boar takes aim.

Boom! The dying squeals of the boar thrashing in the grass echo death-shrieks through the fog. A shotgun blast brings the fallen, tusk-filled, dark mouth of a bloody, black bristling, four hundred pound carcass inches from Rene's face.

Rene looks up as Don Frye rides up.

Don Frye tucks his smoking shotgun in his saddle pouch, and jumps down, "Are you all right?" Rene nods. He helps Rene up, "What the hell's wrong with you!" Don Frye's boot spreads the boar's bloody mouth revealing its ten-inch, white tusks. Pissed, he shakes his head, "*You're the one* that almost became extinct."

Stretching his bruised bones, Rene dusts himself off.

"You got to look him in the eyes all right."

Thunder rumbles as lightning flashes overhead. Raindrops tap the leaves. Gripped frozen, Rene is fascinated by the dark-hearted, primeval beast.

"C'mon," Don Frye grabs Rene's arm and walks him away, "Leave it for Paolo. He'll come get it." As the fog swirls overhead, they thread through the tall trunks of Cyprus and edge out of the forest. Don Frye peeks at Rene, "You're not yourself. You're being careless." He puts a loose arm-lock around Rene, "Stop it. Be careful."

Walking side-by-side, their horses behind them dragging loose reigns, they walk down a long-winding, empty, gravel path, the Tuscan sky's low-hanging, ominous clouds blurring their background. Rene and Don Frye walk silently, like they have done a thousand times, comfortable with each other in the solitude of their own thoughts. In the stillness of the secluded road and fine rain, as the horses clop along, Rene is lulled into his childhood. He reminisces the first time he saw the boy Don Frye. His sleeves up over his brawny arms, Don Frye was in the garage watching his dad work on Rene's father's cars. Because of his size, Rene was sure he was twice his age. When they were introduced, Rene didn't think Don was a big enough name for a kid that size so he called him Don Frye. It stuck ever since.

Rene smiles remembering how the two of them filled up an empty house. He tries, but it seems he can't remember much of anything else before Don Frye. Rene steals a glance of the serene, wide-faced, high-cheeked, bastion of strength next to him. Don Frye's big-boned hand wipes the rain from his moustache and then adjusts the shotgun over his shoulder. Brothers in arms, Rene boasts to himself. The solitary life they existed in, and their community of thought, had given him all the sustenance he needed until now. The absurdity of life clearly taught him the value of a best friend. He smiles at Don Frye but doesn't let him see it.

Don Frye suddenly turns, as if he feels Rene's thoughts.

"Thanks, buddy. I know..." Rene searches for the right words, "I know I haven't exactly been at my best." He sighs, "This whole thing must be rough on you too."

Don Frye puts an arm around Rene, "It was fast for her. Give her time to sort it out." His Stetson drips rain as he tilts toward Rene, "I miss her too."

Rene looks ahead at the grey, solitary path, "Do dreams never come true?"

Don Frye stops walking and catches Rene's arm, "Look at what you've done. The hospitals you've financed. Your museum donations. The children's research."

"You know what I mean."

Don Frye puts a hand on the back of Rene's head, "Don't worry. She loves you. She'll come back."

FIFTY-TWO

A classic, mahogany Riva runabout, carrying waiters dressed in the red-crested, black supper coats of the hunting club of Castilion del Bosco, cuts across a smooth, nighttime, dark-blue lake and pulls up in front of an isolated stone lodge. The bloodhound puppy, Bo, bellowing as the waiters pull ashore, brings Don Frye to the door. He waves them forward. Carrying a row of sterling platters into the lodge, the waiters parade by with trays of the gourmet meal prepared for Rene and Don Frye's dinner. At the end of the line, the huntsman, Paolo de Vecchi, lifts the lid of the largest domed tray revealing the head of Rene's boar.

Dressed in a wide-wailed, rolled-collar, black cashmere sweater, white t-shirt, jeans, and white sneakers, Rene puts another log on the fire. "A second later and that could've been my head."

"Avevi ragione," the huntsman criticizes loud enough so Rene can hear that he agrees. "We found a brown, felt hat in his stomach. Your boar was tracking you."

Like two school kids busted for misbehaving, Rene and Don Frye look at each other and shudder with feigned surprise and amusement in provoking the over-serious huntsman.

Paolo de Vecchi places the boar's head down on the center of the table. With wounded pride, the huntsman looks down his nose at the impressive size of the boar's head and squints beginner's luck, "La prima rondine ne fa primaverile. Signors..." he perfunctorily nods, "enjoy your feast." He turns on his heels and walks out.

As the waiters smooth out a white tablecloth, and place silverware and glasses, Rene asks the headwaiter, "What did he just say?"

The waiter looks for approval from the others. They just smile. "He said…" it comes out with a thick, Italian accent, "one swallow doesn't make a springtime."

Rene and Don Frye look at each other and fight laughter. As soon as the waiters leave, Rene and Don Frye sit down on brass-studded, red, leather-backed chairs before a candlelit dinner. Their stone fireplace crackling in the background, Don Frye lifts his wine glass, "To the best dressed hunter in Tuscany."

Rene looks at the boar's black, beady eyes staring him down. He turns the platter toward Don Frye and self-effacingly toasts, "One swallow doesn't make a springtime."

They both crack up. For a fleeting moment, the laughter pacifies Rene's despair. The candlelight dinner and long day tug at Rene's vulnerabilities. He looks at the empty two chairs alongside the table. He got so used to one of them being filled by Saira. From across the table, Don Frye smiles resilience. The puppy runs and sniffs a breeze at the door. Rene sarcastically laments, "She ain't comin' Bo."

"Well," Don Frye holds up a nine-inch, meaty rib, "mine certainly doesn't have any lactic acid from running up hills," he smirks, "it chased you more than you chased it."

Rene manages a smile.

The two men eat silently, yet voraciously. Knowing Rene is the easiest sell; the bloodhound puppy waits dutifully at his side for a bone. After an elongated whimper, Bo gets a bone half as big as he is and carries it to the privacy of the fireplace. A shared bottle of wine, the heavy meal, the trauma of the day's hunt, and brisk lakeside air take their toll. Rene goes to lie down in front of the fireplace on the rug next to Bo. He pulls the brindle puppy onto his lap and feels his protruding belly, "Ca'mere you little fatty." Bo scampers up to lick Rene's lips. "Yikk," Rene wipes the bone grease from his mouth.

"He's paying you back for not taking him along."

"Don't worry," Rene cups Bo's face, "your time will come."

Pulling on his white Alabama Crimson Tide sweatshirt, Don Frye goes to the screen door and shuts the wooden door behind it.

"It's getting a little brisk in here." He looks at Rene snuggled up with the puppy at the fireplace, "You cold?"

Rene moans cryptically.

Don Frye goes to the fireplace, opens up the etched-glass ash guard and pokes the logs that are crumbling to embers. He looks at the log bin; only a couple logs are left. "I'll go cut some wood." As he reaches the front door, he stops and turns. The late night's air and the flickering fireplace behind Rene, take him back in time. He's flashed back to when Rene's parents died, and a barefoot, pajama-wearing, traumatized, nine-year-old Rene would sneak into his room and spend the night cuddled up with his dog by the fireplace. His moustache lifts with the warm memory. The secluded isolation, quiet mellow hour, and a lifetime of kinship roll off Don Frye's lips. "Rene...."

"What?" Rene murmurs, half-dozing.

"Nothin'...." Don Frye stares at Rene as his eyes close, "Sweet dreams, partner."

Rene's eyes struggle to stay open. The logs flicker dancing their light-show of shadows on the cantilevered, wood-paneled ceiling. Rene transforms the shadows to shapes suiting his own alchemy. He and Saira are alone in the lodge, entwined before the fire, their enraptured-silhouettes dancing on the ceiling. Looking up, he strokes the puppy's soft head, and floats with the sensate tactility and the last warmth of the fire. His elixir of life waning, Rene vainly tries to relish his imaginary moment with Saira; wishing life could linger like that forever. Embers stop crackling. All that's left is a warm orange glow. Rene focuses on it and closes his eyes trying to remember the feeling of how, in the bask his life's most perfect dawn, Saira put her finger to his lips sealing his proposal. The pleasure of the memory eludes him. The white silence of the lodge haunts him. His eyes open to take in every inch of the room, trying to tire themselves. The lacquered-wood walls, red leather chairs, and printed-russet rug lose their color. The drill doesn't work. He takes out his phone for the thousandth time and checks it for messages. None. His life is so private he's more isolated than even this remote lodge. He looks down at his hands and turns them over -- he doesn't recognize them. His dedication to a lifetime of uniqueness has failed him. This is the moment Rene's convinced God has abandoned him. This is his night of spiritual desolation. His eyelids get heavy and close. When all else fails, he performs all he has left -- he does his childhood Rene Sorrell ritual. He whispers, assuring himself, “This to shall pass.”

Bo perks up his ears. He thinks Rene’s going to take him out. He whines.

“Not now, boy,” Rene murmurs, struggling to get more comfortable.

The willful puppy sparks up even more. Darting back-and-forth across the room, his stick-hard, wagging tail whips the furniture.

“Okay....” Rene sighs. “All right. Settle down.”

As Rene goes to get up, he realizes how hard he fell off the horse. He moans out loud. Stiff, he leans on the fireplace and pulls himself up. Bo thinks Rene’s playing a game and gets more excited. He runs up on the bottom ledge of the fireplace and jumps down by Rene. Nipping at the fringe of Rene’s blue jeans, Bo whimpers as he gives him fast nibbles. His whipping tail bangs into the fireplace irons tipping them into a cheap porcelain vase on the mantle. It falls.

Rene lunges for it and catches the vase in his palm.

His wrist comes down on the glass ash guard. The glass shatters slicing his wrist open. Blood pours profusely from the wound.

The shadows on the lodge’s ceiling dance no more. The room darkens as the fireplace loses its glow. Embers turn to ashes.

Don Frye’s boot bangs the door open as he enters with an armful of sliced wood. “Sorry I took so long. I couldn’t find an axe.” Wood crashes at his feet seeing Rene lying face down in a pool of his own blood. His breath sucked out, Don Frye rushes to Rene and scoops him up. Rene is pale and unconscious. Don Frye gasps. “Oh God no. Please God.” His voice cracking, he strokes Rene’s face, “No. No.” Blood oozes from Rene’s wrist. Don Frye rips a sleeve off his shirt and tourniquets it around Rene’s wrist. He cradles Rene’s limp body in his arms.

Rene’s head sparrows back.

Don Frye scoops Rene up and rushes him out the door.

Disoriented, one hundred eighty pounds of a limp Rene in his arms, Don Frye starts running toward the clearing down the road. He looks down at his sweatshirt and hands -- they're full of blood. His eyes fill with tears, "C'mon partner, talk to me. Don't leave me."

Rene's comatose. His breathing stilted.

Don Frye's chest heaving, his lungs gasping for air, he sprints. "Rene, please." He cradles Rene's face against his cheek and cries, "Rene, you promised..." he keeps sobbing, "you promised nothing would ever hurt us." Tears running down his cheeks, heaving for breath, struggling with the lifeless weight in his arms, Don Frye pushes harder to make it to the helicopter.

Gasping for breath, Don Frye yanks open the helicopter's door and rushes Rene inside. Pulling off his sweatshirt, he lays it under Rene's head. Strapping Rene in flat across the back seats, Don Frye jumps into the pilot seat. Yanking on a headset, clearing the tears from his eyes, his soaked hands smear blood across his face. He pushes the starter button.

The helicopter's blades whorl on.

As the helicopter jerks into the air, Don Frye holds the headphone to his mouth, "Mayday! Mayday! Mayday!" Wiping his eyes with his sleeve, he squints at his GPS. "This is helicopter position North 43-37-16 East 11-26-7 leaving Tuscany's Val d'Orcia. I've an emergency request for the closest hospital that can handle a severe loss of blood. Mayday! Mayday! Mayday!"

FIFTY-THREE

In the early morning hours, a light remains on in one of the tabernacle windows of a long, two-story, grey, stone building whose nine semicircular arches face an empty, expansive piazza where a helicopter sits. In the spaces between the arches are glazed terracotta medallions with a baby in blue swaddling on a wheel. A steady breeze chills the air; the flapping of the City of Florence's red fleur-de-lys and Italy's tricolor flags, side-by-side, the only sound punctuating the still peacock-blue sky. Once an orphanage centuries ago, the early Italian Renaissance structure has now been converted into the Ospedale degli Innocenti (Hospital of the Innocents). In a dedicated high isolation unit, with a hemolytic laboratory next door to it for immediate blood diagnostic assays, Don Frye and a white-coated Pakistani doctor huddle in a high-arced, ceiling-blue-lit hallway outside of Rene's private room. Their hushed conversation is interrupted as Saira comes running down the hallway to Don Frye.

Before she can speak, Don Frye's arms envelop her. Fighting tears, his eyes close as he holds her shaking frame. It takes awhile but Saira finally lets go of Don Frye. "Tell me," she pleads drawing deep breaths. Grasping Don Frye's arms, her eyes consume every expression on his face. "Please tell me he's alright."

Buried in Rene's pain, Don Frye's silent. His hope appears to be broken. All the good in the world lost to him, his face is desolate.

Saira gasps. "What? What?" Saira is visibly shaking.

"Ms. DuFour," the bespectacled, Pakistani doctor from the French Red Cross that Rene met with in Paris, steps in and touches her arm. "We've been waiting for you." He takes both Saira's wrists in his hands, holding her, steadying her. "I'm Dr. Akbar Sharif. Rene's physician," he smiles, "and friend."

"Doctor," Saira nods. Placing her fingers against her lips, she hesitates but asks, "How is he?"

Akbar Sharif pushes his thick glasses up and sighs.

Saira holds his eyes, "Tell me the truth."

The narrow hallway seems to close in on Dr. Akbar Sharif. Screwing his lips tight, Akbar Sharif looks up the arched-ceiling and searches for the way to explain it. He sighs while batting his eyes, "It's called exsanguination." He tilts his head softening it, "A severe loss of blood."

Saira hangs on the doctor's expression seeing that there's more coming. "But…?

"But…." Akbar's eyes wince darting from Don Frye to Saira. "That's not the real problem." He takes off his thick glasses and rubs his eyes, "As unique as we all are." He holds his glasses in front of him as he musters a weak smile. "Rene is really unique."

Saira can't wrap her mind around what she's hearing. She looks to Don Frye for more. He's numb. He holds her hand drawing her closer. They both turn to the doctor.

Akbar puts his hand behind Saira's back and guides her forward. Opening the hospital suite's door, the doctor escorts Saira and Don Frye into the room. Bags of French-labeled blood hang over Rene. Catheters rest on either side of him. His skin appears golden, almost yellowed. Eyes closed, he's still in a coma.

Taken aback, Saira covers her mouth in anguish. Raising the sleeve of her simple black dress, Saira buries her head, hiding her eyes from the sight, as she fights sobbing. She tries to clear her throat as her knees buckle. Breathing heavily, she steadies herself on the door frame. She rushes to Rene's side and kneels alongside the bed. Her hand trembles as she slowly caresses his forehead. He's burning up. She starts to sob.

Don Frye goes to Saira and gently moves her to a chair. The

doctor pours her a glass of water and stands over her. After a few deep breaths and a sip or two of water, Saira looks up at Don Frye, "What happened to him?"

"I found him lying on the floor." Don Frye exhales deeply. "In a pool of his blood." He turns from Saira's stare as he shakes his head. "The glass fireplace guard was tipped over next to him. It was shattered. I don't know how it happened. Rene must've accidentally cut his wrist on it. The puppy was just sitting there licking his face. I..." swallowing his guilt, he struggles, "I was...out getting some wood for the fire."

"Wood?" she squints. "Where were you?"

"In Tuscany." His head shakes with the absurdity of it all, "Boar hunting."

"What? Rene doesn't...." she mutters, staring glassy-eyed at Rene. "Hunting?"

Don Frye winces and looks at the doctor with remorse.

Saira seeks Don Frye's hand, "How did you know where to find me?"

Don Frye takes out his wallet. He unfolds a hand-painted, royalty playing card with Tookie's phone number penned on it.

Saira's eyes take in the sophisticated level of medical apparatus in the room. "Why here? Why is Rene in Florence?"

Don Frye slides a chair next to Saira and sits down. He looks up at the doctor.

Akbar Sharif's head drops. He stares at his feet and then looks up. "Florence," he winces, "this hospital, Ospedale degli Innocenti, was the closest trauma center for Rene's very special condition."

Saira repeats it, "Special condition?"

Akbar is expressionless. "His blood." Akbar looks around at the state-of-the-art room provided for Rene. He murmurs to himself and ironically shakes his head. "This hospital is a member of the American Red Cross Rare Donor Database."

Saira shakes her head not getting it, "Rare donor?"

Akbar walks to the bed and checks the central venous catheters monitoring Rene's fluid intake and outtake. He taps the outtake line and scans the kidney monitor -- it reads the same. He sighs. The elevated rapid beeps of the heart monitor draws his attention. He examines the wrist Rene cut -- the arm is hot, its veins enlarged and transfused. He hides his displeasure by keeping his back turned to Saira and Don Frye. He pulls up a chair and faces them. Pausing for a moment, he calculates where to begin. "The vast majority of all humanity falls into four blood types. A, B, AB, and O. Blood types are inherited in the same way as eye and hair color. Blood, as it courses through the body, contains…" his hands animate in the air, "defenders…called antibodies that are attached to the surface of red blood cells. There is never a problem unless you need a transfusion. In a transfusion, the body immediately recognizes blood cells that are foreign. Not their blood type. The antibody defenders will attack any foreign blood cells it doesn't recognize as its own blood type."

Not liking where this is going, Saira deeply sighs. Her face flushed, barely able to hold up her head, she loosens the top buttons of her silk dress. "What does this have to do with Rene?"

Reaching for her hand, Don Frye turns to Saira, "Rene's got a rare blood type." He shakes his head with defeat, "But he was secretive about it. He never let on."

"How come? Why?"

"He must've viewed it as a weakness." His head shakes denying it, "A flaw."

Saira looks to the Dr. Akbar Sharif. He doesn't comment.

"Just once," Don Frye's eyes narrow to the memory, "when Rene acquired this Ming vase in Cotswald, he laughed about it and said it was just like him." He repeats it with the same mystique as Rene did, "Sui generis. He said it's Latin for one of a kind." He shrugs and looks at Dr. Akbar Sharif. "He just never told me how rare."

"Not rare…." Akbar's eyes narrow, "The rarest. *One in a million.*" Akbar Sharif looks at Saira for the first time analyzing her ethnicity, "It's called Bombay Blood Type."

"Bombay?"

"The Bombay Blood Type derives its name because it was first discovered, just a few decades ago, in Bombay." The doctor scrutinizes Saira and answers more precisely, "Mumbai now. The belief is that it was the result of the segregated caste system in India, possibly from noble inbreeding." Akbar gets up and squeezes the top of one of the French-labeled bags of blood.

"Why are the bags labeled in French if we're in Italy?"

That gives Don Frye his first semblance of a smile. He looks at Saira and his eyes get watery again. "That's why he loved you so much." He turns away hiding his tears.

Akbar explains, "When Don Frye called me, I brought the blood from Paris."

A seasoned, sandy-haired, pigeon-chested, Italian nurse, with a large silver cross around her neck, comes in to monitor Rene's statistics. She takes his pulse. It's rapid and feeble. After documenting on her clipboard the high level of Rene's fever, her eyes dart at Dr. Sharif. He nods he's aware, and stares at her impatiently, making it clear he wants to wait until she leaves to continue his conversation. As the nurse exits, she shrugs sympathy, but more so regret.

Dr. Sharif gets up and closes the door. "Beyond being that Rene's blood type is so extremely rare, it's hard to detect."

"That's the problem." Don Frye takes Saira's hand and holds it tighter. "When I first got him here, and they saw that he suffered a severe loss of blood, and how weakened he was, they immediately needed to give him a transfusion."

"Ospedale degli Innocenti did what all immunohematology laboratories do. They screened his blood for a match." Dr. Akbar stalls. He goes over and looks at Rene's central intravenous catheter. As he checks it, his eyes narrow. Feeling Saira's impatience, he turns, "But routine blood typing won't identify the Bombay Blood Type."

Saira's stomach sinks. She looks to Don Frye for support.

The doctor continues, “Bombay blood cells, being so exceptionally rare, test out just like type O when tested for antibodies. Specialized reverse grouping screening tests, involving cross comparisons and serum grouping with type O blood, have be to be done to discover the unique Bombay identifiers.”

Saira’s words come out slowly, “What-are-you-saying?”

“Due to the exigency of the situation, the lab had to give him blood immediately or he could’ve died.” He exhales, “Their tests analyzed he had type O…and they transfused him with that.”

Saira holds her hand to her mouth. Denying it, she shakes her head, “No.”

Dr. Akbar Sharif slowly nods, affirming her fears.

“But….” She points at the French-labeled blood bags on either side of Rene’s bed.

“Cryopreservation.” Frustrated, Akbar blankly stares at the pale-green hospital wall. “Rene had frozen blood banks in America, London, Mexico, Paris, Hong Kong,” he shakes his head, “and some other far away places.” He looks at Don Frye, “But not in Tuscany.” He sighs, “I got here as fast as humanly possible. But….”

Saira looks to Don Frye for security. His head hangs.

“But, the amount of frozen blood that Rene had stored was for any possible planned surgeries that may have come up.” Akbar unconsciously darts his eyes to Rene, “Not for the severe loss of blood from an accidental injury like this.”

All sound is sucked out of the room. All that can be heard is Rene’s heart monitor’s steady accelerating beep, beep, beep.

Akbar breaks the sterile silence, “Of course, before I left Paris, I alerted the American Red Cross to search their donor banks to identify other rare donors. Since blood types are inherited, I had them look for siblings and parents.” Akbar shrugs, “There was only one other genetically-matched donor.”

“Yeah,” comes out of Saira like a surrendered, graveside eulogy. "His parents died in a car crash when he was nine."

Dead silence.

Don Frye goes to the window and parts the blinds. Dawn's sunlight razors in. Squinting outside, he takes off his Stetson and sets it on the counter. His hand tugs his hair as it goes through it, "No, Saira." He turns to face her, "I swear I just found out."

Dr. Sharif delivers it, "The only genetic match died in a casino fire in Linz, Austria a month ago. The Red Cross records indicate his name was Andre Pope. He was Rene's biological father."

Saira looks at Don Frye, and crumbles. She runs out.

Don Frye goes after her and finds her sitting on the floor, huddled in the corner of the blue-lit hallway, in a high-arched doorway, shaking. He gets down on the floor next to her and wraps his arms around her. He gently moves her head to his shoulder. As Saira whimpers, he rocks her, "There, there, darlin'." His hushed, deep voice soothes her, "I know, I know." Holding her, Don Frye's head shakes, as it all becomes clear, "All these years," he emotionally releases an ironic titter, "all the competition between them." His head drops, "They were exactly alike. It all makes sense now." As Saira's breathing settles down, Don Frye shares it with her, "Just before we left for Linz, Andre surprised Rene with a Sunday morning visit."

Saira sparks a little and looks up, "At the house?"

He nods. "You had to see them. They were like two little boys sitting cross-legged on the floor, each trying to outdo the other with their expertise on Vermeer. Andre had never seen the Vermeer."

"The Girl with a Pearl Earring...that's why he came over?"

"No." He moves a loose curl away from her eyes. "No. I'm sure the real reason Andre came over was to talk to Rene about you. I heard him say it." Don Frye smiles assurance, "Don't ever let her go. Saira," he leans into her and whispers, "Rene loved you with all his heart. You were his whole world. When you left he died a little." He coaxes her back up. "Rene's a fighter. He'll open his eyes. You need to be there when he does. He has to see you."

When they walk back in, Dr. Akbar Sharif is opening the blinds. The bright light of the Florentine sun fills the room. He cracks open the window and lets a crisp, cool breeze into the room. All three sit by Rene's bedside, watching, hoping.

Hours later, mid afternoon, the old Italian nurse comes in to monitor Rene's stats.

Chipping away at her thumb's nail polish, Saira gets lost staring at Rene. She hangs on every draw of his breath. She realizes now that all the fears of her life have been a distraction. They seem pointless compared to this. Her most sacred beliefs lose their moorings. Every truth she's ever known becomes unsettled. With every pained breath Rene takes, she feels her body quiver -- its tremor a recognition of the depth of her feelings. What she held as so divine was now fleeting. She surrenders and finally forgets herself. Rene Sorrell had opened the eyes of her heart, his love changing her destiny. Rene's voice echoes inside her. *I am the only one that knows him, her mind whispers.* No matter what, she knows she loves him.

Saira breaks the silence. She turns to the nurse. "Why a baby on a blue wheel?"

"What…?" The nurse stares at Saira, distracted at the random question. "Oh, the reliefs in the spandrels above each of the arches on the front of the hospital. This was originally a children's orphanage. Centuries ago, unwanted babies could be dropped off in a basin located at the front of the porch." She sneers at the farce of it, "Later on the orphanage made it easier by replacing the portico with a secret door with a horizontal wheel that spun the baby into the building without the parent being seen." The nurse shakes her head with pity of it all, "Anonymous abandonment was easier."

Saira's eyes close.

The nurse realizes her words haven't made things easier for Saira. She feebly tries to assuage her. "Such a handsome man," her eyes turn toward Saira, "it's a shame he didn't have any children."

"You're wrong," Dr. Sharif corrects her. "He did."

"What...?" Numb, it doesn't register with Saira. "What are

you saying?"

"He had fifty," the doctor boasts to the nurse stopping her at the door. "I knew him for such a short time, but I witnessed his love give so much."

"Fifty?" the nurse scoffs not taking him seriously.

"He was like the cobbler that made shoes for everyone else but himself," Akbar smiles at Saira. "When Rene found out that there were others exactly like him, Bombay Blood Types, he brought them from as far away as Mumbai, New Delhi, Islamabad, Kandy, Manila, everywhere we could discover them. He single-handedly financed the Paris Center for Immunology Research, and had the children flown in from all over the world to undergo research to help protect their lives." Akbar beams at Rene, "As part of his Parisian Rive Gauche development efforts, Rene helped us build this expansion bridge, The Passerelle Simone de Beauvoir Bridge, to connect the research center with the rest of the project." Akbar nods, "It was Rene's idea. We had fifty kids, in white shirts and stethoscopes, try to rock the bridge. Their little, brown hands above their heads, they swayed in unison and...as the bridge wobbled, their laughter was divine."

Saira illuminates loving the vision.

"It was their present for undergoing two days of pesky, needle-poking research." Dr. Akbar Sharif looks at Rene and shakes his head with gratification, "As we watched, Rene asked me if I thought they would remember it."

"What did you answer him?"

"They'd remember it forever." He holds her eyes. "That his love would endure."

The accelerating pitch of the heart monitor ignites into a rapid staccato. Red warning lights flash as it blurs into a constant beep. The acidification of Rene's blood and elevated potassium levels trigger the kidney monitor. Its alarm blares signaling renal failure. Rene's back arches as his chest constricts. The rare antibodies in Rene's blood serum attack the incompatible blood in his system.

Doctor Sharif rushes to his bedside, "He's going into acute

hemolytic shock."

The hospital staff rushes in. A flurry of white-coated nurses attends to Rene. Regulating the catheters and increasing the blood flow does nothing. Flushing the lines entirely, Dr. Sharif releases a massive transfusion of Rene's French-bagged blood. The blare of the kidney monitor and heart machine become one.

Saira pushes in between the hospital staff.

She takes Rene's hand. Rene's eyelids flutter. He opens his eyes. Seeing Saira, he looks at her with love. The heart monitor flat-lines. Rene's heart stops. In that moment, Saira sees the tenderness on his face. Her love and his death entwine.

Saira lays her fingers on Rene's eyes and closes them.

Tears falling down his cheeks, Don Frye stands over his brother. He kisses Rene's forehead. Sighing, looking at his face one last time, he places his Stetson at Rene's feet and walks out.

FIFTY-FOUR

The bows of paused violinists from the Boston Symphony Orchestra wait in anticipation as the hand-picked guests inside the Isabella Gardner Museum stare over the shoulders ahead of them as Rembrandt's stolen, sepia-toned, self-portrait is fit back into its empty, tiny frame. The pump of an organ, flutter of flutes, and the metronome stretch of violin strokes, mix with applause filling the timbers of the self-styled, fifteenth century Venetian palazzo. From the wood flooring to the paving stones, railings to pillars, tapestries to murals, and the rarest of Dutch master painters, the four-story castle, designed around a sun-filled, central courtyard, is a monument to the passion of one woman, Isabella Stewart Gardner's, travels around the world.

In the back of the ballroom, watching the crowd's reaction, Saira DuFour, in a three-quarter length, military-cut, leather-belted, dark-brown, sheared-beaver coat, matching Cossack hat, and dark sunglasses, turns to her right and asks a turquoise leather-clad Tookie, "Well, what do you think?"

"Ghanaian by birth...but New Yorker by the grace of God," Tookie sighs assessing the conservative, up-tight Boston crowd. She does a jitterbug-shiver, "It's cold and old, straitlaced and starchy, and downright puritanical here but..." she tries but can't suppress a high-pitched shriek as she holds out her hands, "I love it!" With the squeal, prim-faced guests and two guards turn to appraise the Gardner Museum's new, twenty-eight-year-old, cheeky curator, Ms. Tookie Mills. Tookie's fingers flick, waiving her uniformed guards to turn back around. She smirks at her old roommate, "Cute guards, huh?" Cocking her tightly rolled, Nubian curls upward, she loud whispers, "I can't believe I'm living in Isabella's apartment on the top floor."

The audience pushes forward to see Rembrandt's missing miniature masterpiece. As Saira and Tookie take in the blue-blood crowd, a black-turbaned and tuxedoed Maharaja Ravi Rajmar trickles a flirtatious waive from the front row. Saira nods.

"So…." Patient as she could be, Saira asks Tookie again, "What do you think?"

"Well..." Tookie drops her British accent and imitates a tough New Yorker, stretching it for all she can, "we're gonna' havta' change a few things."

Saira takes off her sunglasses and drills her with a look.

"You can't appreciate art in window illumination." Still playing it serious, Tookie looks up at the old, lighting fixtures, "The lighting's gotta go." Tookie can't role-play any longer. She throws her arms around Saira and hugs her, "Thank you, thank you, thank you!"

With that, more of the crowd turns and notices who is there. A gaggle of reporters try getting to Saira. She immediately puts her sunglasses on and kisses Tookie, "Best of luck Madame Curator."

Tookie whispers in Saira's ear, "I want to get married here."

As four, stalwart, security guards intercede, heading off the phalanx of reporters, one of the reporters sneaks out a camera. A tall, broad-shouldered, Dutch guard stands in front of him and blocks him. "Sir," he puts his hand over the camera's lens, "Ms. DuFour is a very private person. She never allows photographs."

Saira heads for the exit. Just as she pushes down on the bar of the door, she turns to smile goodbye at Tookie.

Tookie bows and mouths the words 'thank you'.

Saira notices a bespectacled, East Indian reporter being pushed back. She points at the guards, "Let her through." A gangly, brown-skinned, young girl, barely twenty-one, looks back at the others as she self-consciously approaches Saira.

"Tuhada naan ki hai?" Saira asks, waving her forward.

The girl lights up hearing Punjabi. "My name is Ajeet." She

looks down at the ground, "It's supposed to mean I'm popular." She laughs at the folly of it. She smiles at Saira, "Tussi kiwen ho?"

"I'm fine." Saira takes off her sunglasses. "How can I help you, Ajeet?"

"How...?" Ajeet transforms as she takes out her reporter's pad and looks back at the crowd surrounding the stolen Rembrandt. Her stance is professional as she zeroes in on Saira with her question, "It was missing for twenty years. With all the law enforcement agencies looking for it, the five million dollar reward, and the U.S. Attorney's offer of immunity for the thieves...nothing made a difference. Ms. DuFour, how did you do it?"

"Collecting is a small world." Saira scans the gathering and spots the dark-skinned, polished, young man she met at the roulette table in Linz, Austria. Standing in between his four guards, Sheik Rashid looks back and bows his head with reverence.

Saira nods back. There's a twinkle in Saira's eye as she educates the young girl, "Someone found out it was in his country's best interest to acquire natural gas rights."

As the young girl furiously tries to scribble down Saira's answer, Saira's French-manicured hand stops her, "Don't spoil a good story by telling the truth." She winks at the girl, "Leave a little something to the imagination."

As Saira walks out into the snowy courtyard, Maharaja Ravi Rajmar surprises her by coming out of the shadows. Holding his close-trimmed beard, stepping back, looking Saira up-and-down, Ravi Rajmar makes it no secret he's assessing the new Saira, "Wow." He smiles sarcasm, "I heard a rare piece of turquoise and diamond jewelry hit the Indian antique market recently." His penetrating, brown eyes ooze charm, "In our country it's bad luck to return a gift."

"It went to the right place." Saira steps around him. "Your Highness..." she nods respect, "enjoy the evening." She keeps going.

"It seems to be rather slippery out here." The Maharaja smiles and steps in front of her path, "I was thinking I'd walk you home."

"Thank you," Saira points at the silver Bentley Brooklands,

fogging the winter air with its dual exhausts, and keeps going, "I'm all set. Oh...you know there is one thing...." she turns back to Maharaja Ravi Rajmar. "How come in India there are laws to protect the rights of children condemned to penal institutions, but no comparable standard exists to protect the rights of abandoned or orphaned children?"

Ravi Rajmar is stunned, but intrigued. He smiles sincere piqued interest. "Main ki kar sakda haan?" (What can I do?)

"We shall see." Saira bows slightly. "Good evening."

As Saira crosses the snow-covered terrace of the courtyard, she takes off her sunglasses, closes her eyes and breathes the day's events out. Walking a confident stride, she smiles. Her breath fogging, her gait suddenly slows a little. She stops, catching her breath as she leans on a frozen light pole. A stream of sunlight peeks out from the late afternoon Boston clouds. Her mind races back to the time she found herself waking up in Rene Sorrell's bed. Her shoulders relax. She sighs. Her eyes flutter with the memory of how she raced back to bed hearing footsteps. How Rene leaned in close, his fingers touching her temple as he whispered, "Stay as long as you like."

Her gloved hand blots a tear in the corner of her eye.

Seeing her coming, Don Frye opens the door to the Bentley, "Ms. DuFour," he dips his Stetson and grins, "how did we do?"

Sitting up front, she answers with a British accent imitating Tookie, "The Gardner Museum's new addition was *the rave*."

They both laugh.

"And...?" Don Frye puts the Bentley in gear and points at her unfastened seat belt.

Uncomfortable, struggling to get it around her full coat, Saira shakes her head with frustration. She lets the seat belt go, it zips back in place. Starting with the collar of her coat she starts unbuttoning it.

"Well...?" Don Frye keeps his foot on the brake. "What did the doctor say?"

Saira stares at his determination and sighs. She reaches in

her coat pocket and takes out a small envelope. She stares at it before opening it. A wry smile comes over her mouth. She pinches out a black and white negative image.

Don Frye looks at the ultrasound photo and stares at Saira.

She holds up two fingers.